FATE
of
STORMS

FATE
of
STORMS

BLOOD OF ZEUS: BOOK THREE

MEREDITH WILD
& ANGEL PAYNE

WATERHOUSE PRESS

Copyright © 2021 Waterhouse Press, LLC
Cover Design & Images by Regina Wamba
Interior Cover Images: Shutterstock

ISBN: 978-1-64263-248-4

For Angel…

Thank you for everything.

— Meredith

For Thomas…

Because you are written in my cosmos.

— Angel

"Take heart. Nothing can take our passage from us when such a power has given warrant for it. Wait here and feed your soul while I am gone on comfort and good hope, I will not leave you to wander in this underworld alone."
— Dante Alighieri, Inferno Canto VIII

CHAPTER 1

Kara

"QUITE THE VIEW, ISN'T IT?"

Hades murmurs it in a much too silky tone as I dig my fingertips deeper into my bare arms. I refuse to look at him and gaze blankly out the window instead.

I'm beyond numb. I think I'm dead. All I can feel is endless icy pain. Knives of despair stab at my insides, all the way down to the invisible depths of me. If I still have one, it's never been clearer who it belongs to—the devil whose soles click slowly across the bloodred marble toward me. The god whose voice echoes seductively off the massive room's stone walls and gothic arches.

I shudder hard at his slightest touch, the hand of the devil himself, warm and gentle over the ball of my bare shoulder.

"Oh, Kara, my love, you're freezing."

"I'm fine."

It's not like I can freeze to death, but I'd rather feel like I am than accept his comfort.

Despite this, the fire in the room's wide hearth roars to life. I keep my teeth clenched tightly, but the sudden heat melts some of my raging resolve. Until now, I've held on to it like a death grip, watching the hours pass with no change, no hope.

There's no time here. No sunrise or sunset. Just a never-ending landscape of misery. The grim, formless city lies beneath a gray roiling sky, both seeming to stretch over eternity.

"There…" He presses his lips tenderly against the place where his hand was.

When I tense, he grips hard enough that I feel the pinch of his rings and the edge of his nails into my warming flesh.

"Now, now. Don't be difficult. We don't have much time. Let's not waste it."

I whip my stare to the ruthless blackness of his. "What are you talking about? All we have is time."

He releases his hold on me to stroll the few paces to the fireplace. The fire's amber glow deepens. Its flames blaze beyond the hearth, as if reaching for their lord.

"Not so," he mutters. "Only a couple of weeks. After that, you'll no longer be the lady of my house."

I piece his meaning together quickly. Time may not exist here, but back in LA, hints of autumn were already beginning to show. "Persephone."

"I long for her half of my days." There's a faint but discernible crack in his voice. "Once she returns, I intend to give her all of my attention."

A hard gulp swells in my throat. "Then what happens… to me?"

He shrugs, and the light shimmers off his expensive crimson jacket. "Then you'll go where you should have gone all along. Before Maximus's memories of you called to me so strongly, I wouldn't have given the matter a second thought."

I fix my focus on the canals snaking around the base of what I can only assume is the castle of this terrible kingdom. Below us, nothing's changed. The distant drone of souls in pain—the indistinguishable but unmistakable sound of pure agony—is only interrupted by the boats thudding against the moors and their gaunt captains bellowing at each other in every imaginable tongue.

Hades draws near again, following my gaze below, then higher.

"I really do enjoy the view from here," he says lightly.

I don't want to share words with him, or a moment more in his presence, but curiosity wins out.

"Where are we?"

"The capital, of course. Every kingdom has one."

"Dis," I supply.

He shrugs again. "Judecca. Dis. This place has many names. I call it home. For now, you will too."

For now…

"And the rest?"

"Oh, there's much more." With his finger, he traces the visible edge of the city where the miles of canals and structures break with a wide river. Beyond it, barren land stretches endlessly in varied states of emptiness. Trees rise out of charred fields like smoking sepulchres. A broad expanse of black mud appears alive with the tired crawl of Hades's subjects blanketed in its filth. In the far distance, mountains of jagged rock cut into the bleak sky, and without being able to see those ridges up close, somehow I already know some degree of torture is being carried out in those places too.

My hunger to know more is insatiable now. I can't escape the disgusting but pressing need to understand this new place. "Are there circles?"

Hades crosses his arms and leans casually against the window's edge, bringing himself into my view. "More like districts—each one designed for the brand of punishment that fits the crime of the damned."

"Which one will I go to?"

He hums quietly again, a sound that seems too thoughtful for the devil himself. "Well, your ancestors help oversee the third district. But since your true sin is betraying fate to your lustful appetites, perhaps district two is more fitting. I understand you're quite the expert in this field, though, so perhaps you could tell me."

He studies me for a long moment. I decide not to take the bait or entertain him with my academic theories that are just that—theories. Loose concepts and retellings of an odd dream of hell. Nothing compared to the real thing, which he knows with terrifying intimacy.

With that same eerie surety, he tilts his head. "You must be more curious than that. Come, Kara. Ask me your questions. Show me your mind. Let me into all of your thoughts."

In any other place and time, I'd actually be seeking out the same thing. But I don't want to know the feelings of even one of his fingernails, let alone his whole being. Though some instinct, crawling from the darkest parts of me, whispers that might be exactly what *he* wants.

I tense more and clutch my arms with painful desperation, as if I can somehow keep him out that way. But at once I recognize it's foolish. I'm powerless against him and the ruthless invasion of his will.

I'm alone here. I have no allies. No friends. No hope.

But I do have family. That could count for something, or nothing at all.

"You said my ancestors oversee the third district."

A long moment passes. It's like torture, and I hate feeling like he somehow knows it. If he does, there's no outward gloat about it. His expression tightens with concentration as he gazes out over his vast dominion.

"It may seem like chaos here, but we're rather organized. I can't maintain order single-handedly, so I rely on those who've proven themselves to be worthy leaders in each district. Of course, only the most shrewd and merciless creatures can rise in the ranks here." He smirks a little. "Hierarchy has a way of bringing out the worst in everyone. There's nothing quite as satisfying as watching a mob of miscreants claw their way over each other for such meager advantage." After a long moment, he shifts his gaze back to me. "You look rather like her, actually."

I frown. "Who?"

"Charlena. Your grandmother. She's been very valuable to me for a very long time."

I've always known my grandmother's name, and that, demon or not, my mother, my siblings, and I were brought into the world because she deceived my grandfather. Reconciling my memory of a few old photos of her with this new information inspires more strange, unsettling feelings. And significant doubt that she could be anyone who might care for me enough to help me out of this fate. As cold as my mother has always been, I fear Charlena is likely far worse. If she's as heartless as Hades says, I could never count her as an ally.

"If she's so valuable here, why was she selected to trick and punish my grandfather?"

He shrugs. "She's served me well. Getting to leave this realm for any length of time is a little bit like a vacation."

"A long vacation..." Long enough to produce my mother and her siblings.

"Indeed." He pushes off the wall and walks toward me. "But she was eager to return once her duties were fulfilled. Enough time on earth can feel like hell after a while. Trust me."

I turn and clamp my eyes shut when he reaches for me, but I can't escape the warmth of his touch along the line of my jaw. "I consider you *my* subject, but I do appreciate how your humanity preserves your earthly beauty here. You are as lovely as you are fascinating."

I exhale a shaky breath. From his touch or the chill

leaving my bones, I'm not sure.

"What do you want with me?"

He draws his finger in shrinking circles over my shoulder, slowly, patiently. "You're a sin I've yet to taste... I can hardly wait."

I recoil then, taking a step back and daggering him with a glare. "That's what you want? To take advantage of me and throw me away?" I gesture angrily toward the grand four-poster bed that's draped in velvet and silk, its warm colors contrasting against the otherwise cold and largely empty space. I've yet to sleep, dedicated as I've been to staring dismally into eternity. Now the opulent centerpiece of the room is even less appealing when I think of sharing it with the king of hell.

Another long, cruel moment passes before he breaks into laughter. It's a booming, condescending kind of thunder, making me feel even more insignificant in his presence.

"Oh, Kara. I assure you I'm nothing like my lecherous brother. Indulging the temptations of the flesh is a tired sin. I grew bored of it ages ago. You're a beautiful creature, but the other things you've inspired in Maximus are what truly draw me to you."

Strangely, his declaration doubles my shivers. Giving him my body would've been much simpler than this, I'm sure of it.

"The feelings you can capture..." He shakes his head like a kid beholding his first fireworks. "So *many* of them. And so rich and rare and vibrant. It's no wonder he's addicted to you. Now, I'm greedy to experience it all for myself."

I drag in a ragged breath. "But you'll never have it. Don't you understand that? What exists between us, exists between *us*. Maximus and me. It's never happened with anyone else."

His stare flares wide with intrigue. "I welcome a good challenge. Perhaps my touch alone won't kindle this anomaly the way it has with him, but I'm sure we'll find a way to recreate it. And once we do…once I reach inside your mind, we'll have something I've never experienced before."

I shake my head violently. "What? What could I possibly offer that you haven't already seen through him?"

He licks his lips. The flames flicker on their wetness and inside the coal of his eyes.

"That infinite loop… That circuit of connection. I want to see the colors myself through *your* experience. What a fascinating mirror to look upon. To see it through rapture would be divine, but if you won't give that to me, I can inspire so much more in you. There's fear…sadness…anger. So many unpleasant possibilities."

I take another step back, knowing the small retreat is futile. Everything is. I can't fight him. I can't hide from him. All I can hope is to disappoint him so he'll leave me be. Send me off to whatever awful, unending fate awaits me. It's going to take building some walls inside. As high and as fast as I can. I slam my eyes closed again, hoping I can start this very second.

"Perhaps you can think on it," he adds gently. "We do have a little time. It could be a wonderful surprise to have you choose. I try to advocate for a little free will wherever

I can." Then, extending his arm, he offers me his upturned palm. "Come, Kara. I'll give you the tour."

CHAPTER 2

Maximus

FOR THE THIRD TIME in less than an hour, car tires scream on the soaked street below my apartment's window. This time, the chaos is followed by an angry horn and a loud crash. Nearly at once, the drivers are slamming doors and ranting at each other.

I click the TV remote, cranking up whatever's on to drown the din. Jesse's had the box on all day, claiming to like white noise despite dictating that the volume stay at zero. I've readily obliged because right now I need him. More than I ever have before.

My best friend, seated in my dining nook, jogs a brow in my direction. "Think you can shut down the celestial water works for a little while so I can concentrate here?"

I frown toward the stormy sky and wince at the deafening thunderclap that follows. "It doesn't have an off switch, okay?"

Thankfully, the collision below seems to be nothing

more than a fender bender. The drivers and their volume levels have dimmed to half-civil tones. I mute the TV once more, trying to ignore how my blood's consumed by ice, my gut's on fire with dread, and my thoughts are repelling magnets.

Jesse seems to pick up on all that already. "Damn, dude. Too bad I'm in the know about Rainageddon now. Otherwise, I might be having some actual fun with all this wild and crazy weather."

I shoot a scowl over my shoulder. Jesse remains diplomatically placid, his gaze glued to his laptop screen. The man and his computer have had barely a moment's rest since last night—all in the name of helping the friend who spilled a barge's worth of tea on him and then begged for his help.

He has a point, though. The distraction of the freak storm I've caused being rabidly covered by every news team in the city isn't helping either of us focus. And I need every brain cell Jesse has to spare right now.

And luckily, my front door hasn't yet been pounded in by a half demon in head-to-toe Prada yet.

"You're right," I mutter. "Last thing I need right now is a face-to-face with Veronica."

He chuckles. "Do you really think she hasn't found out by now? You know she's likely gotten the spill from Z. Hades is his *brother* after all. Moreover, Zeus is *the* All-father. He's probably got little spy minions all over hell reporting back to him with game-changing scoops like this."

"What makes you think this is a game changer for my father?"

"Eh?" Jesse snaps. He pushes the laptop aside, all ears for me.

A twinge of guilt hits. I'd really hoped to keep Jesse far away from this wild tangle that's become my life. Now, he's in the thick of it like kindling in a bonfire. I couldn't yank him free if I tried.

"Even if Z does know about this, he's not going to just jump in and play benevolent savior. Not even for me. Not anymore, at least."

A dozen furrows appear in Jesse's forehead. "Dude. He's your *dad*."

"And I honestly think he's burned out."

"How is that a thing? I mean, for a god."

"He's been alive for a long time, Jesse. There's not a lot he hasn't seen or done, including acts in the name of doing some good. Not to mention, the human race writes him off as a myth. His wife is jealous, bitter, and demanding. His brothers are headstrong bastards in their own rights. The subjects of his own kingdom are all creatures with their own unique powers and likely the egos to match. Now try thinking about managing all that, day after day, with no end in sight."

"Yeah. Damn." Jesse nods. "Guess they can't impose term limits for the king of the gods."

"Don't think that's a thing in Olympus—or probably ever will be."

One side of his mouth hikes up. "Why, Maximus Kane. Are you *defending* your pops?"

"I'm defending the fact that everything in the

Olympians' world isn't greener grass and sweeter nectar," I rebut. "But that's not an excuse for him. It's an explanation for me."

An inconvenient one. Even when I can imagine no greater crisis than this, Z's top priority will never be his family.

True enough, until last week, he wasn't a speck in my world, and I'd been perfectly happy. Working hard, surrounded by good friends and family, and falling in love like I never knew I could. My father hadn't been a necessity in my world. Not even close.

But without Kara, I have no world at all.

No fire for my shadows. No torch to show me the way through an existence that will never be normal again.

With Jesse's help, I'll find the way to her. And as soon as we find that path, I'm going to march straight into hell. Unlike Dante, I'm not headed there for exploration. Once there, I'll crush every stone I have to. Topple every wall. Fight every damned soul that gets in my way.

As more thunder rattles the city, I rise to pace the room, my fists coiled. "So you're really buying all of this?"

My friend lifts a brow. "That you're a demigod?"

Unfortunately, I'm long past thinking that insanity might not be real. A couple of trips to Labyrinth and a mind probe from Hades knocked those hopes right out of me. I wouldn't wish that experience on my worst enemy, let alone the best friend hunched at the table in front of me. Contemplating this new reality through his eyes is another lash of anxiety that I'm barely able to handle right now.

I pivot in front of the kitchenette. "Sure. And the rest?"

He peers at his laptop screen again before scribbling a few lines in one of the spiral notebooks he's rarely without. "Science studies facts so fiction is believable—even yours. There are just parts of the story, like Kara going all woo-woo empath to calm your stubborn ass, that are easier to swallow."

His declaration brings the temptation to smile. The ache tugs at every corner of my chest, along with the edges of my mouth, but outright strangles the whole mound of my heart. "That's fair," I concede. "She has a good heart, but she's always been tenacious when she wants to be."

"That—and her being a demon—is either going to make your relationship a cosmic game changer or the most insane reality show on record."

With hearing him refer to our relationship as a future thing, I finally give in to a smile. But the moment is quickly swallowed by a tsunami of rage when the full weight of our hopeless circumstances crashes over me again.

I have to find her.

No matter what it takes.

No matter how impossible.

No doubt Jesse can see that much as I push forward and drum a couple of fingers on the table.

I nod toward his notepad. "What have you got? Tell me you have something. Anything." Now I'm tapping so hard, the tabletop gets a few dents.

"It's not that I don't have *anything*. I've got things." The gullies across his forehead get deeper. "But this is more like…everything."

"Meaning what?"

"It means finding the door to hell isn't going to be a flicker in the dark. More like…a pinhole in a corkboard."

During the declaration, Jesse slides his notepad across the table. Eagerly, I peer at the theories he's got detailed on the page—as well as the twelve or more after it.

"Where do I start here?" I mutter.

"There's not an easy answer for that, I'm afraid. For every biblical or literary reference you've unearthed, I've got scientific counterparts in the double digits," he explains.

"But some are debunkers," I counter. "Right? So we can rule those out at once."

"The obvious ones, yes. Area Fifty-One, Stonehenge, Roswell, Eye of the Sahara, Loch Ness, the Blood Falls…"

I cock a brow. "Someone really thinks Loch Ness is a hellmouth?"

He shrugs. "Oh, you know Nessie and her secrets."

I flip the page, scanning his next jumble of notes. "I don't think anything is glaringly obvious when it comes to Hades. Last night, we simply thought we were at an extra-chill beach party." There's a stab in my chest matching the new growl in my throat. "Until we weren't."

"And that's where your mope ends." He pounces a hand back to his mouse like a lion tamer cracking a whip. His rapid clicks through the screens are just as methodical. "No time for brooding in the labor camp, buddy. I need your brain front and center if we're going to figure all this stuff out."

"You're right." My nod is just as much a mental

shakedown. I repeat it, making sure I've hurled out as many dark memories as possible, before offering up the full force of my attention. "Walk me through this. What's your theory?"

"*Theories*," Jesse corrects. "Dude, we're nowhere close to just one yet."

"So how fast can we narrow it down?"

He has to know by now, nonstop rain or not, that my hope is already threadbare.

"Left my crystal ball back in the other mansion," he deadpans. "But hopefully, we'll catch a break soon." He carefully eyes me again. "But first... You're absolutely positive there was no possible egress through Rerek Horne's living room? No other statuary to shatter and break open a dimensional door?"

I force a full breath in then out. "If there were, I wouldn't be here now."

He starts clicking again. "Stands to reason it was probably a king's-only portal. Even palaces in this dimension have them. Or Hades is so damn special he doesn't need a door. He's powerful enough to make one wherever he wants to go."

"There's got to be another way in." I stab a few more dents into the tabletop. "Something more substantial. Something physical. Or even *meta*physical." I'm not going to be picky about this. I don't need a neon sign and golden entrance stairs. I just need a direction in which to look.

"Twenty-four hours ago, I would've laughed at that idea," Jesse says. "But yesterday, I also didn't believe in demons and demigods."

"So what do you think? Where do we start looking for this...gateway?"

Kara's fate rests in the answer.

"Well." Jesse sits back again, letting one of his favorite sticky stretch toys come out for an appearance. He flicks out the long rubber length, letting the little hand on the end flatten to my patio window before yanking it back. "I took your mythological and sociological references on the subject and aligned them with what present-day science and geography can halfway confirm. Your first suggestion, about Hades ruling over a basic but bleak underworld at the outer edge of the sea, matched up to a healthy handful of islands across the globe."

He shows me that specific list by using the rubber hand to lift the top page of the notepad. My first look at the thing is nothing short of an eye-bulger.

"Healthy handful?" I sputter.

"All right, all right." He rolls his eyes. "How about a robust roster?"

"How about something we'll come back to later?" After trying to skim the extensive list, I hurriedly flip the page. "What else?"

"This is the stuff I connected to Elysium," he supplies, "which is technically a section of the underworld but likely not under Hades's direct jurisdiction. Your boy Dante was one of the few who believed otherwise. It's also called the White Island and is commonly known as a paradise exclusively for war heroes and virtuous soldiers."

"So we can probably put this one in the skip file."

"Figured you'd say that." As I turn the page, he sighs. "*Au revoir*, Bora Bora. *Aloha*, Kapalua Bay."

"Saving it, not burning it," I defend. "I've just added it to the bucket list."

In my own head, I think about stretching out with Kara on one of those exotic stretches of sand—with our clothes conveniently stowed somewhere else. It's the motivation I need to face the next page, a crowded mess that matches the first.

"Next, Tartarus," Jesse goes on. "The bottommost wasteland of hell. Aka, the great cosmic pit. It's lightless and deep, supposedly deeper down than the pit of hell itself. It has either iron gates or ironlike reinforcements, with snakes as guardians. Scientifically speaking, that means it's a—"

"Cave," we state in unison.

I feel my face tighten as a mirror of his scowl.

I lift the sheet and groan when surveying the *second* page of his list.

He tics a fast nod. "Those pages are only the caverns above sea level, though I broke out the criterion in two ways. The deepest that are naturally formed take up a good portion of the list. But the iron factor gnawed at me. If it's ore we're looking for, Australia's the obvious leader on that board. There are also extensive pits in Brazil, China, Russia—"

"So what's this second list on these other two pages?" Moving him on is the only way of saving myself from the research avalanche. "The reject pile?"

Jesse shakes his head. "Those are the *underwater* caves."

A heavy sigh rolls out of me. Despite all my best efforts, my mind's already fissuring like mud in the sun, and there's still more content to go.

I remind myself, in lecture-stern terms, that I was the one to call Jesse in the first place. I *asked* for this, knowing my friend was going to go full nerdcore on all the research. I'll be thankful for all this…eventually.

"So what's on all the rest of the pages, then?"

"Miscellaneous theories," he supplies. "Various places and a few phenomena that don't fit the other labels but might actually be what we're looking for. Like the Maracaibo lightning patterns, the Darvaza Gas Crater, and the Kamchatka volcanoes. Worth noting but too obvious, right?"

"Oh, yeah." I'm mockingly indulgent, already knowing he won't care or notice. Sure enough, he doesn't.

"But the others should be considered. The Danakil Depression…that's a special kind of environmental nasty. And Snake Island, Madidi National Park, the Gomantong Caves? Interesting, but likely in the trying-too-hard column, as well."

"And you thought volcanoes were too obvious?"

He *fwips* the rubber hand at the window again. One of the fingers glows for a second, picking up a sliver of sunlight. I can't promise a full cloud break yet, but just talking about all these potential plans has cleared my mind to a better place.

"This is all amazing, man." The words come straight from my heart. "Honestly."

The words feel, and *are*, pathetically thin for expressing my gratitude. First of all, the guy didn't speed out of here the second I hit him with the truth about Kara and me. Secondly, he's not relented on his research since then. We've literally been at this all day. Though the sun is finally making a shy appearance outside, it'll be setting in less than an hour.

"*Pffft.*" His dismissal is thick with sarcasm but diluted by a limp-armed stretch. "Make it even. Order me some pizza and wings, sugar bunch."

"Done deal, sweet cheeks," I drawl, pulling up the delivery app on my phone.

While we wait on dinner, Jesse reaches over and again spins the notepad around. "How are you proposing we winnow all this down?"

"You think *I* know?"

"One of us will have to make the call. Investigating every one of these will take years."

"And we don't even have days."

Irritation and impatience are new nips at my heels. What do we do? How do we start to figure this out? Where do we separate reality from mythology?

Where the *fuck* has Hades taken half of my heart and soul?

Jesse's face contorts as if he's heard my inner tantrum. He leaves the table, rolling slowly across the living room. For a few long beats, he stares at the blank TV screen. "Just when I thought there was a tutorial or travelogue for everything…" A deep sigh blows in then out of him. "Then you had to go searching for an impossible roadmap to hell." He mutters it while wheeling back around.

As soon as his words sink in, my head snaps up. My throat seizes tight. My heart kickboxes both my lungs. Just like before, Jesse's picking up on every shred of it.

"What?" he charges. "Are they out of the good wing spice again?"

I shake my head. "Damn it, no," I blurt. "A travelogue to hell…"

"You know where we can get one?" He snickers, half joking.

I stare back without blinking—because I'm not. "Maybe."

"All right," he says slowly. "Are we headed to Bora Bora or Hawaii for it? If so, count me in."

"Neither."

His face falls. "All right. Where, then?"

"Beverly Hills."

CHAPTER 3

Kara

"NOT RIGHT NOW." I utter the refusal as softly as I can manage.

I can't deny the pieces of me that thirst for more knowledge about Hades's vast domain, if only because I'm holding out hope for possible escape routes, but touring the capital is the last thing I want to do right now. And perhaps the last thing I can bear.

Hades's brows form a puzzled frown. "But there's much to see."

"I'm sure there is, but I'm very tired. Please…"

His voice softens a fraction. "Why have you not rested, Kara?"

Trying to explain my taxed emotional state to the god who caused it seems pointless, but the new concern in Hades's expression tugs on my deep need to be heard and understood, even by my enemy. Meeting the dark warmth in his eyes, I wonder if somewhere in those depths he might be capable of empathy. If, despite my betrayal, we could share a moment of kindred understanding. Even better, could gazing into the mirror of his own kindness be exotic enough to satisfy his fascination with my abilities? But all other traces of hope have slipped through my fingers since I've been brought here. Why would this crazy notion be any different?

The bleak question throbs through my mind, wilting my impossible optimism with its cacophony. It compels me to release my arms from their panicked grip around myself. "You've torn me from the only life I knew and brought me into this strange new place. I'm…overwhelmed. And until just now, I didn't know my fate. Needless to say, I've thought of very little else. Sleep has been impossible."

His lips curl into a grin that's regal but predatory. "Your worry is to be expected," he says with a condescending lilt. "But surely you must be excited as well? At least a little? This place has been the object of your fascination for so long."

I purse my lips, now relieved he's unable to fully read me. At least for now.

"Well, you're here at last," he goes on. "And I will satisfy all your curiosities. Every one of them. I promise."

That's what terrifies me most. I swiftly shove the thought aside, focusing on returning a tight smile instead. It's my pathetically strained effort to match his enthusiasm, but for the moment, I think I have him fooled.

He takes my hand and brings it up to his smiling lips, kissing it slowly. "For now, though, we will let you rest."

This time, my smile is a lot more genuine. "Thank you."

"And I have just the place to soothe those tattered nerves of yours."

And there I go again with the premature sincerity. "But—"

He *tsks* loudly and tugs me after him at the same time, ending my objection to our new journey. For the first time since arriving here, through what portal I still can't figure out, I leave the prison of my room. The arched door swings open effortlessly as we approach it, revealing a narrow stone hallway. The cold floor shocks the bare soles of my feet. My flimsy robe, despite its long and sweeping train, is little defense against the chill. I do the best I can to manage the garment as my captor speeds up our pace.

More than a few times, I nearly trip as I follow him along the endless halls and stairways that wind through the castle. Swiftly the sounds of the busy moors are replaced with the sharp chatter of the creatures who clearly do Hades's bidding here in his home. I really am curious now, but we're moving so quickly, I can only glimpse flashes of the scenes as we pass.

There's a harshly lit room filled with ghastly demon soldiers, shoving and shouting at each other past mottled maws with rotten teeth.

In a room that offers a welcome blast of heat, a beastly wild-eyed demon berates a small cowering servant, a table of platters covered in decadent dishes between them.

And there's a library. At least I think so. The room looks like a hurricane blew through, with loose papers strewn about and books stacked messily all over the floor.

Hades leads us to the frigid outdoors through an arch-lined breezeway. Far below, there's a wide, fully frozen canal. Even from this distant vantage, I peer harder, curious about what's giving it such a strange texture.

Suddenly I see it. I see *them*—the malformed outlines of human figures trapped in the confines of the thick ice, their silent bulging eyes pleading eternally to the sky.

I slap my hand to my mouth, but not fast enough to hold in my terrified shriek.

Hades stops so suddenly, I fall against his rigid body. I shriek again, this time more from fear of him. Of our disturbing proximity. He casts a confused gaze down on me, especially because I can't conceal my own bemusement. His body temperature is neither warm nor especially cold. His countenance is neither benevolent nor betraying his pure evil. Everything about his appearance—from the moment he appeared so coolly at Rerek's party days ago—has struck me as oddly human, which gives him a disarming quality that worries me the more time I spend in his presence.

I can't ever fool myself into believing his deception. I can't ever let my guard down with him. Just doing the same with Rerek, one of his devotees, was the opening act of this nightmare. I can't bear to contemplate what would happen if I offered Hades that kind of trust.

"What is it, Kara?"

I let out a few harsh breaths before my gaze slides to the frozen waters below.

"Ah." He takes advantage of our new closeness to rub

some warmth into my arms. "You must be wondering what these vermin must have done to deserve such a fate."

Actually, I don't need to ask him, because between my first gruesome discovery and this moment, my knowledge has supplied the answer. The horror before me resolves with the cantos and the vision my imagination created of those punished within the desolate confines of Judecca.

I stood now where the souls of the last class
(with fear my verses tell it) were covered wholly,
they shone below the ice like straws in glass.

"The treacherous to their masters," I say with a painful exhale.

Hades's lips curl into a satisfied smile that can only be made of pride. "You're exactly right." He regards me a moment more, his expression more intense than any camera lens I've ever had to face off with. "I cannot wait to see your mind, Kara. Truly."

I tense in his gentle hold: my silent, desperate protest to the suggestion. He answers with a gradual withdrawal, leaving me chilled by the relentless wind tunneling through the loggia.

"And if you don't show it to me…" he warns. "If you dare betray me once more, you may find yourself locked for eternity with them, which I personally would not mind at all. I use this overpass often and would relish the gift of your beauty frozen just below the surface, your gaze locked into mine for all of time."

Every cell in my body grows colder than it was before.

The dread of his threat seeps below my skin, penetrating my bones like stabs of a thousand ice shards. I can't think of a worse fate than the torment he's drawn so vividly for me, but I trust there's no end to his list of awful possibilities.

Will I be subjected to them *all* at some point?

Is this my life for the rest of all time?

He steps back some more, though his cool retreat does nothing to ease my dread. "Come," he says. "We're nearly there."

I follow behind, careful to keep up with his swift steps and grateful he's no longer dragging me to our destination. I should be glad the relentless pace helps to warm me up a little, though I'm certain part of my chill is now bone-deep and permanent.

At last, we stop before a tall arched door, no different than the many I've already passed. But instead of a crush of demon soldiers or a bustle of attendants, the opened door reveals an oddly serene room.

We step inside. I stop abruptly at the motion before me, fearing we aren't truly alone. But the movement is simply our two figures reflected in the handful of tall mirrors propped up against the farthest wall. Each one stands at least eight feet tall and just as wide, ornately framed in gold leaf. The middle one also reflects the gold soaking tub that faces it.

"Wow," I breathe out.

The room is strikingly different than anything else I've seen in the castle. It's beautiful, even. A massive chandelier hangs from the vaulted ceiling, shooting prisms of light off the two shallow pools set into the marble floor. Two waterfalls feed seamlessly into them from golden spigots set into the polished stone walls. The same luxurious color is threaded through plush bathmats in front of each tub.

"What is all this?" I ask.

"A place to reflect. To wash away what ails you."

I don't believe him. As alluring as these new surroundings are, the overwhelming energy of the castle still screams death and deceit. The walls alone, though cleaner here, are eons old and etched by sorrow. They speak to my senses more strongly than any human ever has.

Hades circles around me, his bold survey of my figure obvious in the mirrors before us. "Too, it's a place to celebrate and revel in one's beauty. In your case, in all its earthly grandeur." He sweeps his hand broadly, gesturing toward the display of mirrors. "You must enjoy it, no? Vanity is a Valari favorite, after all."

I barely hold back the urge to roll my eyes. The design of the room makes such hideous sense now. What creation of Hades wouldn't cater to a cardinal sin?

"I'm not like the rest of them." The words hit the air like a reflex from years of believing the sentiment in the depths of my soul.

He quirks a brow. "No?"

"No."

He reaches out boldly to toy with the ends of my hair. "You don't appreciate these thick locks of hair?" Our gazes meet. "What about those eyes that arrow into one's soul? Skin like spun silk. A body that millions covet. Some people would kill for what you have, you know."

His eyes glimmer, like the prospect of that excites him. Murder in the name of envy.

"Luck of the draw, I suppose. None of it has any bearing on what truly matters. A truth my family has yet to realize."

He chuckles at that. "Enlighten me, young Valari. What *really* matters?"

I swallow hard, wary to give him my answer but committed to the truth I know in every cell of my being. The truth that, in so many ways, keeps me sane through this very moment.

"Love," I declare, firming my stance and raising my chin. "Love is always what matters most."

His arrogant grin curls into an unattractive grimace. "Does it now?"

"*I* think so."

No. I *know* so, but saying that out loud probably isn't such a wise call right now. I'm challenging him when I'd be wise to make him think he has me under his spell.

"Love. That's all of it?"

I cast a fast glance at him via the mirror. "That's all there needs to be."

"Then why is love so easily consumed by greed and power and pride and envy?"

"Why indeed—though I strongly suspect that might have something to do with you," I snap.

Instantly I regret the words and the passion behind them. The feeling worsens as his nostrils flare and his gaze intensifies.

"I don't create the darkness, Kara," he utters, his voice low and dangerous. "I respect it. I see it for what it is."

"You do more than that," I accuse. "You give it power."

He shrugs. "You could say I'm heavily invested in it. But it's your human friends who power the engines of hate. Don't blame *me* for their inherent weaknesses. I'm only here to collect the trash. It's an unsavory task, but alas, the one I was given."

Without another word, he strolls toward the tub. I follow, as if pulled by an invisible string behind him. Bending, he trails his fingertips across the glassy surface of the water, eliciting an eruption of steam from the fragrant water.

He turns on his heel, gazing directly upon me once more. "Anyway, perhaps it's for the best that you don't stay in the castle long. No doubt the others will soon resent you for the human beauty you retain here."

True enough, every face I've seen except my captor's has been gruesome to behold, distinct in deathly pallor and rotten flesh. So that must mean I'm not actually dead, though I'm not exactly part of life in its purest form either. But looking into the mirror gives me no easy or clear answers. All that's changed on me is the red garment draped elegantly off my frame, replacing the expensive party dress I wore when Hades captured me.

Against my will, the backs of my eyes start to sting. Forever gone are the days of gowns and stilettos and servers with champagne. I never thought I'd be so mournful of it all, but I'd happily go back to mingling among the social sharks of LA if it gave me another chance at life. *Any* chance at life...

Hades makes a concerning point, however. I may be sheltered and protected until Persephone returns, but my appearance is bound to create problems as I journey to other parts of the underworld.

"You could change that. You could make me like the others."

I swallow hard. Did I really just say that? Am I really considering relinquishing my earthly body to wear a face of the damned for the sake of survival?

"I wouldn't dream of it." Hades moves closer again until he's only inches away. He draws the backs of his fingers down my cheek, following the line of my jaw down my neck, stopping at the collar of my robe. "I'm far too selfish to not want to look upon it every time our paths cross. Whether you end up in your family's district or frozen in the ice beneath my feet, this is what I shall see. No matter what we do with you, whatever unending torment comes your way, nothing can mar this face. It's mine, and so are you."

I close my eyes, forcing away the truth in that self-imposed blackness. I'll never be his. I've only ever belonged to one man…one god. Maximus. My lover, my hero.

Emotion burns thick in my throat to remember his touches, his love, his passion. More tears threaten. Tears I refuse to show Hades for the pleasure they'd give him.

"Come now. Open up. Look at me."

I turn my head away, refusing his demand.

His sigh mingles with the quiet gurgle of water rolling into the pools. "Have it your way, then. Languish here as long as you'd like, and I'll have you brought back to your chamber when you're through."

I release some tension, hoping he'll soon leave me be. But when I open my eyes again, he hasn't moved. The quiet but aggressive expression across his features hasn't changed.

"Just remember, Kara, that everything you see… everything you are…all your gifts, all your extra senses…are mine." He pauses, his eyes endless tunnels boring into mine. "Your time on earth was a privilege you never earned. You belong here and nowhere else."

CHAPTER 4

MAXIMUS

"**Y**OU'RE AWARE THAT IT was easier to hear that you're a bastard of Olympus in love with a demon than wrap my head around what you're attempting *here*, right?"

Jesse backs up the charge with what must be his hundredth double take between me and the wrinkled paper brochure on his lap, fronted with a bold headline *See Where the Stars Sleep!*

I ignore him and keep going west, pushing the speed limit and testing the yellow lights.

He begins folding the map as the clubbing district gives way to wider streets and manicured greenbelts. "Hook a right on Roxbury."

Very soon after I do, we're rolling up in front of a sprawling Mediterranean complex fronted by an ornate iron gate.

He drums his fingertips on the center console. "What do you think?"

"I think we're in the right place," I say, putting the truck in park.

Actually, I *know* it as we study the mansion from our vantage across the street. It's not the gate itself, even though it's centered by dramatic iron wolves that fit together to embrace in the middle. It's something else. A vibration, unconventional but exceptional, that clings to the air. It's as revealing as petrichor after rain or cocoa after Reg has made her special Barbajada.

Kara has been here before. Many times.

I'm as sure of it as my next breath, which doesn't enter my chest without some taut resistance. "Yep," I murmur, leaning over the steering wheel to gain a better view of the multifloored mansion beyond the well-developed olive and palm trees. "This is it. I'm sure of it."

Jesse nods while applying the last fold to the tourist map. "Are you as certain of how we're going to get inside now? Because something tells me that little guy has plenty of friends." He gestures toward the small security camera atop one of the gate's support pillars before joining me in focusing on the mansion.

There's no screaming bustle of activity inside, leading me to believe Veronica is still in the dark about the trouble two-thirds of her children have stepped into, but it's obvious the matriarch is still home. Her pristine Bentley is parked out front, and most of the mansion's windows are glowing with gold-hued light.

I push away from the wheel with a peeved grunt. How could I have not accounted for security cameras? The old me, controlled and cogent to a fault, wouldn't have. But that guy was also only half of me. The man who'd never actually allow his stronger side to take over, even for six seconds.

The half dozen beats that it takes me to speak now-familiar words, "*Ex ignes victoria.*"

"From fire, victory?" Jesse returns with a rough chuff. "Do you really need the translation again, man?"

I toss him a fast side-eye. "Of course not."

"Then…what? Because I'm not sure the Valari rally cry is the *Alakazam* you're looking for. As magic spells go, that's—okay, *whoa.*"

During his snark, I've been focusing harder on the security camera: willing the powerful Latin creed to fill my mind and senses. The harder I concentrate, the thicker the air swirls directly over the security camera. Soon, it forms a thick, dark cloud. The small nimbus starts to overflow, dumping out a three-foot-wide downpour. Within seconds, there's even a triple feature of lightning.

Jesse chuckles in time to those electric charges. "Professor Kane says lights out, bitches."

After a moment, I get out and make short work of setting up his chair on the truck's passenger side. As soon as he swings down and gets settled, we go into stealth mode that's been well-practiced since fifth grade.

We slip past the sprung gate with less ruckus than a pair of alley cats and then cautiously proceed down a wide flagstone path alongside the main mansion. The outdoor lights ahead are already making it feel like a direct way to the backyard.

Thankfully, we're right. Soon we discover an enormous pool, a large stone fire pit, two marble fountains, and a scattering of Caesar-worthy loungers. More importantly, I spot the guesthouse and the narrow pathway to it.

Once we're side-by-side in front of the door, I hesitate to knock. But why? I *am* the one who insisted we walk out on hot pizza and reliable scientific research to come here. But for a split second, I doubt the call. I worry it won't be the Valari elder on the other side of this door. Or worse, it will be, and he'll refuse to help us.

"Seriously?" Jesse mutters it as if all my thoughts have turned into holograms across the small stoop. He spares me the lecture and leans forward to level a forceful knock on the door.

There's an answering rustle from inside. And then, "In the study!"

Following instinct, I try the doorknob. It's not locked. "Come on."

Inside, the furniture is well worn but clean, and the air smells like herbal tea and biscotti. Already there's a pang in my chest. Just by inhaling, I can discern why Kara treasured her visits here. As Jesse and I take a slow perusal through the place, I envision her hanging out with her gramps at the small table in the kitchen or snuggling under the thick blanket on the couch while trying to convince him to watch a film from this century.

I miss you, little demon. With every cell in my being.

"Dalton! Christmas on a cracker. I already told you I'm back…"

As the man's voice fizzles, I'm finally able to follow it to one of the rooms at the back of the cottage and step into the doorway of a sizable study. The figure in the leather chair is an odd but ideal match for the scene, with his wrinkled pants, argyle sweater vest, and tortoise-shell eyeglasses.

Glasses he uses to size me up with eerily calm thoroughness. "You're not Dalton."

I shake my head. In return, he draws in a long breath.

"I know who you are. I just always thought Kara would be the one to introduce us when the time came. And since you're not here with her and you look like you're about to start a tsunami in the swimming pool…"

With traces of Kara's presence all over the air, I'm reminded again of how far away she really is. My scowl becomes painful.

"What's wrong?" he chokes out at once. "What's going on? Is she in danger?"

I take the room's other chair. As Jesse glides across the threshold, I plant both hands onto my knees, squaring my posture to fully face the only man who might understand how deeply I love Kara Valari and how dire these circumstances truly are.

Jesse rolls in a few more inches and pulls out his spiral pads from one of his wheelchair's saddlebags. "We need your help, Giovani. Kara needs it."

Gio drags his worried gaze from me to Jesse, who offers a small wave of introduction. "Greetings. I'm Jesse, by the way. This dude's best friend, which defaults me to the front of the line for Operation Find Kara enlistment."

"Find her?" Gio's eyes bulge wider. Harsh air snags in his throat. "What's happened?"

"We were on a date," I begin. "Actually, Jaden invited her to a party he was co-hosting with his friend Rerek."

The old man's growl says enough about his opinion of Rerek, so I don't elaborate further on that part of the story. The snake will get what's coming to him one day, but finding Kara is my first priority.

"Rerek was in on it. Hades..." I sigh heavily. "My *uncle*...he took her."

"In the middle of the party?" Gio demands. "With mortals watching?"

"Nobody in that room was pumping warm blood," I say. "The whole thing was a setup. Hades had the upper hand from the start. He took us by surprise, and his strength and powers unfortunately far exceeded my own. We didn't have a chance of saving her."

"Are you saying—"

"We're pretty sure Hades dragged Kara back to hell... so to speak," Jesse supplies. "Which means someone needs to find a way down there. And we're lost, man. There could be a million paths to take. Or none."

"No." Valari snaps his gaze, already filled with so many haunted shadows, between the two of us. "There's only one. That's if you haven't lived a life of sin or plan on meeting an untimely end and intend to arrive there with no hope of getting back."

A weighted breath leaves me. I'd actually considered my own death as a possibility of fast-tracking myself to the underworld but truly hoped there were alternatives.

"Thank God."

But I double take when the old man seems to think that's worthy of a chuckle.

"What?" I demand. "That simplifies things, doesn't it?"

When he raises his head, I assume there'll be more of his rheumy gaze. But his pupils are practically blown, pushing at the boundaries of irises that gleam like irradiated glass.

"You've been acquainted with your uncle already then, yes, Professor?"

I nod in reply.

"So tell me… In what world would you consider Hades *simple*?"

I rock back, tempted to blow off my nervousness by tapping at the edge of the desk, but its particleboard surface won't weather my stress like my mahogany dining set. "Point heard and taken. So does that mean you can't help us? Or you simply won't?"

He shakes his head. "You and my ladybug really do share similar wiring."

A quick chuff from Jesse, and then, "You mean the single-mindedly stubborn part? Or the won't-take-no-for-an-answer part?"

I surge to my feet. "I'd love to bask in the compliment cavalcade all night, gentlemen, but every second we waste is another moment the woman I love remains prisoner of the hell master she's defied."

Both men stare at me as thunder rumbles overhead.

"So you do love her."

Gio issues the observation with a mixture of ferocity and calm. I meet the challenge of his gaze without a flinch of my own.

"With every cell in my blood and throb of my heart."

He pushes up from the desk and stiffly turns, pacing over to a tall teak display hutch fronted by glass windows. He tugs open the cabinet's doors, triggering the built-in lights to flare to life. Occupying the top two shelves are bound screenplays much like the ones I already studied at Alameda's library. The bottom two tiers are cluttered with an eyepopping array of trophies and awards, including a couple of iconic gold men with crusader swords.

But Gio's attention isn't on his screenplays or the accolades they've earned him.

He's fixated on the middle two shelves, where there's an intriguing collection of knickknacks and photographs. Among them is an aqua apothecary vial that looks like it was preserved from Vesalius's own laboratory, kept preserved and upright in a customized wire holder. In a red velvet box rests a sizable gold coin that's definitely rarer than a double eagle. I lean in to get a better look. The writing on it is foreign, which has me wondering about the distinct chill I get when gazing too long at it.

Time to move on. *Now.*

Next, I set my eyes on an array of elegant cufflink sets, dusty and neglected, obviously cherished from long-ago special occasions. Beside it is an ornate gold ring, set with diamonds and rubies that remind me of Kara's heirloom earrings.

But my interest in the story behind the thing doesn't come close to my fascination with the framed photographs crowding the next shelf down. More precisely, with Gio's fixation on them. At once, and even just viewing his profile, I know the man might as well be showing us the inside of his hidden treasure chest. In these images, in the laughter and smiles and achievements of his family, we're beholding the most valuable pieces of his life. His world.

Inside that unmistakable truth, there's another fact to acknowledge. Kara's photographs outnumber everyone else's. And not by a little.

"I can see she's been your favorite."

Our stares engage via the hutch's polished glass. I'm close enough to watch as his irises turn a texture that can cut that glass, and his angled cheekbones protrude along with his deeper frown.

"Bah." He throws a stiff arm up. "I love all my grandchildren!"

"But not like you love Kara."

When he whirls on me, there are still dark diamonds in his eyes and deep crevices across his face.

"Is that what she told you?"

I drag in a deep breath. "She's told at least a dozen stories about the ways you've inspired her to be compassionate, humble, hardworking, and kind. Judging from how different she is from her siblings, I'd guess the special attention she received made all the difference."

"She has a natural capacity for all of those things… and a great deal more. I simply recognized it in her from an early age and tried to lovingly guide her talents. God knows, Veronica couldn't see the ways to nurture them."

Now doesn't seem like the right time for listing the many strong traits his daughter *has* imbued into Kara, especially as he trades his combative gleam for a sad wash of nostalgia. I'm not going to get a better advantage to press him on the mission.

"Gio. There's a good chance you know exactly what I want here and why I've come directly here for it. Why I've come straight to *you*."

He reaches out, bracing a bony hand to the hutch's polished frame. "Certainly not because you have an ounce of sense in your head."

"I came here for your insights, not to celebrate mine."

"Wisdom comes at a price. I earned the bells on my fool's cap quite a long time ago. Undoubtedly, you've been apprised about how I've been paying the price for it since."

I grimace. "So what are you saying? That I'm not ready to pay my own price?"

"That's an assumption I can't—and won't—make for you."

"Where does that leave us?"

He lifts a solid grip to my shoulder, even as both of his slump. "I escaped hell once and paid the dearest toll, short of death, for it." His next sigh is full of resignation. "I regret nothing, of course. My family is my whole world. But if you think my part in the Valari dynasty is the bargaining chip you need, you've knocked on the wrong door, boys."

Jesse rubs an impatient palm along the top of his right

wheel. "Okay, so that means exactly what?"

Gio steps to an arched window with a deep ledge that supports a small stack of books on one side. As he rests a hip into his makeshift reading nook, weariness seems to settle over him. In direct proportion, my anxiety climbs.

"It means that in terms of hellbound strings getting pulled, you're hitching your wagon to a nonexistent star."

Forget about the climbing dread. I've already reached the peak, and it turns out it's a roaring volcano.

"Mr. Valari, the other half of my soul is a hostage in hell," I utter with the force of a desperate man. "So if you think I'm after a *star*, check your cosmic compass."

He winces. "I…well, I assumed…you have access to a number of resources now. If not your father himself—"

"No," I bite out. "Zeus is about as reliable as a mall phone repair guy."

Gio's salt-and-pepper brows jump up. "But he knows, yes?"

"Wouldn't matter if he did. According to Hades's ledger, Kara is his subject, not Zeus's. Pressing the issue would mean certain catastrophe for the mortal realm."

Clearly, my elaboration isn't necessary. Gio's face is back to contorting as tightly as mine. "What about the woman who helped raise you? The Olympian guardswoman? The one who was even spying on *us* for a while."

"Regina." I blurt it before thinking. "How'd you know?"

"I didn't," he admits. "Not for a little while, at least. I put it together eventually, and by the time I confronted her about it, I think she already counted me as an ally." A corner of his mouth tilts up. "Never mind her ultimate intentions. With three kids so active all the time, it was comforting to have her around, helping out however she did. I was truly disheartened when Veronica let her go." He shakes his head, refocusing on me once more. "So where is she now? She can't have returned to Olympus so soon."

"Eleven years isn't exactly soon," I say.

He shrugs. "Time is a unique construct for every realm."

"Regardless, Olympus isn't where we need to go right now," I volley. "So Regina isn't my hitching star either."

"All right, then." He stands once more, pulls out a journal from the chaos across his desk, and scribbles in it with stubborn deliberation. Across his hunched back, I trade another assessing look with Jesse. Are we being dismissed, or will Gio give us more? Anything that will bring us closer to finding Kara?

I'm ready to beg, when Gio finally straightens. In the same motion, he tears the page free from his journal. With sharper resolve, he thrusts the sheet at me.

"Take it before I convince myself how crazy this idea really is."

I snatch the paper before he can consider second thoughts. On it, there's an address not far from here. Five or six miles, straight up Sunset.

"Crazy idea how? What do you want me to do with—"

"Meet me there in an hour," he grates. "You'll have to change first. This isn't a stroll through the farmer's market. This is a journey into hell. You should dress for it. Leave any valuables behind. If we're successful, you won't need anything but your wit…and a strong stomach. No doubt the gifts you've inherited from your father might come in handy as well."

Before I can fully process the importance of the words, Jesse rolls forward. "Ten-four," he says. "He can leave it all with me."

"No way," I say. "You're coming with us."

"Come on, man." With his elbows on his armrests, Jesse spreads out both palms. "I'm not going to do you any good on the flip side. For all we know, every concept of *our* viable physics are wrong there."

As if nature wants to prove the point already, I can't seem to get in a full breath. My lungs hurt. My heartbeat is a worse pang. "God*dammi*t, North."

"I'm right and you know it. Besides, you need a wingman up top, yeah?"

"Right," I mutter. "Yeah."

No sooner do I finish processing the bad news than Gio is on the move again, rushing out of the room. By the time Jesse and I get to the bungalow's hallway, Kara's grandfather is already in the bedroom, flinging clothes out of the closet like a teenager on a hunt for perfect date attire.

Only this excursion sure won't be date night. I have no idea what it *will* be, but in the end, the reward outweighs the peril. Any of it. All of it.

Whatever it takes to have the woman of my heart back in my excruciatingly empty arms.

CHAPTER 5

MAXIMUS

I'M PARKED DOWN THE street from the address Gio gave me on Sunset, which in theory puts me one step closer to Kara. But right now, I'm doubting everything about the quest I initiated in the first place.

By Kara's own admission, during one of the most memorable moments I've shared with her, Gio is the closest person in the world to her. But at this point, we're no longer talking about anything involving *this* world. And this latest development has me questioning not just Gio's ability to help us, but the possibility of his senility.

The faded red lettering plastered on the iconic building facing us couldn't be more appropriate—or mocking. Of course, Crossroads of the World, the faded and nearly forgotten Hollywood landmark, would be a perfectly themed spot for a dive into Dis if it weren't such a ridiculous notion.

"This has got to be a joke."

"I don't think it is, man." Jesse nudges the straw of his fast food drink toward the facade of the church next door. Its ornate arched window is flanked by narrow stone alcoves that house equally slender statues. Those stone representatives don't look like tea companions for Hades. That quickly, Gio's meeting point makes a lot more sense, even if it's doubling my anxiety. Suddenly a stroll around an abandoned outdoor mall sounds a lot better than a trip to church on a Sunday night.

"Why is this idea already giving me hives?"

"Huh?" Jesse swings his stare around.

I punch the button to drop the truck's back gate. "You know what places like this do to me."

"Because of ancient history?" he shouts as I pull his wheelchair out.

"It wasn't that long ago."

"It was eleventh grade youth group, as I recall."

I set up the chair next to his open passenger side door. "And you weren't the one being called Satan's freakboy after saving the pastor's kid from being crushed by the altar cross."

My mumble is mostly swallowed by the roar of passing traffic as Jesse descends into his chair, and maybe that's for the better. If I've learned anything over the last ten days, it's that I'm a different person than I ever thought I was, including the warped perceptions handed down by close-minded individuals. Maybe it's time to put that recognition to a solid test.

The reflection, though brief, is a nugget of well-timed fortification as I wheel Jesse across the street. We're nearly to the entrance when I hear a definitive creak from the church's wide doorway. There, a figure appears. He's dressed nearly identically to me, in a long-sleeved hiking shirt, khaki cargos, and thick-soled boots. But unlike me, he's pressing one hand to a leather messenger bag that rests against his left side. The bag isn't big but bulges enough that I give it more than a passing glance.

"Told you he was serious," Jesse drawls as we navigate the tight turn onto the wheelchair ramp.

"Guess so," I bite back, more curious than ever about why we're here. In a few seconds, I'll get the information I need from the source who'll be able to explain it best.

The man who holds the door open as Jesse and I pass through.

Inside, the air is quiet and cool. It smells like old wood, floor wax, and candle smoke. We're in the main sanctuary, where more tall archways face each other from the sides and lead our gazes up to numerous stained-glass windows and the Renaissance-inspired ceiling. At the end, seemingly miles away, a larger archway frames a circular nave housing a polished marble altar.

"Yep. Hives," I mutter. "What are we doing here?"

And why right now?

Keeping that part to myself doesn't negate its relevance. It's early on a Sunday night, and we're in a place that was clearly built for a thousand. How the Valari elder pulled enough strings to totally empty the place... Does "knowing a guy who knows a guy" apply when said "guy" is the patriarch of a half-demon dynasty?

I decide it's better not to know, but that doesn't stop me from subjecting Gio to my fresh scrutiny as he walks up to us. His jaw is firm, his demeanor resolute.

"I'm afraid you can't take this particular journey alone, Maximus. And despite everything, I've decided that I'm willing to take you—"

"But?" I interject with the word he was getting to anyway.

"But I'm not the only ticket you need to get there. Consider the magnitude of what you're asking. What you're ordering the universe to do for you. To bend. To even crack. To let you walk through the boundaries of reality."

He's still so serene, I anticipate angels to swirl around his head at any second. Good thing, since I'm actually starting to follow where he's going with this.

"So that's how this works? Like a doorway we've got to crack? Using a code or something?"

The man inhales with determination. "As best as I can figure, yes."

A headache forms behind my knitted brows. "You mean you don't kn— *Ouch!*"

I'm the victim of a Jesse wheel butt, backed by the pound of his hard glare. "Dude, you need to open that mental hymnal and borrow a few lines about calming your soul."

"What does my soul have to do with any of this?"

"Your soul has *everything* to do with this."

Gio's claim, spoken with the reverence of a vow, does more than jerk my head back up and around. It jabs at something inside me. A new…awareness? Like a sunbeam through one of the stained-glass windows overhead, my senses sharpen in a new light. A special truth. A strand of the same bravery that answers me from Gio Valari's wise eyes.

"I escaped from hell once, Maximus. That doesn't mean I thought to drop breadcrumbs along the way or that they presented me with the key to the city when I was voted Fugitive of the Year." He lifts a small but knowing smile. "So I really can't just wave a cursed wand or toss some magic stones and instantly deposit myself there once more."

"But you have some way, right?" I insist. "At least one?"

Granted, the man likely hasn't spent the last fifty years pondering how to return to his worst nightmare, but to think he hasn't given the subject *any* consideration before now… I can't go there. I refuse to.

"Yeah," he finally utters. "I believe I do."

"Thank God." Since I've never meant it more, I throw a grateful glance toward the stately crucifix at the end of the aisle. "So what do we do now? How do we start?"

Gio pulls in another long inhalation. "Actually, by obeying your friend's advice. By finding as much serenity in your soul as you can."

Jesse chuckles. "Maybe you *do* need to keep me around."

I chuckle softly. "For *a lot* of reasons."

"Here." Gio gestures for me to step over to the stone pedestal at the rear of the sanctuary. As we approach the round font of holy water, he reaches into his bag and pulls out a strikingly familiar object. It's the aged glass vial from his cabinet of collectibles.

"I thought that looked important."

He grins. "It's from the collection of a seventeenth-century monk who also secretly dabbled in chemistry and physics. Unlike many at that time, he saw subjects as companions to spirituality, not opposing forces. He was so convinced about the relationship, he snuck into the baptistry at St. Peter's Basilica and rinsed seven of his vials in the waters there. Only four of them still exist." He holds up the glass container in one hand and a cork stopper in the other. "After today, perhaps only three."

So maybe he *has* given this a little thought.

I'm assured of that conclusion, and several more, as Gio pivots and extends the bottle and stopper to me.

"Best not to leave anything to chance now," he says.

"Damn good thinking," Jesse concurs, rolling up behind me. "God's magic elixir, gathered by a god."

"*Demi*god," I counter, though it takes my mind off arguing as Gio presses the bottle and stopper into my grip.

"Last time I checked, that still beats fugitive from hell," Gio rebuts.

Stepping up to the font and scooping the vial through the blessed water is like a swim across the shallow end. Quick, thoughtless, effortless—until the second I'm jamming the stopper into the vial. While doing so, I take a last look into the shallow waters in the font. Back at my reflection—

Which *isn't* my reflection at all. The visage belongs to someone else. The one soul who won't leave my mind, my memory, or my heart.

"How can she—"

The shatter of glass resounds through the church. Vaguely, I recognize Gio's shouted curse, as well.

"Kane!"

And now Jesse's too, rasped as if we're in the middle of an actual mass. But he's wrong. It's better than that. A much bigger miracle. Gio yanks at my arm as an agitated priest barges in from a side entrance. I don't care if he's called out the national guard and a handful of SWAT teams. I'm not moving from where I stand. And I'm *not* taking my hand out of this water. Not until I reach deep enough to touch her.

"Kara." I splash in again, desperately reaching for her face. My fingers stretch, begging for the silk of her hair between them. The fullness of her cheek. The strength of her neck. She looks cold. Defeated. Alone. If I can only touch her for one moment. Just one…tiny…moment…

"Liar!" the priest yells at Gio. "You said you wouldn't touch anything!"

I lift my head and growl hard. It makes him hesitate. The poor padre. I hate doing this to him, but not as fully as I need to keep reaching for the face in the water. The woman of my obsession. The reason for my breath. The love of my existence.

"Kara. Baby, I'm right here…"

But her stolid expression tells me she doesn't hear me. She doesn't feel me. I hate this. *I hate this.*

Gio links his elbow through mine and leans back for leverage. "Come on! We have to go now!"

"Hold up," Jesse says. "We can't leave without the water, right?"

"Too late for that." Gio's tone is grim and defeated. "The vial's destroyed."

I let that much through the background haze of my head as I sift my fingers back into the water, desperately trying to reach the woman who's already vanished in that impossible liquid shell. Jesse's right, but so is Gio. The water *is* the most important thing, to the point that I'm not leaving until we get what we need. But the vial... The remains of Gio's precious container are no more than scattered shards on the church's art deco floors.

"Here." Jesse sounds just as resolute as before. "It's only been blessed by the girl at the order-out window, but it's better than nothing."

Gio flashes a glance up at the fast-approaching priest. "Very well. But we must hurry."

The last thing I want to do is look on as Jesse's plastic fast food cup invades the watery heaven where I've found my love again. But as I learn the next moment, it has to be an illusion for my senses alone. A chimera that's been placed there, perhaps by Hades himself, to waylay me from the quest at hand. Ignorant of the vision I've just had, Gio plunges the cup into the font until the only face I see is the superhero embossed on the side of it. Then the certainty sets in as real.

She's gone.

And once more, I come to grips with the brutal truth at the center of my existence.

There really are no shortcuts to hell. We're figuring out the path, one agonizing step at a time.

The sooner I accept it, the sooner we'll be able to get there. I'm committed to the purpose now and tell Gio by way of my determined stare as I turn around. Barely taking a second to accept the full cup from him and then the snap-on lid from Jesse, I set my jaw, steady my breath, and shoot the full force of my respect into the equally determined man before me.

"Where's the yellow brick road taking us now, Gramps?"

*✳

Since Gio's in the front row with me, Jesse issues his verdict about our new destination from the truck's back seat.

"This is making a hell of a lot more sense."

"Underworld humor intended, Professor?" I ask.

I don't give him a chance to jibe back as I hop out, approach the thin chain and lock binding the cemetery's filigreed black gates, and snap them with an efficient twist.

"Great security system," my friend says after we've driven in. "And there's the humor for the night."

Ignoring our banter, Gio leans forward and peruses the expanse of green lawn dotted with pristinely kept headstones. "Stop here for a second."

I slow the truck next to the long oval median just beyond Hollywood Forever's entrance area and join him in peering around. The silky rays of early autumn moonlight are like atmospheric symbolism, coating everything around us in silvery reverence: a reminder that Hollywood's history has now reached triple digits and has its fair measure of diplomats, dissidents, and debutantes to honor.

"I came to one of the summer cinema showings here once," Jesse says wistfully. "But that was a date with a dancer who really believed in the back row necking tradition, so I never got a chance to look around. Did you know Fay Wray is buried here? And Johnny Ramone?"

"And the wildest random statement of the night goes to the honorable Professor North," I mutter, glad when Jesse takes the hint from my taut tone and lets the banter die there.

Right now, I'm not so mired in the dark about Valari's intentions, only the finer details of the plan. That thought smacks the reality of this endeavor to the forefront of my mind.

I'm seriously about to do this. Take a nosedive into hell. If that's even possible...

I almost give in to a shudder but am saved by the only image with enough force to crowd everything else away.

My Kara. I think back to the church and seeing the vision of her shimmering and amazing and *alive*. A demon hidden in waters reserved for angels. Baptizing me into new hope and fresh courage when I'd needed it the most.

I draw greedily from that fortitude now. Even impatiently. A surge of restlessness pushes new words to my lips.

"All right. So which way should I head?"

"I think...over to the left," Gio says. "I remember the lake when I was stumbling around..."

"Stumbling?" Jesse reiterates. "Were you here on a date with a dancer too?"

"I was here because this is where hell spat me back out."

"Huh." Jesse settles back as the lake comes into view. "I'll remember that one the next time I need a conversation killer."

Chitchat isn't the only thing dying off at the moment. The bravado I had in such spades starts to curdle in my gut, especially as we travel deeper into the cemetery. Never mind that this place is a Tinseltown historian's dream. Graves are graves in the dark. As the moon rises higher, fingering the trees with beams resembling old-time movie projections, I'm vividly reminded that Gio and I haven't come here to casually drop a wreath on Judy Garland's crypt.

I jab my chin back toward my best friend. "You sure you're good from here?"

"If you ask me one more time, I'll sneak into your place and rearrange your books according to the Sinhalese alphabet." Via the rearview, he answers my glower with an I'll-do-it-and-you-know-it grin. "Seriously. I'm good. You two kids just go and have fun storming the gates of hell."

"Here," Gio calls out, shooting his finger up. "This is definitely it."

I stop the truck, wishing his enthusiasm for the words matched his certainty. But would I trust a guy who looked downright gleeful about all this?

He cants a somber stare back toward me. "You ready?"

I drag in a long breath. "As I'll ever be."

My words are as much the polar opposite of a rah-rah as his were, but he nods in understanding.

"Good enough," he says. "Let's go."

After inserting the manual controls for the truck and then tightening them for Jesse's preferences, I quickly carry him around to the driver's seat. "Everything feel okay?"

He pumps the brakes, revs the engine, and then jabs a thumb up. "Right as rain. I'll let HR at Alameda know you caught the plague and have to quarantine."

I shrug. "That excuse works for half my seniors..."

"Yeah, but only half." He winks, then sobers his expression. "But seriously, don't make me come in there after you. No sightseeing, man. Get Kara and get back home. I already don't have to tell you that the excuse will work for Alameda but not Reg. After a couple of days, she'll be pounding on your door—and then mine. You already owe me copious amounts of alcohol for braving her fire and brimstone about not getting an invite to this shindig."

"It is what it is, all right? I still don't know how many ties she still has with Olympus, and the tighter we keep this box right now, the better. Even Regina will understand that." I pause, clearing my throat. "Eventually." A grunt escapes as I retie my boot. "Who knows? Maybe a face-off with Hades *won't* be the most exciting event of my holiday season."

At some point, he's taken his long rubber sticky hand toy back out. It *thwacks* the side of my face before he mutters, "Just get your ass—and your woman—back here in one piece, please."

As I peel the sticky hand away, a chuckle fights its way to my lips. "Only because you asked nicely..."

It fades away as soon as I look across the hood to observe Gio's departure. I expected him to make his way to the sizable lake on the other side of the road or to the large mausoleum about twenty feet ahead. Instead, he's descending the concrete steps toward the memorial down the nearby slope. After a last wave to Jesse and then a careful grab of the superhero holy water, I follow.

At the bottom of the steps, a wide patio leads to the edge of a long reflecting pool. As soon as I pick out the name on the memorial at the far end, I twist my lips.

"Douglas Fairbanks?"

"Senior *and* Junior," the Valari elder replies.

"Zorro, Robin Hood, and Gunga Din? Those Fairbanks?"

"Impressive." He reaches to take the fast food cup from me.

"Good action and adventure stories are the same in any century," I say.

"Keep that one in mind, son."

"I will. But every story's better if it all makes sense." I point to the extensive length of the reflecting pool. "Are you sure we're in the right place?"

"Following the logic that the way out is also the way back in, yes."

Though it's the answer I half expected, it's far from reassurance. If anything, the enormity of this whole undertaking, beginning here in the actual world of under*takers*, sets off warring alarm clocks through my senses.

Some beg me for more time. So many others proclaim that time has long since run out. Just one glance at Gio, and I know he's dealing with the same unnerving chaos. As he pulls the plastic lid off the cup, his fingers tremble. But he continues to move, wasting no time to lean over this end of the pool. Then farther. Just when I think I'll have to yank him back from accidentally tumbling into the murky thing, which is two feet deep at most, he mutters something.

"Perhaps even these things, one day, will be pleasing to remember."

I'm so taken aback, I pause. "Funny time to be quoting Virgil…"

"It's what I said when I was close," he rebuts.

"To what?"

"To death. What I thought would be mine, at least."

Something about the familiar words of the poet inspire the peace I need in this moment. Because I know, whether I'm going to live another three seconds or three centuries, that my parting thoughts from this world will remain the same. With one person's name on my lips.

"Kara."

I whisper it at the same moment Gio empties the water from the cup into the reflecting pool.

I repeat it as those waters start to pulse with light and bubble with energy. And now, remarkably, begin to glow with depths that look endless…boundless…

Merciless.

Waters into which Gio takes a full header. And just as quickly, disappears.

"Holy sh…"

The rasp extends, continuing at full force on my lips, as the waters close over him at once, almost like a canvas curtain on a stage.

Swiftly it turns into another kind of canvas. A stretched one, like an artist would use on a wooden frame. The surface takes on myriad new colors, textures, light, and beauty. Mediums that, again, coalesce into one perfect portrait. One extraordinary face.

"Thank you." I wrap the words in the same soul-deep gratitude that blanketed me in the church. I repeat it as the features of my beautiful angel get sharper, more intense.

My breath snags in my throat. Kara looks so similar to how she appeared in the font back at the church. So gorgeous and naked and wet. Her lush, inky tresses trail over her shoulders, parting alongside her high, firm breasts. And this time, she's silently calling out for someone.

One heartbeat...

Two...

Three...

But then the organ stops altogether, freezing deep inside me. It's not from the fact that I see my name so vividly on her lips. It's not even that I can also see the wobble of her chin, the fear in her eyes, and the defeat in her posture.

Her eyes are frighteningly wide. She's bewildered. Lost. Searching. And reaching...

For what?

Or maybe...for whom?

Her fingertips are so real but not real enough to breach the canvas of the illusion. Her palms meet the surface of the water, as if it's made of glass between us. The same glass silences her words, whatever she's trying to say to me.

As sure as my heartbeat swells through my chest and

echoes in my mind, I'm sure of her presence. That she sees me too. That I *am* what she's fighting to touch. My spirit throbs, pushing new power into the sinew of my muscles and marrow of my bones. My instincts swell, bound to her call. Hearing her prayers. Seeing the empty circle of her arms. Swearing I'm going to fill it.

"Kara!"

I fortify myself with one last gulp of evening air, never more scared or driven or determined than I've been in my life. But trusting in the shimmer of hope I glimpse in the eyes staring back at me. I take a step closer, the last step toward a fate unknown…calling on faith and the gods and the poetry that has always given me solace in dark times.

"*I come from the blessed height for which I yearn. Love called me here,*" I whisper.

Then I utter her name one more time, binding its magic to my heart and its strength to my soul, before I plunge forward. As my body breaks the water, my spirit declares one last vow to the fabric of the universe.

I'm going to find her.

No matter how dark this ocean, how vast this hell, or how many times I have to give up every breath in my body.

CHAPTER 6

Kara

I STARE INTO MY reflection too long. My eyes burn, and another wave of hopelessness cascades over me. Part of me wants to leave here against Hades's insistence and rush back to the familiarity of my bedroom, cold and miserable as that place is. Another part of me wonders if this could be the last indulgence I enjoy for the rest of eternity.

So I stay in the opulent bathing room even if I feel frozen in place, frightened to move. Frightened of everything...

The once still water of the soaking tub ripples, sending a soft swell against the lip, as if calling me toward it. But I still don't move, not before daring a nervous glance over my shoulder. Hades is gone, but I can't escape the eerie feeling that I'm not truly alone.

I exhale a shaky breath and force myself forward. A sheen of steam now hovers over the bath water. I can feel its heat curl against my palms.

So what if Hades wants to lure me here into some

blatant appreciation of the physical body that will only curse me for the rest of time? I release some tension in my shoulders, ready to resign myself to that curse, but am snapped back to the moment when the steam begins to whirl. I pull my hand back, consumed with wonder. Are the vapors somehow responsive to me or my closeness?

It forms a thicker mass until it doesn't look like steam at all but soft clouds. I squint as they shift and arrange into shapes that almost feel familiar.

Instinct tells me to step away, or run, but I'm too fascinated, which seems to be my weakness in hell. Despite knowing that, I can't seem to control my curiosity, which has become an odd piece of companionship. It's a sad highlight in my thoughts… Thoughts that reach always for my old life, for Maximus. I'm staring as intently into the steam now as I was the mirror, this time convinced I'm seeing something more. Particles twisting like tendrils of honey locks that, once upon a time, I'd tangled in moments of lust and abandon. Glimmers of the water cutting through like the icy-blue gaze of my beloved.

I slam my eyes shut and step away from the tempting illusion. Maximus is gone. That beautiful life I knew with him…is *gone*. Forever.

"Don't be afraid." A rich, arrogant laugh echoes off the walls.

I jump back and swing my gaze toward the door. An elegant feminine figure stands at the threshold. She looks like a designer's sketch, draped in tight black leathery fabrics. Her sharp shoulders and bony hips make a waif-like silhouette as she walks toward me like a feline. If I weren't in hell, I'd peg her for a runway model. That, and her entire face and head is wrapped in black muslin, obscuring her finer features. All I can make out are her wide, dark eyes that can't seem anything but enormous and foreboding behind the scarf.

I'm so busy sizing her up, I forget to retreat until it's too late. Now we're face-to-face. A subtle shift in the muslin hints at her smile. Everything else about her posture is regal and assured.

I realize I'm holding my breath. I exhale only to suck in another one.

"I told you, Kara, no need to be afraid," she murmurs this time, though the laughter stays in her voice. Like all of this is so amusing. At least it is for one of us.

"Are you saying I shouldn't be afraid of you...or...?" I look over to the now calm waters of the tub.

"Either. Acceptance would be my advice. Fear only begets fear here."

I have no idea who she is or why she's come to see me, but through the whir of my thoughts I decide her advice is sound. No point cowering in fear at every turn. Easier said than done, of course, in a place so foreign and fearsome.

"Who are you?"

She makes a small sound of understanding. "Of course. You wouldn't recognize me this way."

Slowly she unwraps the covering, letting it collect in a dark swath around her neck. She's gaunt but strangely beautiful. Her short dark hair is slicked tight against her scalp. And her eyes are as deep and penetrating as I suspected they were behind the veil.

Do I recognize her? How could I? I have no friends here.

All I have…

"Are you—?"

"Yes, of course. I'm your grandmother."

I nod mutely, reconciling the creature in front of me with the few photos I've seen of her. In most of them, she's arm in arm with my grandfather, playing the part she was sent to play. I always wondered at what point in their history he realized her betrayal. Were his smiles in those photos truly loving or a classic Hollywood facade designed to fool the cameras and all the onlookers on his highly publicized life?

But after one look at the woman—the incubus who gave my mother life—I can clearly see how she could bewitch my grandfather. Yet her beauty only spurs more questions.

"You look like me. I mean, you're…" I nip nervously at the inside of my lip.

She laughs again. "Are you trying to say I'm not a heinous ghastly beast?"

I can't fight the returning smile. "Well. Yes. Basically."

She glances over my shoulder briefly and winces before carefully winding the scarf back over her face, her humor fading. "Little side effect of my time on earth. Sometimes… Well, sometimes we just don't come back the same."

"That's not completely terrible." In fact, the circumstance gives me hope. Maybe I really can navigate hell without the face of a demon.

"Depends how you look at it." She sweeps her hand over her face, then gestures to the mirror behind me. "It's certainly nothing to celebrate. Not here anyway. You'll learn soon enough."

For a second, nothing's remarkable about our reflections. I'm the same as I was moments ago, but she isn't. I truly see that now. She's all sharp lines and waif elegance, but something's wrong. Her nails are grayed and jagged. Her skin is bruised with rot. Her clothing, sleek and sensual, looks ridiculous on her sparse demon body.

I swallow hard and look back at her, meeting her eyes through the veil.

There's understanding there but also a shared misery. I'll have to hide too.

"Mirrors are the carriers of truth, Kara. The eye of a little god. Remember that," she murmurs quietly.

I nod, committing her sad wisdom to my mind. It leads me to another recognition. The mirror isn't the only truth bringer in the room. Something in her voice carries it too. I can feel it, for the first time since finding myself in this cold, sad place...the palpable energy of another. It's oddly invigorating. All I've been able to feel in Hades's presence is my own wild fear. It's been so overwhelming, wielding too strong a hold for me to access anything else. It's like Hades himself is an impenetrable wall, which poses its own problems for my purpose here.

Fresh worry lodges in my gut as conflict takes over my mind. I hunger for more advice from my grandmother, so many more answers to all my questions, but I dread what those answers will be. I'm tempted to wade in my ignorance the way I'll soon languish in these baths.

But how can I, with my grandmother inches away? What if she can help? Or at least be my guide, easing my way into this new world. Isn't that what an elder is for?

As I ponder all this, she crosses her arms—a motion that makes her look important and impatient at once. "You may call me Charlena. Familial names and endearments aren't quite the norm here, as you might imagine. Even if they were, we're hardly familiar."

"Of course," I manage.

Being forced to refer to Gramps by his given name was strange, but calling this woman any version of *grandmother* would be far weirder. Past that, I have no idea what attachments if any she might have to me. She's a demon, and I defied her ruler.

Still, she's here. That could mean anything, and I won't take for granted that it's for my benefit.

"What's brought you here?"

She sighs, looking me over. "Existence here affords us few delights, but I'll admit that seeing you is one of them. Time means little here, but I expected the wait to have you join us to feel longer."

I startle, though I fight to hide the violence of my jolt. "Am I going with you? I—I mean now?"

Or even eventually? And shouldn't that idea make me happier, not spike me with worse dread? I don't even know how to ask what the rest of this existence will look or be like. It's the question I've likely been avoiding the most, for what feels like good reason. I'm cold with fear. Shivering with trepidation.

She shakes her head. "No, not now. He's…" She glances over her shoulder briefly, then back to me. "The fact that he's given me any time with you surprises me, to be honest. I expected him to want you all to himself, in consideration of the time constraints. But I also underestimate his laziness. He's given the task of touring you around to me."

I widen my eyes. "He has?"

My trembling abates, at least a little. I can't know what that means, or if suddenly I should feel differently about an introduction to this awful place now that it's being given to me by my demon grandmother.

Charlena makes a small humming sound. "He scares you, doesn't he?"

I expel a heavy sigh, filled with relief that she might empathize.

"Of course. He's…the devil."

She laughs softly. "Right. He'll never get what he wants from you if you're paralyzed with fear, though. And it seems to me, you should figure out a way to give him what he wants."

I nod in agreement, even if I disagree in my ice-stricken bones. I don't want Hades in my head, but I'm more worried about the horrible, and eternal, alternatives to that invasion.

"Smart girl," she says. Her gaze flickers to the mirror, then the tub. "Take your soak and get some rest. You'll need it. You'll end up looking like the rest of them if you never sleep. I'll find you afterward."

I nod, cherishing the advice now only because it comes from her. "Thank you."

She doesn't move, as if the gratitude strikes her like an insult. Perhaps here it does. A moment later, the woman dips her head in a silent goodbye and slinks away as gracefully as she arrived.

Watching her leave fills me with mixed emotions. I decide to take Hades's advice and wash away what ails me—the turbulence of my time here and all the uncertainty I can't shake. Silently, I undress and lower myself into the tub, grateful for the warm embrace of the water. I sigh and let the heat work its magic on me. With my eyes closed, I can almost imagine I'm not here. That I'm home and safe. That this is all a dream. A terrible nightmare that I'll forget with time…

A long time passes that way. The peaceful reprieve is everything that was promised. Relaxed and ready for sleep, I open my eyes and lift myself to the edge of the tub, lazily gazing upon myself in the mirror before me. It isn't vanity that holds my attention there. I find myself searching for Charlena in what I see. And wondering if her half beauty is a blessing or a curse, same as mine.

In the end, why does it matter?

The mirror carries truth, she said—and at once, I know why. Ultimately, her beauty is an elaborate illusion. A grand lie. But if her demon appearance is her true self, what does that say about her heart? Her soul? Can she love? Or feel anything important at all?

My eyes droop with sleepiness. The bath should be cooling, but another unexpected ripple in the water brings a wave of heat with it. Thick steam rises off the water, swirling up and collecting on the expansive mirror next to the tub. I rise to my knees and wipe at the condensation. A childish instinct, maybe. But I'm uncertain because the water seems to be acting on its own. But why?

I'm not given a moment to fathom that answer. Whorls of steam billow up between the wide mirror and me, seducing me with shapes and movements once more. I'm like a little girl staring at the clouds, trying to make sense of them, except this is more than whimsical imagining. Quickly, it becomes alarming. I push back a little, even admitting I'm afraid. Is the vapor going to solidify? If so, into what? Or whom?

I keep staring intently—and am finally rewarded by an answer. A feeling that starts in my soul and, like the fragrant steam, puffs to life in every corner of my mind. And it makes me smile.

I'm no longer looking for signs of Charlena in my visage. I'm looking for a sign…

I'm looking for Maximus…

And the vapors don't let me down. His face appears through the steam. Clear enough to make out but distorted, like he's underwater. I rise up quickly and press my palms to the mirror. The water sloshes around me.

His lips move, but I hear nothing.

"Maximus!"

My smile dies. Once more, my desperation sets in. It

echoes off the walls. All my panic. I slam my palms against the mirror once more, the only answer I can muster.

CHAPTER 7

MAXIMUS

C AUTIOUSLY, I OPEN MY EYES.

With even greater care, I roll my head to the side. No way do I trust my neck to hold it up if I lift it. I feel like a cat who jumped in a swimming pool, only to learn the water was actually fire. I'm not ruling out the possibility. Just a month ago, I was teaching plots like time travel, talking forests, and themed hell circles as fiction. None of it compares to my strange truth these days.

Illustrated clearly by this moment.

I jerk back to awareness when my right ear is inundated by slopping noises. After a couple of seconds, I realize it's the mud bath I've landed in.

I have no idea where I'm at—or if this nothingness qualifies as anywhere at all. I stand and try to reset my bearings, but nothing registers as familiar anymore. It's quiet to the point of *dis*quieting, and my stare can barely penetrate the thick fog. When it finally does pierce the damp view, I don't make out much except tall, leafless trees that seem to be returning my intent stare. I breathe deep but am penalized for it with nostrils full of sulfur. I grimace and emit a few favorite cuss words but barely to the point of being audible.

A groan off to my left sounds like a weak but clear response to my eruption. I rise and walk that way, my bootsteps making prominent *schlop*s through the mud while I hope—and even pray a little—that the source of the sound is Gio and not some stranger or strange *thing* for which I'm unprepared.

Relief doesn't come a second too soon. Gio's covered in more mud than me. Despite the groan that brought me over, he seems mostly unharmed—except for a dark scrape up the left side of his face. As soon as I see it, I grimace.

"That bad?" He gingerly fingers his wound. "Ah, it's just a scrape but a fair reminder of why I never tried out for baseball."

I extend a hand, ready to help him stand. "Some guys were meant to be baseball stars. And some were given the gift of golden words."

As I pull him all the way up, he actually chuckles for a few seconds.

"You're being kind, but you don't have to be."

"It's the truth," I say. "I read your screenplays one afternoon. The trophies in your cabinet are well earned."

If the compliment has sunk in, he has a strange way of showing it. "You read *all* of them? In *one* afternoon?"

I flash a lopsided smirk. "I was on a mission."

"To stuff a load of Hollywood schmaltz into your head?"

"To learn as much as I could about Kara. Which meant learning about the people she loves too."

A good half of his tension fades. "Good answer." But the stiffness quickly returns, back up his spine and across his shoulders while he opens his crossbody bag and efficiently checks the contents. Then he cocks his head toward the mist that's doubling as a sky. "So if my estimations are right, we've officially reached the Vestibule of Hell."

"Which apparently…is a swamp. And that's a gigantic compliment." As we've been sinking slowly into the putrid mud, many other designations have definitely come to mind.

"*I found myself in dark woods, the right road lost.*" He punctuates the Dante quote with a surprising smirk. The springs in his next steps are equally interesting. I don't remember noticing them before we left.

He strides past me as if an inner compass has just dinged in his head. Perhaps the same hypersenses drive him toward the moans and cries that cut through the fog and trees. It's a sound for which I have no accurate earthly comparison, each scream a unique wraith on the merits of its agony alone.

And it's merciless.

Endless.

A din of despair that invades my ears without mercy—and without stopping.

As the fog dissipates, the wails worsen. And now I'm trailing a good ten to fifteen feet behind Gio, pushing through the roars and sobs and screams as if they're a howling wind. The metaphor isn't far off, since my eyes are watering, my hair is whipping behind me, and my face stings from brutal chapping.

How has anyone ever survived this?

The answer is dauntingly clear.

By the time someone tromps this way, they're not usually concerned about survival.

By the time we reach the edge of the forest, I'm gazing at Gio Valari with new respect. All those years of hiding out in the granny pad behind the fancy villa, when everyone thought he was filling his time with random writing projects and old movies, the man had already earned stripes like none other. I want to tell him he deserves another gold statue for his impressive performance as a ditzy old man—but as we approach the far riverbank, I suspect the decibel levels will climb. We're in the chat-free zone now.

Luckily, that doesn't preclude conversations with myself as I follow him into a dip between two steep slopes. The valley is freezing in these dark shadows, temporarily distracting me from our tenacious trudge—until I'm stopped where I stand by a slam of blazing insight.

I lift my stare to Gio, who has thankfully waited up for me ahead. Even so, I suddenly understand all the reasonings for his incessant rushing.

The second I emerge from the tiny valley, onto the marsh that leads up to the shores of the river ahead, every tormented scream from the banks coalesces into a chorus of immutable misery. They join together to form just one line of shrieking sorrow.

"All hope abandon, ye who enter here!"

The chant is such an invasion, I swear I can taste it as well as hear it. I sway in place, fighting the onslaught. Gio isn't so lucky. He's knocked to the ground, doubled over as if kidney-punched in a bar fight.

At once, I sprint to his side. "You okay?"

He nods while finding his way back to his feet. "Nothing I wasn't prepared for."

Just like my moments back in the cemetery, I'm assured and unnerved at once. But maybe it's a teaching moment too. Like him, I order every instinct in my being back to high alert—and command my brain to be ready for anything.

I'm able to accomplish that task as the screaming souls back off, perhaps convinced that their message has been delivered. Or perhaps by an edict from the boatsman waiting on the shore up ahead.

He's a nameless gondolier. Except every step I take toward him, matched to the rising banging of my heartbeat, confirms that he's not nameless at all.

If this place is anything like the hell I've already come to know on the page, I'm about to come face-to-face with Charon.

As Gio and I approach the shore, my curiosity has moved in to throb along with my nerves and awe. I've imagined this moment in my mind a thousand times or more. Now I'm truly living it. Taking in the captain's eyes of fire and haggard beard, as long and red as an ancient Scottish laird's. The ginger lengths on his head are interspersed with long braids fashioned around sets of teeth that chomp at empty air and eyeballs that dart around with vacant purpose. He's wearing nothing but a low-slung kilt, its pattern made up of colors to match the sludge at our feet. Every inch of the hem is tattered beyond repair.

"That's him, isn't it? Charon?" I say it barely above a whisper, too scared I'm right.

Gio pushes me along with nervous energy. "Yes, that's him. Now hurry, son."

By the time we get to the slick waterside, the infamous boatman is clearing the path, beating back the souls clawing through the mud with the flat of his oar.

"Don't look at them," Charon dictates.

I wince, disturbed equally by the desperate beings reaching for us and his violence toward them. "Why not?"

"Because they know you're not like the rest. They can smell it on you."

Once that thought reaches full fruition in my mind, the crowd of futile souls and doomed angels presses in like I'm a cup of tasty Darjeeling, this time without the burly boatsman to beat them off. I slough them off my back and legs, but Gio's begun a strident string of nonstop Italian. There's enough of the filthier words for me to pick out what he's getting at, but his panic isn't what spikes mine all over again.

"Don't hurt them!" I bellow at the incensed ginger who's barreling back toward us, his oar raised again. But my appeal is unnecessary. The moaning wretches skitter away, leaving Gio and me alone in the middle of Charon's brutish assessment.

"Well, well, well," he drawls in his smoky semi-brogue. "Woe to *you* wicked spirits."

"We're not here for trouble," Gio says breathlessly. "Just passage across the river."

Charon thrusts down, giving his oar enough footing in the ground so he can lean on it. "Which I should grant to you two reprobates because…why?"

"We've got these."

Gio steps up and extends his palm. In its center is not only the coin from the velvet box in his office, but another form of payment: an obolus in amazing condition. I have no idea where he got the ancient Greek silver in the hour between his place and the church, but I'm damn glad he pulled the necessary strings.

Charon snatches up the coins and quickly bites into them with pointy teeth, testing their authenticity.

"This is an agreeable start," he grouses, as if meaning just the opposite.

Gio huffs. "A *start*? That obolus is worth thousands!"

"On earth maybe." He holds up the coins, one in each hand, and they twinkle in the weak light from the dock lamp. "Two coins for two souls is usually a fair deal. But I can see as plainly as these coffin rockers that neither of you are average souls."

"We're asking for simple passage, not special treatment," Gio argues. "The task for you is no greater. The journey no longer."

Charon answers with a snide chuckle, his eyes fixed on the obolus now shimmering in his palm.

"A devious mortal should have a better mind about these things. Taking bribes from deserters isn't exactly what I'm paid to do."

Gio's expression turns weary. I cut him off before he persists with his persuasion.

"If the coins are of no value to you, then give them back. We'll find another way."

Charon tears his gaze away from the coins, only to clutch them tightly in his palm. "I said no such thing. And mind you, there *is* no other way."

I shrug, confident Charon's already received all the payment he needs. His posturing is just wasting our time.

"Maybe there isn't," I say, not backing off from his scrutiny. "But maybe there is. Have you ever had anyone down here actually exploring the matter?"

The boatsman flares his nostrils and lunges a few inches at me. Gio steps to the middle of the fray, slamming his hands to our chests.

"Here, now!" he shouts. "We could stand here arguing about all of this a little longer, or you could accept this generous payment and we could all be on our way."

"All right, then," Charon snarls, already knowing he's been outsmarted. At least for now. "All aboard with you miscreants," he barks. "The sooner I'm done with your sickening swaggers on my river, the better."

As we hustle toward the gangway, Gio stabs me with a new look over his shoulder. This time, the injection spreads warmth through my chest while I give myself an inner high-five. We're really doing this now.

Just as Charon hoists the vessel's sails—one big, one small—a warm wind flows down the river, filling them both. Despite that, the voyage feels slow. Just when the opposite shore feels close, it seems to scoot back by matching increments.

What is going on?

I don't dwell on the frustration. I can't. It's wasted effort, and that's the last thing I want or need right now. I walk to the boat's rail and brace my elbows. Peering into the dark waters, my thoughts drift to Kara again. It feels like a million hours since Saturday night, when she and I were snuggling, watching the constellations from the Malibu sand.

What I wouldn't give to know those moments now. To feel the soft rain against my extremities. To breathe in the salty air. To gaze up at the stars in their spectacular peace, their serene sparkle...

Do you remember it all too, beautiful? Or has Hades already stolen all the memories he wants? Every thought of me from your incredible soul...

No.

I can't start thinking that way. I have to try harder. To believe stronger. To remember the spirit and spice and strength of the woman who has made me love her for all three. And to worship her for so much more.

I *have* to have faith...

I tighten my grip on the boat rail and urge the damn thing on in my mind. If only the peculiarities of this place lent me the ability to fly.

Then, suddenly, it feels like I'm doing just that. But

that's not my power at work. It's the stunning vision that the water gives to me again.

It's Kara. She's wrapped in red satin, and she's reaching out again. She's seeking me again. But her fingers are slicing empty air…

Until she's not.

When she seems to see me, she cries out with such joy and relief that my own eyes get watery. I don't waver my returning stare—wishing I could tell her, with the love that brims from my gaze and the faith that permeates my soul, that we're going to make it. But I already know if this is real, if *she's* real, she won't hear me. She's shaking her head, as if pleading for more words from me. And now she's so close, just below the water's surface. I can see her fingertips graze the waves next to the boat…

Can it be real? Can she be this close?

The need to touch her is too strong. I fold myself over the edge of the boat and reach out for her. She's so close… Just a little bit farther…

Just a little…bit…

Until I'm learning, the hard way, that gravity works in hell too. And I'm tumbling over, covered at once by the wild tides of the Acheron. And I don't even mind. Not if this is where Hades is keeping Kara.

CHAPTER 8

Kara

I'M DRAINED, PHYSICALLY AND EMOTIONALLY.

It's not what I'm supposed to be thinking right now. Hades granted me this respite in the tub room in his perceived spirit of generosity and benevolence. But I also have no doubt that he cleared Charlena's visitation for the exact same time, officially slashing my tranquility by half. My grandmother is gone now, and as odd as our conversation was, I already hope to see her again. Maybe that's exactly Hades's plan: I'll get more time with Charlena if he gets a chance to stroll through my mind.

And what about the unexpected visions of Maximus? Is Hades behind those too? Was I experiencing a real connection to him in those mystical vapors, or was it an elaborate stunt from my cunning host, orchestrated as yet another bargaining tool for my surrender? How do I know if Maximus is really in distress now?

It all felt so real. He felt so close. His heart, and all its desperate energy, was all mine too. For a few amazing but agonizing moments, we were together again.

Keeping my hands flat against the mirror, I wait through awful minutes. Then more. Even as the wall spigots shut off. Even as the water turns cold enough to make me tremble.

I'm on the verge of succumbing to more violent shivers, when a scratchy voice over my shoulder breaks apart my brood. "It is time to return to your chamber."

I gasp and protectively shield my breasts. The servant demon glares as if she couldn't care less. She's standing there with a towel, alarmingly close, looking like she wants to turn the thing into a sheet of steel wool.

"Th-Thank you." I barely rasp it out before snagging the cloth from her. I manage to get most of my body dry without showing her too much of it, though she sees enough that the envious green glow in her eyes intensifies.

A gut-deep grunt is her only response while she holds out a cut glass bottle of glowing silvery liquid. "The master wishes you to apply this before re-donning your apparel."

"What is it?"

"He wishes you to wear it," she repeats. "A gift perhaps."

She attempts a smile, but it comes across more like a grimace. She's likely comparing my luxurious robe to her tattered attire and loathing me for complaining about the request.

My quick thanks softens her a little, however. More importantly, it compels her to turn around and shuffle elsewhere in the chamber as I unstopper the bottle and take a tentative sniff of the glowing oil, which has nothing close to the scent I expected. This aroma is more like…a forest. Maybe a meadow. I pull back, stunned by the overtones of juniper, clover, and pine. Though it's markedly different than what I'd pick out at a perfume counter, it's not unpleasant. I pour a measure into my palm and test it over my skin. It lends a sheen that's nearly translucent, an effect so odd that my fascination nearly overrides my apprehension again.

An instinct tells me to savor this moment a little while longer, but I turn and reach for my robe, pulling it on once more.

As the maid leads me out of the pool room and hands me off to a pair of Hades's guards, I cross my hands over my chest and grip the satin lapels with white-knuckled ferocity. I manage to keep hold even while scurrying four steps for every one the stern soldiers take, one in front of me and one behind, as we head back out to the massive bridge across the awful canal.

I steel my nerves, knowing I won't be able to escape at least a glimpse of the tormented souls below, but a relieved breath rushes out when we get to the loggia. This time, the overpass is engulfed by dense fog. I'll be lucky to see my own two feet in front of me.

Which in this case is completely fine by me.

As soon as we step outside, though, a deep chill invades my bones. My still-damp hair doesn't help matters. I clench my teeth to keep them from chattering and force myself to keep moving on. I'm thankful that I can keep my head down without seeing terrifying faces before my eyes.

A conclusion issued too soon. Because suddenly I'm confronting the most horrifying sight of all. The thick mists along the left of the bridge mold themselves into new substance. Into an actual form.

The striations of muscle, power, and vigor that I recognize all too easily. Even the tears beneath my burst don't alter this new apparition of him. But is that what this is? He's so clear now. So *real*. Only the edges of his form are shrouded in mist now. But instantly, I wish for more of the cloud cover. Something to tell me this is just a fabrication of my wearied mind.

Once more, he appears underwater—though this time, he's frantically swimming. He's stretched out over the loggia, seemingly immersed.

"Maximus…"

I reach out, but he doesn't see me. He doesn't hear. His eyes close as if I've called to him in lust instead of alarm.

With his next exhalation, I can finally hear my name on his lips… For the first time, the watery depth of his voice hits my senses. But all the joy of the moment is lost as he drifts farther into the clouds.

He's drowning.

I know it. I feel it. My lungs ache and burn because of it.

I sob his name once more.

"Subject Valari! Move along. Now!"

I wrench my arms, battling the soldier who clutches my shoulders from behind. There's pain as I finally free myself, but the price is worth it. I'm able to charge ahead, spreading my arms and praying for the ability to somehow yank the center of my world out of his watery prison.

"Don't you dare give up. Maximus, please!" I cry.

Though the first escort doubles back and helps his partner with shoving me to my knees, I refuse to give up. With desperate abandon, I stretch out my fingers again. They brush a sworl of Maximus's wet hair. Another. A sob bursts from me. I can't hear it, but I feel it. All of it. The joy of finding him. The completion of touching him. The fullness of his love.

Then, as soon as it's all there…the desolation of his departure. Like the mists that formed my vision to begin with, he has evaporated once more. Vanished back into the realms of my fantasies.

"Nooo!"

It's my own keen on the air, but I barely acknowledge it past the gash in my soul. Oozing from that aperture is a toxic energy I've never encountered before. A psychic bomb has been set off in my spirit.

Though tears still gush from my eyes, I order them to pry open. I stare at my hands, still coated with Hades's silver-infused oil, planted but quivering against the bridge's icy stones. There's nothing I can do because my mind is still on a wild hunt for my sanity.

"Kara!"

I recognize the voice as Charlena's, infused with surprising alarm. Still reeling from my vision, I jerk my head all the way up. And then gasp in new terror.

My grandmother hasn't returned by herself. Hades

glides closer, his eyes dark and pinned on me.

"It's working, Kara," he suddenly exclaims. "It's working!"

"It's...what?"

"The silver." He reaches out, and all my nerve endings order me to flinch away, but I can't. I'm helpless and motionless as he runs the tip of a finger along the back of my left hand.

I blink, confused.

"It's increasing your psychic sensitivity and energy," he goes on, barely missing a beat, "but also lulling your conscious, so you're more receptive for this."

"More receptive for..."

I lurch away at last and curl both hands against my chest. What I really want to do is peel every inch of my skin away from my bones, now that his "gift" is revealed for its true purpose. But I also have to look at the whole picture. Was I able to see Maximus more clearly because of the silver infusion in my senses?

"You can feel it, can't you?" He scoots close again.

"I can feel...what?"

I demand it of him but shoot my desperate look to Charlena. She remains steadfast several paces behind him. Even through the dark veils, I pick up the ripples of her concern. It's as confusing as the mix of Hades's hopeful words with his eyes' predatory eagerness. I can't figure any of it out. Not fully. My heart pounds like a rabbit's, and my instincts scream a command to run, but there's a vast disconnect across the switchboard of my brain. I'm moving but not fast enough. I'm panicked but not wild enough. All I can do is whimper as he completes his approach and reaches for me again.

But not for either of my hands.

This time, he grips my head by both temples.

A scream, primal and petrified, rips up from my belly. I scramble backward, pumping my feet to hasten the escape. I only stop when the back of my head collides with a bridge balustrade and it looks like Hades won't be taking up pursuit. Every muscle and nerve ending of my body remains on high alert, trying to stay ready for him again.

Ready for...*that.*

What. *Was.* That?

I can't begin to work out an answer. My mind is still razed. My senses are still numb. Every inch of my skin is ready for another bath. This time, scalding hot. Or in acid. If only Hades's unblinking stare didn't feel like exactly the same thing.

"Kara, please. Don't fight this."

When he accents his mystified sigh by leaning toward me, I scrape up a few pebbles and hurl them. "Stay away from me!"

He pushes back on his heels with a chuckle. If I could magically manifest a dagger and hurl it through his chest... But talk about wasted dreams. Whoever Hades was before inheriting hell, he certainly didn't have a heart in that existence either.

"You're rattled. That's understandable."

"*Rattled?*" I normally use the word for missing an A on

an exam by one point. Or tumbling into a sanity-shattering crush on my literature professor. Not *this*.

"I mean, just look at you," he goes on. "All that rosy life in your cheeks. All that captivating breath on your lips."

What he fails to highlight is all the fury and loathing roiling through me. It's dark, humiliating…devastating. Up until now, I've clung to composure by threads thinner than strands of the corner cobwebs, all of them spun from a sanity called Maximus. Gone now. All of them, gone. I might as well be stripped naked.

Another thought, though silent now, that I yearn to snatch back. So much further back. But the corners of Hades's lips curl up as if his mental hooks are still invading my head. Detecting every thought, big and small, that I have.

"Kara. What is it? Talk to me. What has you so out of sorts?"

Besides the fact that you're driving me out of my mind?

Instead I frantically mutter, "I'm fine." I cross my arms again, gripping at the robe's collars like they're life ropes. Maybe they are. Nothing else feels balanced. Nothing feels like reality.

"Shall I take you back to your room now?" he asks with what sounds like forced politeness.

I don't even care. Nothing matters but finding silence to recover from his tap of chaos.

"Yes, please."

Hades dismisses Charlena and the guards, personally walking me back through the dismal palace. Thankfully, he keeps his distance and his silence during the journey.

Once inside my chamber again, I sweep a fast gaze around. It's not the opulence I'm seeing now. It's the chance to transform any or all of the decor into a possible weapon against my captor. I've never fantasized about murder with more desire in my life. I've never been more certain that I'd carry through on the temptation.

But how does one kill a god? Certainly not with an implement so simple as the hot poker glowing in the fireplace.

Again, as if I've accidentally blurted my thoughts and not known it, Hades tucks his hands into his front pockets and regards me with maddening calm. "*Kara*. Don't be foolish. I know you're upset, but you risk upsetting me, as well. You *must* know that is far worse." He widens his stance in response to my ongoing glower. "I am doing my best to ease you into this, but I would not test my patience if I were you." As he hauls in a deep breath, his posture relaxes but his scrutiny hardens. His stare is the texture of twin onyxes. "You should rest now. When I return and we try again—"

"Again?"

My recoil is met by matching degrees of his raised chin.

"*Again*, Kara. I have already told you: I *will* open you. Whether that happens next time, or a thousand times from next time, is solely up to you."

He means it. I know it. Beyond any doubt, down to every petrified nucleus in every horrified cell of my body, I know it.

For long moments, none of those cells are able to move. Not even to budge the small strands of my sanity. Not that Hades notices or cares. He's already gone, punctuating his decree with a decisive pivot and a direct exit out the chamber's arched portal.

Leaving me to dread the next moment he stalks back through it.

CHAPTER 9

MAXIMUS

M IND OVER MATTER.

It's cliché, but right now it's the backbone of my survival and the incentive that keeps my senses straight despite the shocking cold that bites at me from every angle. Somehow, I make it to the surface and gulp in a huge breath—only to be hauled right back under by the Acheron's ferocious waves.

Ferocious—and freezing.

How do I have any sensation left in my hands and feet? And how has this river not hardened into a glacier? My numb senses struggle to reconcile the anomaly. Disconnected words race each other in some semblance of order—*not… earth…logic…none*—but I push them aside. The *hows* aren't important right now. All that matters is the *why*.

The only *why* that matters is my fiery angel. My heaven in the depths of hell.

Where is she?

I refuse to surface this time. Not unless I do so with Kara in my arms. Giving up is out of the question. *Any* question. There has to be a reason behind these continuing visions. It's a message. Another force on the cosmic energy grid, bigger than anything Hades can throw at Kara and me, showing us the way to each other.

I have to keep believing it. I have to keep fighting for it.

But after I've fought the currents to conduct a full circle, my outstretched fingers still come back with nothing but filthy flotsam. I'm ready to join a furious bellow to the screams of Charon's masses. Maybe I even need to. Maybe that's what I need to blast back the dirt and gloom. Maybe this damned world needs to know exactly how serious I am about defeating it.

Just when I'm at the edge between raging contemplation and serious deliberation, I go numb again. Icicles form along my shoulders and in my beard. When they solidify around my legs, starting to weigh me down like concrete blocks, I resign myself to being a dead man. Unbelievably, that's not the worst element of this surreal moment.

My eyes slip closed, but even in that darkness, Kara's nowhere to be found. My last cry is my last breath, released into the water with her name on it.

The river drags me farther into its liquid mire. In seconds, I'm swept into a psychic bog too. A torment more terrifying than a nightmare, more acute than a triggered phobia. It's sharper than either. Clearer.

It's a…memory.

I know that now, without a shadow of a doubt. This

is from the corner of my brain I've just written off as irretrievable, perhaps because I'm dead now, or dying. It's a chunk of myself that I once demanded so desperately, I reduced my mother to tears.

Now I see why.

She wanted to keep me from this…

It's a glaringly bright afternoon, in which I'm tossing a ball of some sort with Regina. The orb is clear and filled with points of light that chase each other in different directions depending on how we throw it. It's warm to my touch, a contrast with the cool grass beneath my bare feet. There's a balmy wind that smells like the nearby fruit trees, and it blows my hair into my face, causing me to miss a throw from Reg. But since Mom is laughing about it, I don't care.

Mom…. Wow. She's so different. Her shiny curls are piled on top of her head, held there by jeweled pins and shimmering ribbons. Like me, she's wearing draped white clothing so bright that it hurts my eyes.

But what irks me is the quiet conflict in her eyes—eyes that never seem to gather up the joy of her smile…

They flare weirdly wide now, as I turn to retrieve the ball from beneath a bush with lush red flowers.

"Maximus, no! Forget the ball!"

I careen into an obstacle that wasn't there before. I stumble back, stunned to see it's a person. A woman. She's with several other females, all dressed in dramatically draped red gowns.

"Titans," Reg hisses under her breath.

I don't understand what that means. Only that these women aren't friends. I know that just by listening to the scary snags of

Mom's breaths. And now with certainty by the distinct shing of a broadsword being released from its scabbard.

Reg never pulls the weapon out for anything but cleaning.

Her hard expression and the taut clench of her muscles tells me she hasn't drawn it to clean it.

One of the women in red flashes her teeth like our cat after I've stepped on its tail. "You should be glad I'm in pleasant humor today, Miss Nikian. Put that thing away, or I'll ensure you're reduced to your true sentry origins and withered back into a skeleton."

I back away even more, forgetting the ball and wanting only to run to Mom or Reg. But the hissing lady slings a hand down to ruthlessly pull me against her legs, making me wince as her knees jab between my shoulder blades. Now I can't breathe either.

"Let the boy go, and I'll put the sword away," Reg offers with forced calm.

"Put the sword down, and I shall think about letting him go."

"He's not yours to taunt, Clymene. Don't be reckless."

She laughs, tightening her grip on me. "Do you think staking your claim on one of Zeus's bastards will endear you to him? Perhaps you want him for yourself?"

"Let him go! The child is mine!" Mom's proclamation—and it is that—has me staring agape at her. She's never sounded so angry. Or looked more ready to do something terrible.

"And he's mine to protect, Clymene," Reg adds. "So say what you will. I'll make sure his father knows of this. You can threaten me all you'd like, but I'm sure you're not immune to his retribution. And if you hurt a hair on that child's head, I promise there will be retribution."

I try not to wince as Clymene curls in her fingernails and

pierces through my tunic, breaking the skin directly over my galloping heart. As I grunt and frown, she does it again. Liquid brims in Mom's eyes—and it's not the kind that comes before her declaring how proud she is of me.

I don't think she's very proud of me now. And it's the worst feeling in the world. This is my fault. I shouldn't have ventured so far.

I have to fix this.

I'm done with this strange woman and her stupid claws. Sinking my teeth into her wrist is so satisfying, I do it again in spite of her shrill shriek. Mom's yelling just as loudly, commanding me to stop, but I don't want to. It feels good to be this mad and even better to do something about it. Mom and Reg are always making me stay controlled. Calm. Peaceful.

But losing control is nice.

Especially when I watch as Clymene gawks at her wrist. The joint that's just a few strands of flesh now, barely keeping her hand attached to her arm.

But the satisfaction drains once Mom frantically grabs me back. We're running for the villa as Clymene screams on.

"He won't get away with this. I am a titan of noble lineage! Mark my words, I will ruin you all. Everyone in Olympus is going to know about your boorish brat and his violent ways. Then we shall see how tolerant Hera will be of your bastard!"

It doesn't feel awesome to be angry anymore. Not at all. Now I'm nothing but afraid and sick, to the center of my stomach, as Regina hustles me inside the villa. But that doesn't help. I watch in helpless horror as Mom rushes forward, standing her ground against the awful titaness—and pays for it by bearing one brutal lash after another. *My head is a terrible sting and my vision clouds from wet grief, but I can't look away. I don't dare. What if the shrew doesn't stop? What if she beats Mom so hard that—*

No matter which way I struggle through the tides, the vision torments me. I can't think about it. I beg to forget it all again. The despair consumes me. I'm going to die like this, I know it. Weighed down by my sorrow. By the memories I never reconciled. The forgiveness I never got to plead from my mother.

There's blackness all around. I can't see my own hand in front of my face. It's quiet now. As silent as a tomb.

"Maximus."

The softest of whispers. It's Kara's…and it's incredible. Beautiful. Like heaven.

"*Maximus.*"

The kind of heavy sigh I'd expect to rustle through my hair and into my ear as I plunge my body into hers. To be repeated, pitching higher, as I slide against the trembling nerves at her center. So much need in her rasp. So much connection in her heart. I feel it all…

I need to live for it all.

I…must…live…for her.

Kara.

I can only answer her from inside. There's no breath left to do it now, not even from my preternatural lungs. Every ounce of strength left in my body is focused on simply opening my eyes. On seeking her light in my dark liquid eternity. And then somehow, I don't know how, swimming for the pinpoint of dawn on the horizon of this disgusting night.

I start rotating my arms. Kicking my legs. It gets easier as soon as the ice chunks break off. I let the violent currents help me along too. The light seems to approve, getting brighter as I flow along. Brighter and so much better...

Because now I see her again.

She's sparkling. I swim faster, yearning to caress every inch of her burnished skin until I'm filling the air around her with my nonstop worship.

I'm close enough to lunge for her. To finally, *finally* wrap my arms around her...

I break the water's surface. Blessed oxygen—or whatever's standing in for it here—douses my lungs. Though it hurts so good to take it in, more air in my blood means more power in my grip.

But instead of grasping Kara in my arms, I'm crawling up the Acheron shore, looking at nothing between my fingers but inches of stinking mud.

She's gone. Once more as if she's never been here.

And I don't even have the strength to roar about it.

What I do is roll over onto my back and beg the mist, now a shade of bloodred, to just take me. Wherever the destination, it has to be closer to Kara than this forsaken bog. The mist doesn't answer. Before I can issue the plea again, it's eclipsed. Two faces, one from the right and one from the left, move in to fill my vision.

"What the hell were you thinking, Maximus? How could you be so foolish?"

Charon chuckles hoarsely. "First dafty since Achilles who's survived that stunt."

Gio snaps a stunned stare. "Achilles? You're serious?"

"Do I look like a teller of tall tales?" The boatsman doesn't wait for an answer. He swoops his oar over his shoulder and turns back toward the boat he's run up into the mud. As he shoves off into the ruthless current, I push up until at least my torso is vertical.

"You all right?" Gio murmurs.

"Not sure," I answer truthfully.

"What hurts?"

His tone is so tender, I actually force myself to look at him. For a second, I'm seeing things differently again. The smile and worry lines have almost fully faded from his face. His trimmed beard is black instead of gray. He's the Gio of long ago, as Kara must remember him. A grandfather helping her up after a scrape.

Suddenly all I want to do is sit here and waste some more of our time letting him give me all the warm praise that was missing from my own paternal contributor.

Or was it?

I don't have the time or energy to dissect the memory— or any others it could lead to—now. "I saw Kara again, Gio. In the water. She was right there. She was *here*, in front of me…"

He frowns. "Again?"

"In the font at the church, I swore I saw her face. Then again at the reflecting pool. On the river, she was so close, I could have touched her. I swear it. I'm not crazy. It was too real."

"I know." There's just as much comfort in his tone,

though it's now backed by some mature force. "Believe me, son. I know."

I take another moment to catch my breath and absorb his words. "You do?"

He nods somberly. "For me with Charlena, it was the same. You might have noticed, there's not a mirror in my little backyard abode. Visions of her haunted me for years, and I let them until I couldn't take it anymore. I couldn't bear seeing her…without feeling her, hearing her, and even tasting her…"

"Wow," I say, openly empathetic, though I privately wonder if the torment of missing her ever really abated. Perhaps he's just gotten used to avoiding mirrors instead.

Just when I think he's about to wax nostalgic a little more, he rises and offers a hand to help me do the same. "I speak from experience in saying there's no useful purpose in wallowing about it. Come on. I know a place we might be able to rest."

While my body protests the idea of any movement, even toward respite, I couldn't be more mentally on board with the idea of getting away from the river. And if we move on, even if it's to slog through more of this land that feels like the Everglades invited Antarctica for a sleepover, we're that much closer to Kara.

The motivation carries me forward through a countless number of miles. I'm so focused on my feet now, angrily ordering them into every lead-filled step, that it takes plowing into Gio to realize he's stopped. And that he's done so in a new bath of light.

The soft amber glow pours out of a structure that's broken through the ice and begun to rise, reminding me of some grand set piece from a pricey Broadway musical.

"The noble castle," I blurt.

The place has walls and a roof, even if they don't come with the sprawling meadow and pretty stream from the cantos I've memorized. In a way, that's encouraging as long as it isn't packed out with a crowd of virtuous pagans either. In any other time and place, I'd brave the crush for a chance to trade ideas with the likes of Homer, Socrates, Orpheus, Hippocrates, and the notable cast of so many more. But right now, all I crave is a clean place to drop my head and make friends with subconsciousness for a few blessed minutes.

"Depends on what you mean by 'noble,'" Gio says. "But at least we've got the place to ourselves."

"I'm not interested in noble so much as safe," I return. "I mean, it looks empty—but are you sure?"

The old guy snorts out a laugh. "You asking if I'm *sure* about absolutely anything here?" He rolls back one shoulder and then the next. "The only answer I can give is that this is what worked before. If we encounter a different game now, then we'll roll with those rules."

I accept that with a tight nod. "Fair enough."

"Of course, we won't stay long—"

"Ten minutes is all I need."

A small smirk takes the place of his laugh. "Let's try to get in a little more than that."

"All right. Fifteen but no more." Now I almost laugh too. Are we negotiating nap time in a place where fifteen minutes or fifteen days might have already passed?

The answer doesn't matter once we push past the castle's looming entrance doors. Inside, the place is brighter than it seems from the outside, though the Italianate accents are gaudy reminders of what I've glimpsed so far in the Valari compound. A look in Gio's direction brings confirmation that he's not a fan of the decor either.

I can't bring myself to be that bothered, though. I'm ready to sleep on a bed of nails. The massive leather lounger that I do find is like reclining onto a cloud. Within seconds, I've hauled off my shirt, shucked my boots, and am fully down for the count.

But my mind doesn't let me stay that way for long.

CHAPTER 10

Kara

IT'S DISTURBING THAT I'M taking one shred of Hades's words as constructive, but he's right about the fact that I need some rest. Correctly translated, some hardcore getting-to-know-you time with the big pillows on the huge bed in the middle of my chamber. Fifty percent of my DNA is one hundred percent human, confirmed by my overriding exhaustion level. And as beautiful as this draped thing is, I desperately don't want it to be my death bed, as well.

This time, I just have to make myself do it.

Encouraged by the impression that my host will be leaving me alone for a little while, I approach the high, plush mattress. I release a blissful sigh from the mere thought of finally shutting my eyes and escaping into nothingness.

Into peace...

The thought is better than the thickest blanket, enveloping my senses as I drop my head to the pillow. For the first time since Hades seized me at Rerek's party, I'm able to fully breathe. To feel free. Free enough to let my mind fly to thoughts of Maximus.

He's in the clouds again. The beautiful thunderheads across the landscape of my memories. Air, water, and wind collaborate to create his hair and smile and eyes. Soon, his shoulders fill out too. Then the magnificence of his chest, the firm waves of his abs, and the stunning lengths of his legs. They're all here before me. But...*how*? He can't really be here, can he? Not in this dark suburb of hell's desolate capital.

I wish I could celebrate the possibility, even just a little. That I could welcome the vision of his light shining into the gloom of my fathomless prison. He's so beautiful, I can't help but shed tears. Because to think he's actually nearby, having survived a journey into this realm on his way to find me, is foolish. To keep contemplating that I'll ever see him again, let alone have him...

New agony tears through me, ruining the descent into sleep. I push up until I'm sitting again and open my eyes into the mostly dark room. A fresh sigh spills out of me.

Right before a small rustle shivers across the air.

After a silent startle, I straighten even higher. My gaze darts to the rich red couch on the other side of the room.

"Huh?" I ask beneath my breath. This is so strange. I don't remember the lounger being there before.

Fantasy and sanity are still dancing flawlessly together, because Maximus is there now, reclining in what looks like a fitful rest. The waltz gets even more beautiful when he lifts his head to meet my stare, which fans his tawny mane across the rich mahogany cushion.

At once, my skin breaks out in aroused perspiration. I tremble from the need to surge forward, stretch myself across him, and bury my hands in his thick, luxurious strands while kissing him with all the need in my soul and desire in my body.

But I don't.

Because when I do, I'll know it isn't real.

Just a little while longer, I beg to the outer reaches of my mind. *Please, just let us have this for a few more moments.*

If only the dream will allow…

"*Kara?*"

But, pathetically unable to resist his call, I rise to my feet. At the same time, I let my robe slide off my shoulders. It whooshes down to create a silky crimson puddle from which I step with seductive slowness.

"Kara," he rasps again. "This…*you*…can't be…"

I secretly bow to providence in thanks while quivering from the fresh dew across my skin. And collecting along the walls of my core…

"It's me," I answer in a rough whisper. "Is it really you?"

He pushes up, showing me more of the breath-halting mounds that compose his upper torso. Unable to help myself, I roll the tip of my tongue between my lips. He's that mouthwatering. That stunning. That incredibly close.

"It's me."

I don't know how it truly can be, but everything feels too real between us to convince me otherwise. I've never wanted a dream to be more real.

"I miss you…so much." My confession is broken apart by a jittery sob. Every inch of my body, from the roots of my scalp to the valleys between my toes, aches so exigently for him.

"Then come here," my lover husks. His hands, splaying his massive thighs, now slide to his sides. It's not just a physical opening. His eyes well up too, vulnerable as lakes beneath lightning. He swallows with raw uncertainty. "Come here and find me."

A smile breeches my lips. But I can only take one step. "I…can't," I rasp.

His eyebrows dive toward each other. "Why not?"

"I'm afraid."

"Of me?"

"No." I chide him with a small laugh, and it feels so damn good. "I'm afraid…"

"Of what, then?"

"That you'll disappear. That you're…"

"Not real?" His sleek mouth gives way to the small smirk that always makes my pulse skip. "You mean like the persimmons we swore we bought at the farmer's market that day, that never made it back to my place?"

My heartbeat isn't skipping anymore. It's fully stopped.

I dare another step forward. With equal deliberation, I say, "I've never told anyone else that story."

Maximus fully locks his stare with mine. "Neither have I."

I'm taking my own turn to gulp hard. But to hope with the same magnitude. "I totally forgot about them until we got back home."

The lightning finally touches down in his gaze. His eyes are agleam with dazzling light. "I like it when you call my place home."

I scoot ahead by another step. He's still here. I force myself to believe it. "*You're* my home."

"And you're mine. Forever and always."

His vow is a fervent force on the air, to the point I'm longing to reach out and capture it like ribbons. I look around, battling to make sense of where my chamber ends and his room begins. But he's not there either. At least not the retreat in downtown LA where our love began and flourished in such magic and passion.

"Is this an accident of reality, or a collision of dreams, or...?"

"I don't know. But does it even matter?" he implores. "It's a gift, Kara. A gift for which I've been begging fate since you disappeared."

Anguish hits me like a twelve-foot wave at Venice before a storm. "I'm sorry." I wring my hands. "I'm so sorry. I should've been more careful. I should've known Rerek couldn't be trusted. If I'd only—"

"Stop," he orders. "Hades stole you away from me, and in no world is that your fault. You're brilliant and strong and caring and aware, but you're not a mind reader. Neither am I."

I draw in a long breath, ordering myself to pull in all the comfort he intends with that. But my spirit is still dark and my feet are still stuck. "So what do we do now?"

Maximus pulls himself a little higher. Though his shift

seems only a few inches, his presence in our beautiful bubble seems to double. His stare is more intense. His muscles broader. And his voice, deep and sure, is that of a true god.

"Now, we make the most of the moment. The chance we've been given to become stronger."

He bores his gaze deeper into mine, his blues already filled with supernatural certainty. The answers to my earlier questions… He already has them. And he knows that I do too.

"Come to me, Kara. Let me feel you."

And just like that, the reticence of my heart is lifted. The doubts in my mind are gone. And the shackles on my ankles, invisible but heavy, are snapped open.

And I'm all but flying to him.

Reaching for him.

Falling across him on the couch and rejoicing in the glorious heat of his body. The mighty cocoon of his embrace. And yes, at last, *at last*, the exquisite explosion of his consuming kiss.

I'm lost again—but now, in all the best ways. I'm helpless in the wilderness of his beautiful mouth. Basking in the torrid waterfall of his tongue as we crash into each other while craving more.

More. I need *so much more*.

And I take it.

I absorb his velvety moan, letting it power my muscles. His hands, now clamping at my waist, jolt my whole midsection with awakening and arousal. I spread my thighs and lower my pelvis to ride the ridge beneath his pants. I'm already so soft and wet and ready for him.

The second Maximus feels that too, his head falls against the top of the brocade cushion. Our mouths fall open together, his to gulp more air and mine to bite the underside of his jaw. Through the wonderful curls of his beard, I taste his unique salt and sweat. It's the headiest aphrodisiac of my existence.

Second only to his growl, full of adoration and destitution. It's a call to every intrinsic instinct in my being. My human's heart is a sensual celebration. My demon's soul is an illicit inferno. I'm full of desperate fire. Beyond possessed.

"Maximus," I plead, beyond dizzy with that lust. It's so hot now. So layered. That can only mean one thing. He's with me, in every sense of the word. His heartbeat at this speed. His desire at this demand. But it's still not enough. Not nearly. Only one force will fill that need now. Will complete me now.

"Need you," I pant out.

"I know, my love." His voice is steamy and hoarse in my ear. "Help me."

We fumble together at his clasps and buttons before our fingers mesh to lower his zipper—and then the barrier beneath. Then he's springing free for me, so huge and swollen and erect. He's groaning and straining his hips, seeking me with such urgency, I forget to move or blink or breathe.

"Find me," he husks out. "Come home to me. Kara…"

As he fills me, his name is nothing but stretched air in my throat. I'm still gasping it as he moves with me, blooming inside me, giving me the heat I need to know. No place else will ever be my shelter like this. My strength. The beacon of my spirit. The center of my storm.

I tell him all of that and more with the force of my eyes and the thrusts of my body. He answers with a grip at my nape with one hand while driving our primal rhythm with the other. In the flower of light that spreads in the middle of my chest, I feel every nuance of his response. Every drop of his desire. Every flicker of his reverence. Every inch of all the beautiful ropes that bind us.

It all grows, expanding like sunlight behind billowing clouds, until I can't hold back the brightness anymore. There's too much pressure in my body. There's too much demand in *his*. But I try to delay it. I try so hard, even compelling broken words to my lips.

"I...love you."

Maximus lifts the hints of a smile. "As I...love you."

"Forever."

"Forever, my sweet demon."

His declaration is the ultimate flint to my kindling, igniting my body in a blaze of completion. I drop my head back and squeeze his fingers as a scream of rapture begins in my pussy and spirals out of my throat. The moment is all the better when Maximus emits a bellow that joins the hot, violent shudders of his body.

The best aphrodisiac of my life has officially been followed by the most magical orgasm.

Until I realize that the light in my mind isn't the breaking sun.

It's a break-*in*. A spy as obscene as he is uninvited. The intruder who's now leaning against the wall several paces away, gazing upon us, tainting every inch of our entwined bodies in the filth of his lingering, lascivious scrutiny.

Hades.

"N-N-No," I stammer. "Oh please, no!"

Maximus blinks sleepily before following my gaze.

Hades slides out half a smile. Once the other side catches up, he murmurs just one word.

"*Fascinating.*"

Four syllables.

Four seconds that change my world from paradise to perdition. From a dream back to damnation. From the heights of my most blinding joy to the abyss of my most dreaded agony.

I push up and away from Maximus in a frantic rush. But the moment I do, he vanishes. And just like that, the agony doubles. And Hades's delight doubles. I'm sure of it. Because at last he's broken me open. He's found the biggest crack in my soul's fortress and broken it big enough to crawl all the way inside.

He's kept his terrifying promise, down to its last disgusting degree.

CHAPTER 11

Maximus

I SWEAR MY HEAD has only hit the lounger's cushion for a few minutes before I'm jerking it back up, called by a million alert zings through my blood. I blink a bunch of times, but my vision is still shrouded at the edges.

As the fog of my brief sleep dissipates, memories of my vivid dream become clearer.

The more I think of it, the more real it feels. No more masquerades as a water ripple or a river tide.

This vision felt...different.

Kara was flesh and substance, movement and matter. Tangible, naked curves and potent, open need...

Need I crave to fulfill again and again.

All of it. All of *her*.

We were talking about the missing persimmons from that day not so long ago...the morning that was so perfect until we had to go to Arden's place. But even that ended pretty wonderfully because we were together. Inseparable. In complete, starry-eyed love.

Remembering all of it... all of *her*... fills me with intoxicating energy and an equally deep need to get back to that wonderful place. Even back to the dream with her nudity all over me and her tongue inside me.

Then, so blessedly and perfectly, being inside her too.

Nothing will ever compare to the heaven of her body. The joy of her passion. Her love is my sustenance. She's the rain in my desert. The summit of my climb. The order in my confusion.

Except when that bewilderment suddenly floods my consciousness. And then hits even harder, as I remember more of the disturbing ending to the dream. Kara's frightened eyes. The tremble in her body. Her terrified rush to leave. For every good reason.

Hades's penetrating gaze is burned into the memory too.

Right before the moment I lost her again. Not just from my embrace. Something came between us, invisible but impenetrable, like a force field only worse. The barrier was sudden and savage—and woven out of pure evil. Nothing can alter my ultimate impression—and lasting fear—about that.

Or the new incision into my mind from it.

The impression is a warning and an affirmation at once. "Shit," I mutter, fighting stunned tremors from my own body. But I'm losing. Miserably.

All of it really was more than a dream. The vision...

wasn't that. It was absolutely real. And now, so are the new depths to which Hades has gouged, courtesy of his simultaneous violation of Kara and me both. Our moment of intimacy and commitment is tainted forever.

Never again.

The shock of his ambush pales against the pain of losing Kara again, but the violation of his lurking presence means there's also hope.

She's got to still be with him. So if I can find Hades, I can find her.

Rage and bitterness climb through my senses now, churning into a storm I can't stop. A detonation I can't contain.

Can't—and won't.

In one motion, I'm zipping up my khakis and bounding up from the lounger. In my wake, the long couch flips and crashes into the wall. My incensed roar is also my self-directed promise to deliver Hades to the same fate. I don't care who he is or what he's capable of. If hell collapses while I'm busy tearing his head off his shoulders, so be it.

I sprint out of the great room and begin scouring all the other chambers until I find Gio how I was moments ago, abandoned to sleep. I hate to wake him, but finding Kara has never felt more vitally urgent. Perhaps even a matter of life or death—though hers or mine, I can't begin to guess.

I shake his shoulder, jolting him awake. At once, his eyes are wide and full of panic.

"What is it? Is something wrong?"

"I saw her again," I say, swallowing hard. "It felt too real.

Hades has her. He's *with* her. I'm sure of it. We're not too late, but…"

His features tighten with worry. "But we could be. Let's go. I'll sleep when I die again."

A relieved sigh rushes out of me. "Thank you."

Within minutes, we're putting the light castle in our rearview. New determination, inspired by dreading fear, drives our steps over the bleak terrain.

"If she's with Hades, she must be in the capital. He wouldn't be anywhere else, would he?"

Gio swats away a swarm of aggressive flies that disappear as quickly as they arrived. "It's a fair assumption. But sadly, it means we're still plenty far away."

I clench my teeth to muffle a groan. We need to move faster. I need to find her. All I have to guide me is a rough mental map of a fictional hell and an old man who managed to jump out of the real one fifty years ago.

"There has to be a better way. A quicker way."

He shakes his head slightly. "I wish I knew one. Sadly, I'm the mere mortal of the two of us." He squints, his focus narrowing on the glowing light ahead of us.

Lights, rather. The glow comes from nine ornate candelabras, arranged in a semicircle around a tall leather throne perched on an ornate dais.

"Speaking of immortals…" Gio mutters.

The dread that's been following me around since we got here is overrun by a strange new sense of caution.

Not even the beast in the chair, awaiting us with casual but careful attention, can change that. An audacious air drips from him like the never-ending wax cascading off the candles. He's dark-eyed and well-muscled, and his skin has a worn leathered look that doesn't surprise me, considering the elements Gio and I have faced so far. An eternity of this would take its toll on anyone. Even a beast.

Even Minos.

The infernal judge of the damned.

He's a nebulous but curious character, watching us with mild interest as we approach.

"Who comes into my house of pain?"

His voice is shockingly refined and echoes across the dead landscape around us.

I'm almost impressed until his tail uncurls, looking like a well-made leather whip. Its massive length creates a wide boundary that stops us short.

"Wellll?"

Minos tacks an appraising brow and a suggestive smirk onto the end of his summons, though I don't mistake either for humor. Once upon a time, he might have ruled one of the earth's leading civilizations, but now he's a beast and a loyal follower of Hades.

The conclusion has me straightening my posture. It's time to prove I deserve to be here. To be taking this full journey. That I can handle whatever this strange savage and any of his other friends dish out.

After pulling in a determined breath, I move forward by a forceful step. "My name is Maximus Kane. And this is my guide, Giovani Valari."

"Valari." Minos slithers a taloned finger across his slimy

smile, continuing until the digit supports the droll cock of his head. "Well, there's a name I haven't heard in a minute. And yet here you are, Giovani, daring to tempt the natural order again?"

"For a noble purpose." Gio is just as regal about it but keeps his voice humble. "This man's dedication to the truest love of his soul."

A hum rises from the rugged figure on the throne. His posture follows suit. "High moral ideals aren't exactly worthy of special privileges here. Neither is love, even in its truest form. In fact, that foolishness is more likely to drive a man to sin than anything else."

"He's not a sinner," Gio argues. "Not as I was, anyway. We simply must pass to find my granddaughter."

The beast's eyes spring wide. For a couple of wild seconds, even his tail whips up to make crazy eights in the air. "The beauty in Hades's custody as we speak? I've heard whispers of this. She is your granddaughter? Oh, my, my, my. Now this smells like some delicious retribution."

Before he's done, I've returned to being a block of seething tension. The words turn my nerves into knives and my throat into an uncontrollable growl. It doesn't surprise me when I look back over to find myself the fresh subject of the beast's attention.

"You, Maximus Kane, have no place here. You've committed no mortal sins that warrant my judgment. Further, you're not even dead." He turns his gaze back to Gio. "Technically neither are you, but you have yet to pay for your sins, Valari."

"I've paid, damn it!" As the shout spills from Gio, he stalks forward with balled fists and a jutting jaw. Both of us have tried doing this the civilized way. Now, we're done with holding back for the sake of appeasing this beast's ego. "A thousand times I've paid! If you ask, even Hades himself would—"

"Hades is not your judge. I am," he drawls. "So give me one good reason why I shouldn't hurl you at once to the fourth circle, where your greed and avarice should've already had you languishing."

I step forward, driven by a renewed sense of urgency. I cannot lose Gio. He's my guide, and he's fast becoming my friend. Beyond that, it'll ruin Kara's heart if the man is restituted to eternal suffering in the name of saving her from the same thing.

"Do you know who I am?"

The beast's tail slithers silently between us as he seems to ponder the question. "You do look familiar."

"Family resemblance, maybe." As easily as the words slide out, a rising tide of horror takes over me. I'm actually bound by blood to this creature—and countless others.

Minos cants his head, silently questioning me.

"Zeus… He's my father." I declare it firmly, owning it more than I ever have.

Minos erupts with a deafening laugh. The ground seems to shake through the aftershocks of it. "Turn back from whence you came, fool. Leave this escape artist to his fate and be gone."

"I told you, I'm a son of Zeus." I say it with more force,

wondering if he really doesn't believe me. I don't exactly have a birth certificate on me to prove the matter.

"Born to a mortal mother, yes?"

"Yes. But the only parentage you need to worry about is the one we share. *Nothing can take our passage from us when such a power has given us warrant for it.*"

Minos's expression turns cold. "And you believe your parentage gives you the right to pass without judgment?"

"Zeus is your god and your father. His blood flows in my veins the same as yours. *At his touch, all gates must spring aside.* I don't know about you, but I call that divine aid."

Minos rises from his throne, showing off the full height and breadth of his body. I'm not as daunted by his physical size as the skepticism that twists his thin lips. "Delusional mortal," he scoffs, squaring his shoulders as if they're about to sprout wings. "You read of things you know nothing about."

When he puffs up more, Gio hastily shifts back by a few paces. I stand wider, holding my ground. Minos's massive tail lifts and slams the ground between us. Without thinking, I lurch forward and shove on it with all the force in my body, clearing it from the space between us. The motion is enough to knock the lumbering beast off balance, setting him back into his throne with a rumble.

"All gates must spring *aside.*" My growl turns into something worse, and small lightning bolts erupt from the cracks in my fists.

Minos seethes as the pace of his breath ticks up. "Do I look anything like a gate, boy?"

"You look like someone who's in my way. That's close enough in my book. But if the blood of a god earns me no respect, you should know I also have the blood of a mother who rarely took no for an answer. This doesn't need to be complicated. Step back. Let. Us. Pass."

He pauses, finally seeming to hear me. Still, he slides his gaze to Gio. "What about the deserter?"

Gio gingerly steps to my side again. "You're not the only one who's determined to see me relegated to this place for the rest of eternity. Trust that this journey won't be over for me until one of your fellow wardens sees justice is done. But unlike them, you have a choice to wield punitive power or memorable mercy right now—mercy that will earn you the gratitude of a fellow demigod, no less. Or have I been away so long that favors owed aren't viable currency here anymore?"

Minos's grumble, long and contemplative, sends more tremors beneath the mud at our feet. At last, he winds his tail in a tight circle, averting his stare. It feels like we've won, but if I've learned anything to this point, nothing is ever certain in this place.

Another rash of flies buzzes across the sky, prompting Gio and I into reactive motion. I'm not about to keep waiting on the capricious permission—or not—from the brooding narcissist on his towering chair.

As we hurry past the throne, there's no ignoring the angry stroke of a sparkling whip, cracking into the dry ground right behind us. And then, "All the powers of the light be with you, Son of Zeus. And if they aren't, then perhaps we shall meet again—and I will *not* forget about that favor you now owe me in such rich spades."

After we leave Minos behind, Gio and I trudge in silence for a while. In the distance, as I half expected but seriously dreaded, is the massive whorl of the Underworld Gale. Sadly, it looks exactly like I imagined. A front of swirling air of biblical proportions, picking up every speck of dirt and ice and mud in its path. But even my inadvertent wit doesn't pierce my exhaustion—or determination. Somehow, I'll dig deep enough and find the stamina to get through this thing—and then every trial that awaits us beyond it.

CHAPTER 12

Kara

"WAKE UP."

Hades's dictate has me flinching and jerking awake—and at once, wondering if he's used my subconsciousness as a new excuse to pillage my mind.

With a sharp gasp, I sit up. My fingertips dig into my scalp, on the brink of splitting it open like a summer melon, but I don't feel ripped apart in any new ways.

The only sensation that keeps stabbing is complete surprise. Seems it's the only blade sharp enough to cut through my shivering despair. I'm almost too frightened to believe it. Has Maximus found a passage here? To hell itself? Is that why he keeps appearing in my visions and why they keep getting more vivid?

But how?

My first thought brings on a growl I can barely suppress. If he's gone and caused his own death, I'll kill him all over again.

"Sweet dreams?" Hades's voice is sugary, but there's nothing genuine about the words. I have his full attention, but he seems edgier than before. Unsettled.

"I... I don't know," I admit.

If it was indeed a dream, my reunion with Maximus was beyond divine—until I realized Hades was lurking. Once Maximus disappeared, I did the only thing I could think of. Run to the safety of the bed and pray for sleep to take back over.

I shake my head slightly, challenging myself to truly believe it. Maximus was here, in my arms. I close my eyes, letting the sweet memory wash over me. His touch, his whispers of devotion, his passionate drives into my body. My heartbeat ticks up as my mind is drenched with intoxicating visions.

He was here. I *know* he was. Somehow I can still feel the pressure of him inside me, the echoes of our lovemaking.

For the first time in what feels like forever, I fill my lungs with as much air as they want. As they balloon, my mind is equally buoyant. Can this really be happening? Is Maximus truly that close by? Is there a chance, however small, that I'll see my love soon, beyond a fleeting vapor or passing mist? And if so, then how soon?

Another inhalation brings sober consideration about that. I'm a hostage in the grand palace of Dis, in the center of hell. And my days here are already numbered. If *soon* doesn't come before my transfer into the city's general population—or worse, into one of the underworld's distant districts—there's a strong chance that Maximus will rush in to find nothing but my decimated carcass.

Yet as urgently as I implore him to hurry, I long to instantly retract the plea. Racing to find me means he'll also find Hades—a connection my captor is already furiously aware of, if his scalding energy is any indicator. It's tumbling off Hades like sparks out of a steel mill, to the point that I hiss in pain when he seizes me by the shoulder.

"Now get dressed," he orders. "I have a meeting of the captains to call. Wherever I go now, you go too. I refuse to miss a moment more of those exquisite gifts of yours," he adds with a sneer.

I can't tell if he's truly angry or if this is an extension of his twisted fascination with me. I fear I'll be banished from this place before I have a chance to fully unravel the mystery of this dark god.

I scramble to obey, all but expecting his edict. Despots are nothing if not predictable, but his chaotic wrath clouds so much of my senses.

We walk down the hall and enter a huge circular space with a goliath black stone table in the middle. The piece is round, its twenty-foot circumference held up by a crowd of hunched, grimacing gorgons. Again, I'm the mouse in the room, but my human side weathers a pang of pity for them. My demon side fights it, keeping the sentiment tightly concealed. If Hades is about to populate the room as I expect, I'll need my emotional walls to be as strong as I can make them. He may have found a way to breach my innermost passions, but I must protect as much of everything else as I can.

Without prologue, he stretches out his hand before the table, palm up and index finger out, until he's covered the whole circle with the gesture. In the wake of his motion, figures appear at the edges of the table, looking like activated holograms before becoming fully real.

The captains have been summoned.

And at once, I'm frowning in perplexity. I count only eight figures around the vast table. If these are the leaders of the districts of hell, my calculations say that someone is missing.

Charlena. She's the one not occupying her seat straight across the table from Hades and me. But why? Our visit was so strange and brief, but I do miss the comfort of her company. Especially now, surrounded by a new set of fearsome strangers who eye me with unfiltered suspicion.

One big-snouted demon is the first of anyone to find his voice. "What is the meaning of this?" he barks at Hades. "With great and due respect, my lord, I have new arrivals due for their *orientation.*" His snicker comes out as a series of loud snorts. "My crew has been waiting all day to introduce them to their new fates, and—"

"Shut up," Hades mutters. "Your wretches can wait, Malacoda. We have a bigger issue to address."

The demon gives me another dirty glare, clearly playing judge and jury based on the first ten seconds of my presence.

Hades grimaces. "We have a breach."

A palpable shockwave takes over every creature in the circle. Everyone's repeating the word, which is clearly a rarity for Hades's vocabulary.

My heart leaps with hope, but I hide it behind a calm facade. The whispers keep coming, along with frantic glances and discomfited squirms. No doubt they're well-justified. Because who would dare breach this realm? My guess is they were all expecting Hades to announce an escapee, not an intruder. The list of souls who'd force themselves *into* hell has to be a short one.

But the more important question is how…and where?

Judging by the stench of stress in the air, I'm certain Hades's most valued commanders are wondering this too. Depending on the answer, any one of them could be in for a worse fate than their underlings. The beasts in the room are as certain of it as I am. It takes clenching every muscle in my body not to let their fear seep in and debilitate me. The last time my extra senses brought me this much anxiety, I was in a lecture hall at Alameda while Maximus tossed a pair of snickering bullies out of his class.

But I have to stay detached. I don't have an inch of choice about the matter.

"What kind of breach?" Malacoda demands. "And what do you need from us now, my lord?"

Hades studies them all with pointedly arched brows. "Perhaps some information from your comrades in the Vestibule and Limbo."

"Minos? Ron?" The demon drags in an ugly snuffle. "But what in all misery is happening?"

Hades tilts his head with eerie intent. "Have you heard nothing? I find it unbelievable that a single one of you would have heard *nothing* of a demigod marching through my kingdom uninvited!"

I shrink back with the others, cowed by his seething accusation.

"Wait. A demigod?" one of the captains dares to demand. "But how?"

I'm uncertain if my presence here is widely known, but eight sets of wary eyes on me are an unnerving answer for that question. Hades darts a quick glare my way, seeming to confirm their suspicions. He's serene but fuming as more stunned whispers take over the small crowd. Those ripples explode into full spurts. Some are openly angry. Most are overtly baffled.

"Because of *her*?" the brave one rumbles, slashing a finger in my direction. "After she defied you with Zeus's spawn?"

"Punish her!" another cries, its voice like gravel and glass. He glares at me with wild, bloodshot eyes while wielding a rusty Damascus blade. "The pleasure would be mine, my lord."

The others rally in agreement. My heart races again but this time in dread. The relief of knowing Maximus is closer than I would have ever imagined is swept away by the very real fear that Hades will hand me off to this horrible mob.

I step back but don't get far. Hades ruthlessly clutches my hand in his own, keeping me from retreating farther. His dark eyes twinkle with knowing calm. Dark satisfaction. Maybe even a hint of mischief.

I barely hold back a desperate sob. He's enjoying this now. The flying of my heart. The blinding fear for my survival. He must feel it.

Recognition of this game of his is almost distracting me from the alarming *tings* of metal against metal, the jostle of weaponry among their angry shouts.

"Enough," Hades says in a biting tone, interrupting our horribly searing connection.

But it does nothing to quell their new hatred for me. Or is it violence? Or all the worst vices in their purest forms combined and embodied in Hades's most loyal subjects?

"She cannot be spared!" Malacoda shouts, now as unruly as the others. "She is the temptress responsible for our shameless violation!"

Hades returns the creature's glare with his own twisted lips and flaring nostrils, taking over the energy on the air and the awareness in my head with his fury. I sway in place, dizzy from the awful *whomp* of it. I debate closing my eyes, certain Hades is about to free everyone of their heads.

"She is not your concern. Finding Maximus Kane and bringing him to me is."

"But the girl—"

Hades waves a hand, which lobs a large wad of flaming pitch at the angry demon's face. His muffled scream lasts a couple of seconds before his mouth and jaw melt into mush.

"My God," I whisper, struggling to wall off my mind from their combined torment. I crumple to my knees from the assault, but I'm sure Hades doesn't notice. His rage is an equal jackhammer of energy.

"You all have voices." He sweeps his black glare around the table. "Let this be a lesson to use them for what they are good for. Finding the intruder by any means necessary and bringing him to me immediately. *None* of you are dismissed," he bellows when they start shuffling after the reprimand. "In case it's escaped your feeble comprehensions, a bastard of Zeus is wandering my land as freely as a missionary with four-color pamphlets. Fortunately, his goal isn't to save every wretch between here and the Gale. He aims only to retrieve one." He answers that by tugging me back up to my feet. "And whoever brings me Kane successfully shall prove you are truly worthy of your station."

Malacoda finishes his moaning as the bottom half of his face grows back. His recovery does little to the spite in his eyes as Hades levels this new challenge and threat. But from somewhere deep within, a flame flares, filling my chest as it drives my shoulders back. With a new swell of pride, I don't shy my gaze from any of the indicting ones that are ready to tear me down. The souls that don't want me to grasp my overwhelming truth.

They can't break me.

They don't even scare me anymore.

And not because Hades is my keeper right now.

Nobody in this chamber can deny—or fight—the reality that brought me here. The destiny I dared to follow. The love that I chose above all else. The power that's so much higher than all of them. They hate me for it, that much is undeniable, but they're helpless in the face of its brilliance. The faith I have in its fortitude.

"We shall seek him out with haste, my lord," Malacoda offers, his tone undeniably more reverent.

"A most passionate plan. Remember, however, that

Kane is not condemned. You are to return him to me unharmed." Hades moves forward again, disconnecting his clutch on me. He leans over to brace his hands atop the dull black tabletop. "And one more thing. Whoever succeeds shall have the added prize of inviting this lovely demoness into their district, to do with whatever you wish."

"No!" I cry, earning no one's sympathy.

The crowd is still rank with contempt. And the room is still empty of Charlena. My one ally. My only family here. While I feared the fate I'd find in the third circle, I had desperately reassured myself that she might advocate for me there.

Malacoda leans forward. The wretch is back to being his seedy, snotty self. His beady eyes gleam. His demonic ears twitch. "Oh, I already like the sound of this game."

Hades is one step closer to manipulating all of hell into taking down the man I love.

I'm a shivering mess from the thought alone, but when he casts an arrogant glance over his shoulder as if he knows it, my blood turns to ice. What is going on in his determined, diabolical mind?

He pivots back around, clearly and completely in his element, holding court with the wicked crew who await his will with held breaths and bright, turbulent stares. He stays like that, sucking every drop he can get of their adoration, before speaking again.

"The demigod is likely on his way to try to kill me."

He finishes with a wide smirk as every creature in the room but me erupts into wild laughter. It's no surprise when

Malacoda bellows over everyone else, his shout as raucous as a frat boy's.

"We can't have lovesick bastards thinking they can wield power in our midst, can we now?"

More laughter ensues, no doubt welcome comedy relief for the fearstruck leaders of Hades's kingdom.

But during the briefing that follows, my premonitions are validated in a thousand awful ways. I force myself to listen as Hades lays out a detailed plan that earns him a rising tide of his captains' approving cheers—and a growing storm of dread in my terrified heart.

I can't endure a moment more of their slimy stares and salivating glee.

So I run.

I run as fast and as far as I can, past brutish guards and whimpering souls, until I reach the one place in the palace that feels like it could be safe.

CHAPTER 13

MAXIMUS

UNLIKE MUCH OF THIS journey, the Gale is exactly what I imagined it to be. Freezing, stinking, and disorienting. Sleet comes at us from all directions, bearing disturbingly dirty flecks along with its giant ice chips. I'm grateful that Gio's inner compass is functioning better than mine, making it possible to dig in and follow his slipstream until we're free of the debris.

When we finally stumble free, we both fall to all fours to get back our breath. I grimace at my hair, most of it pulled from its tie and dripping with muck.

"And I thought a hostile Hollywood press corps was the worst cyclone I'd ever face."

I don't respond to the old man's quip until I can push all the way back to my feet. "Before they threw a three-headed dog at you in the form of a paparazzi crew?"

Gio hurries back to a full stand as well. "Sounds about right. With any luck, *this* beast can be appeased with some smiles and a candid exclusive."

A nice thought, but I'm not placing a lot of hope on it as we trudge forward. With every step, the ends of my nerves and the depths of my blood fuse with fiercer intensity. Nothing like the looming prospect of facing the world's most notorious hellhound to make a guy forget he's not in LA anymore, even if I'm trying to remember every pro tip from every junkyard mutt encounter I've ever had.

"Maybe we caught a break," I say hopefully as we navigate canyons between huge cliffs of calcified refuse. "Maybe having three heads means three times the need for naps?"

"I doubt we'll be so lucky," Gio drawls as we progress farther.

On each side of us, there are steep walls formed from layer upon layer of strange-colored debris, courtesy of millennia of abuse at the whims of the Gale. The peak of every tower resembles a defiant mohawk, and I begin to think that given the right lighting and landscaping, the tapered towers would even be beautiful.

At once, I jerk my head to clear the thought. There are a lot of circles left between here and Dis. I need to be on guard through all of them, not admiring the scenery like I'm planning to write a poem about it later.

An extremely fitting reality check—considering the snarling canine that charges down a scum slope at us.

"Holy ssshhh…" I backpedal a few stunned steps.

Gio's with me but drops into a battle crouch. Lowering to Cerberus's level never entered my mind but no doubt is the smartest move.

I'm pretty sure the hellhound doesn't see or care.

All three of the beast's heads are openmouthed and slavering. One barks nonstop at us. The middle head is already tossing from side to side, as if ready to shred us raw. The third is consumed with gnarls and growls I've never heard outside of horror movie double features.

"I'll try to take the left head," Gio grits out.

"No, I got this," I growl.

Gio may look a couple decades younger here, but his strength is nowhere close to mine. Finding Kara is my first mission. Keeping Gio safe is a close second.

But before I can insist on it, a new din hits the air—the terrifying thunder of massive paws pounding the ground as Cerberus makes a twelve-foot lunge at us.

Gio doesn't hesitate, lurching forward into the attack. But the beast barrels right past him and lands a chomp into my shoulder.

I holler from the blast of pain, but nothing in my life has prepared me for the hound's toxic-waste breath.

"My God, who's been playing fetch-the-corpse with you?"

It's the snark or the quick progress I make unhinging its maw from my flesh that inspires the beast's middle head to come at me with a vicious growl in my face, gifting me with a second dose of halitosis. Past the point of profanity, I grimace and wonder if my skin's about to peel off. I'm dizzy to the point of losing my footing. One stumbling backstep leads to another.

At once, Cerberus senses the give in my balance. I

tumble to my back, overtaken by his savage pounce. With the wind punched out of me, my vision swims again. I barely comprehend one of the heads descending to strike, and my swerve is too late to avoid his brutal bite to my other shoulder. The dog howls again, though I can't discern the difference between its glee and frustration now. But that's far from the important takeaway as it rears back and sets up for another strike. I grimace, preparing to give up my face. Or worse.

Another howl fills the canyon. But not his. The bellow is…Gio's.

I blink, realizing it's killing my eyes to do so. But they're still my eyes, solid in my head and not rolling in the mud. My entire face is still here. My whole head is.

The same head that I lift, wondering why Underworld Fido has suddenly decided I'm not a great chew toy. My view reveals Gio's arms lassoed around one furry neck. The offensive only earns my guide a roller coaster ride through the air as Cerberus tries to buck the old man off.

"Shit," I mutter.

I push to stand and find my balance. I have one goal now: to catch one of the beast's extremities despite its crazy thrashing.

But before I can pinpoint the perfect moment to launch, a deafening crack cuts through the air. Then another.

"Cerberus!"

A deep feminine voice echoes off the high rock walls. At once, we all freeze in place.

The new silence makes room for the sound of footsteps.

A second later, a pair of shiny, stiletto-heeled boots steps into my vision. Because I literally can't gawk at much else, I follow the legs to which they're attached, the thick whip trailing from her elegant hand, and then all the way up a strikingly slender form...

Until I'm peering at a completely black-bandaged face.

"Put him down at once," the demoness barks, shockingly bold with the beast that's at least five times her size.

Cerberus doesn't move, but Gio takes advantage of the pause to release his hold and crash clumsily to the ground. He lands close to the mysterious figure—too close, judging by how he rushes to push back from her. The action stirs up more dust around both of them.

"What's going on?" he demands. "Who are you?"

After a silent moment, the regal female peels the dark silks away from features that should be on a Times Square cosmetics billboard.

Gio's jaw falls. After all we've been through, this is the palest I've seen him.

"No," he whispers. "It can't be."

She visibly startles at the sight of him—but only for a second. Perhaps two. Just as rapidly, she relaxes her stiff shoulders and averts her eyes. "Oh, Gio. You were always so adept at fictionalizing life and wrapping your mind around the impossible. Don't tell me you've changed so much to think you wouldn't find me here of all places."

All he can do is release a painful sigh and shake his head. He's in shock by what he sees, but I can't figure out why. I also can't figure how this slight woman has brought the massive Cerberus to heel with such little effort.

"In any case, you're welcome," she states without a hint of sarcasm. And then extends a hand, hauling Gio up as if there's a truck driver hiding behind her facade. "Come now. If I leave you here, the hound will not take long to chew through both of you. We must go."

"Wait." I scour my gaze across her face again. There's a weird but frightening allure about her. Haunting but familiar. "Go where? And who the hell are you? Why should we trust you or follow you anywhere?"

"Charlena." Gio sounds like he's got a whole screenplay to spill behind those syllables.

"Charlena?" I repeat, already acknowledging a whole string of my own questions for the strange woman.

But I should have saved the strange notation for this moment instead: the pause in which I forget about Cerberus and hell circles to watch the female pivot like the fashion ramp model she so vividly reminds me of. There's an equally urbane half smile on her dark-red lips, but that doesn't arrest me as much as what I glimpse, for the barest of seconds, in her gaze. What kind of light *is* that? Once more, I'm struck with a powerful sense of affinity. No, something deeper. *Déjà vu?* Another repressed memory?

"Should I be flattered that you remembered my face *and* my name after all we've been through?" she says to Gio.

"I remember everything. Every single blessed second," he returns, gaping as if every inch of his body craves to hold her.

But it seems like a stronger instinct is holding him back.

Something resembling…fear, for which I can't blame him under the current circumstances.

"Fifty-one years," he whispers softly. "And not a day has gone by without you somewhere in my thoughts, dahlia."

A softness washes across her countenance with Gio's confession and what I suspect is an endearment he often uttered in her presence. Yet the vulnerability vanishes as quickly as it arrived.

"Your days, hours, minutes, and seconds mean nothing here. *Nothing*." She struts past him coldly, like the fashion show turned edgy and the designer gave her one line of walking notes: *look pissed off and determined about it.*

"Wait. Will you stop and just look at me? Charlena—"

"Stopping for anything doesn't serve us well right now. If you will just follow—"

"I would follow you anywhere," Gio cuts in, his gaze still on her like a riveted dance partner. "Even in here."

"Yes." She blinks slowly. "I know."

"But you must also know that's not what brought me here, don't you? Have you seen her? Our granddaughter?"

And so much for that whole dance.

My thoughts are whirring at five times their normal speed, practically afire from the implosion of comprehension they've just withstood.

Charlena, and all her mysterious effects on me, now make perfect sense. Same for why she's making Gio rush over his words like a lovesick middle schooler.

She's the ex who gave him the trigger about mirrors. The demoness lover he'll never be over.

She's also the underworld side of Kara's DNA.

No wonder the old man looks like he doesn't know what to feel right now. I don't begrudge him. But I also know I can't help him with any of it—especially because there's a higher objective at stake right now. A bigger game to prioritize.

"Kara," I blurt. "Have you seen her? Is she…all right?"

I can't help my hesitation before the last part of it. The words that are practically rhetorical. I already know she's not all right. I've seen her myself, in a way. I've felt her hopelessness and heartache. And now, more than that. After Hades broke in on us…all the horror and violation in her eyes and shaking through her body…

"I mean, is she safe?"

It's a relief when Charlena tics a brief nod, already offering a small balm of commiseration. "Reasonably," she finally shares. "Depends how you look at it, I suppose."

"*Reasonably?*" I hope my echo will turn it into something more hopeful but wind up with the exact opposite. Every syllable is a dig of doubt. "What does that mean? You did see her, right? Did you talk to her?"

"Of course I have seen her." She declares that like a starlet announcing a juicy film deal, with a notable glance at Gio as punctuation. "I am now one of his lordship's highest-ranking captains in Dis. It allows me to request certain privileges inside the castle and elsewhere."

While that earns her another look from Gio that's equal parts desire and disgust, I clench my hands to keep from grabbing and shaking the haughty creature. *You need her, damn it. You need her in a* good *mood.*

As if hearing my silent plea, he reaches over, curling the tips of his fingers around the thin joints near her black lacquered fingernails. "Dahlia." She tenses in new ways. I can't tell if she's flinching from recollections the endearment evokes or insulted by being compared to something so earthy and frail, but her new stiffness is prominent.

"Don't call me that," she finally murmurs, fixing her gaze on the grim horizon.

Gio twines more of his hand with hers. "Give me a good reason not to."

"All right. I'll give you the most important reason of all. It brings you no closer to what you clearly came for. If you wish to see Kara, your only chance of that is with me." She casts an impassive stare in my direction. "Unless, of course, you're feeling so brave and bold you'd rather tromp through all nine districts before you storm the castle and face off with an immortal god with exponentially more power and experience than you."

She tilts her head in a way that gives me flashbacks of Veronica. The resemblance, never mind the words, is enough of a reality check for me to pause and consider what I'm arguing over. I have no idea if we can trust Kara's grandmother, but she's right on one account. Letting her fast-track us to Dis makes sense, even if she's going to drop us into the middle of an ambush.

"You'll bring us to her, then?" I ask, even though I can't count on her to tell me anything close to the truth.

"If she's still in the capital, you may well see her there…"

My eyes widen in alarm. "*If* she's still there? Where else would she be?"

My worst fears take over the dialogue in my head. *Kara's gone. She's fucking gone.*

Why can't I fathom it? Why won't my mind accept it? Why hasn't my soul already confirmed it?

Charlena shrugs. "I have no idea. Once Hades has reached all the depths of her mind, who knows how long she'll hold his interest. I saw her fight him off before, but he's not one to give up easily."

"That's my ladybug."

Gio flashes a grin and pumps his free fist. The other one is soon released to join it, courtesy of Charlena breaking away and folding her arms across her leather-clad chest.

"He saw us," I say. A hiss escapes from my clamped teeth. My eye sockets ache deeper. I can't hide my tension, nor do I try to.

The confession seems to break Charlena's chilly exterior. "Us?"

"Kara and me, together."

She frowns. "How?"

"A dream. A dream that felt incredibly real."

"A dream…is the ultimate open space," she expounds. "The confluence of wishes, desires…vulnerabilities. A place where your protections come all the way down—"

"And assaults can move all the way in."

Only Gio has the courage to mutter it. I'm physically incapable. The only thing preventing my knees from buckling all the way back down to the ground are my hands' brutal grips on them.

"So she's already gone." Every syllable is drenched in my own misery. "Is that what you're telling us?"

"No. But if he's broken into her mind and accessed her thoughts that deeply already, her time with him may soon run its course. Especially now that he's seen you *together*, connecting in an even deeper way that he's powerless to stop… Honestly, I can't predict how he'll react or where his interests will trail…if they don't fade altogether." She flashes a look at Gio. "And you returning when you should have never left… That's certainly salt in the wound. Does he know you're here too?"

"I have no idea, love. I seem to have a familiar face in these parts, so it's possible word has made it back to him."

"News travels faster in some circles than others. Kara's visions had me suspicious that Maximus had broken through to find her. I decided to take up the search myself. When I learned he wasn't traveling alone, I had to come see for myself. I thought it might be you," she confesses. "But Hades may not find out so quickly. Needless to say, most of us are invested in our self-preservation here. Not many are especially eager to dispatch an ill-received message to the king of pain and agony, regardless of one's tenure or status."

Which could rule out Minos or Charon running to Hades with bad news. Or the beast panting not-so-patiently nearby, seemingly waiting for Charlena's go-ahead to chew us to bits. While our tenuous circumstances should have me more than ready for her to whisk us to the capital, something still holds me back. But it's not going to get resolved if I just sit here and brood silently.

"Why are you helping us?"

"What makes you think I'm helping *you*?"

Her somber emphasis has me regarding her with new concentration.

"You've implied as much," I counter.

"You think so because you're a victim of your mortal world's propensity for sentimentality and weakness. Don't be mistaken. I have neither."

The new tightness in Gio's features all but negates the statement. I'm more willing to believe she's telling the absolute truth. She's a full-blooded demon, after all.

"But," she continues with a measure less venom, "Let us say I am not a stranger to his lordship's hobby of collecting mortal experiences." While her tone is subdued, it shouts so much—and exposes another element behind her enigma. She's proud of that captain's symbol embossed in the leather of her jacket but not necessarily of the leader who bestowed it.

"And Kara, with her hybrid blood, must be like a new dessert for him," Gio adds.

She straightens her stance. "Of course. And while I have no interest in forcing myself into her mind as he does, I am interested in her gifts, not to mention our shared curse, if you will. She'll be relegated to the third district when he's finished with her. I've been promised this in exchange for what already feels like an eternity of loyal service." Her gaze, tracking between us, falters even less than before. "Now we really should be going."

I release a caustic laugh. "You really think either of us is going to let you have Kara?"

She appraises me for a long moment. "I think, Maximus Kane, that you are very brave and impassioned, and that has you under the illusion that you can somehow change the natural course of things."

"There's nothing *natural* about a demon breeding out a family's humanity," I snap. "Being a product of that betrayal is Kara's only sin. She's a good person. She doesn't deserve to have Hades violating her thoughts whenever he pleases, and she sure doesn't deserve an eternity in your special corner of hell. Don't you get that?"

She has the audacity to smile. "Taking your anger out on me will do no good. You have to get through Hades first, remember."

"I plan to."

She lifts a shoulder. "Then we should be on our way, don't you think?"

"Dahlia. My darling—"

All Charlena's humor vanishes when she sets her gaze upon Gio once more. But she doesn't admonish him for lavishing her with sweet praises I'm unsure she deserves at this point.

"Please," he continues, "we both know my chances of making it out of hell twice aren't very high. If any of the minutes, hours, or days that we spent together meant a shred of anything to you, do me this favor. Give me a moment more with Kara before Hades tosses me to whatever place I surely deserve. Can I see her again? Can you bring me to her?"

She narrows her eyes. "Do you think you can deceive me with such a simple ploy?"

He takes in a heavy breath. "Charlena, it was you who first deceived me, remember? I only ever saw the best in you."

Her only answer is a tight press of her lips. Such a small move that says so much.

With no reply, Gio presses on. "I beg you. Can we have just a moment with her?"

After several agonizing seconds, she dips a short nod. "It might be possible…to calibrate a small glitch in our return trip."

I trade a glance with Gio. Though I'm ready to give up a minor grin, his features are unsteady. By now, I know better than to not trust that look.

"A glitch like what?" I ask.

"A delay," Charlena says. "*Not* a long one," she qualifies. "I cannot risk the king's wrath by extending it more significantly. Now that I've found you, I have no choice but to deliver you to him myself. But he's not expecting Gio. It'll buy you at least a little time while I explain the situation."

"And then?" I ball my hands into fists at the thought of facing Hades again. After all he's put us through, my expertise at self-control is going to face its most grueling test.

"Well, I suspect Hades will make quick work of you. He won't kill you, of course, with you being the son of Zeus and all. If you're lucky, you'll wake up in front of Honey Bacchus at the Labyrinth in no time, feeling a lot worse than the hell that spat you out. Hopefully, you'll be a bit older and wiser. Wise enough, at least, to know how foolish this quest was to begin with."

We couldn't disagree more, but I'm game for her plan if it finally puts me in front of Kara. I'm even willing to swim a hundred more rivers and brave a thousand more hellhounds, though I hope we're now nearer to the ultimate treasure of my love.

"I look forward to proving you wrong," I say, determined to make her hear my dedication, though it's clear I've lost her attention.

She's busy wrapping her face in its black covering once more, a mystery I can't begin to unravel. Not with this new leg of our vital journey ahead of me.

"Come, now. Both of you."

But the dictate isn't necessary. As soon as she starts swirling a hand in the air, Gio and I are mesmerized. The light trails that follow in the wake of her fingertips are like stars, except they're formed out of razors. As they collide with the moisture in the air, fierce sparks shoot out. The mini daggers fly farther and farther, raining along her sleeve until it's shredded.

Even Cerberus seems impressed, as he's retreated to the far edge of the canyon. Charlena sticks to her task, steady as if she's tracing a line in the air, until she's burned a large hole into the atmosphere.

No. Not a hole.

A doorway.

"Damn," I rasp along with Gio.

In the area framed by the door, the air begins to change.

The sizzling portal lures us into a long hallway. The dismal lighting and bleak stone walls are an upgrade from the canyon we're leaving behind for a multitude of reasons, not the least of which is that I can start to make out our destination.

It's a library.

As the doorway closes behind us, details about the place we're moving toward become clearer.

The room looks like the touchdown target for a tornado, with furniture toppled and loose paper sheets like uncollected leaves across the dusty Persian carpets.

At once, all my senses kick in. My pulse quadruples. My eyesight goes from human to hawk. Both my shoulders are on fire, as I feel my broken skin start to repair itself. The rest of my body is also a blaze of awareness, tormented by an onslaught of need. An overriding pull to get myself all the way through the hallway as quickly as possible—though I'm damn sure it's not for a nostalgic read of Poe or Blake.

There's only one force capable of making my limbs feel like outlaw torches and my brain clamor for a sharp guillotine. Nothing gives away the truth deeper than the inescapable jolts to every vein and the ventricles of my heart.

The heart that's meant to be with only one other.

Kara.

"You all right?"

Gio's question registers in my mind, but when I nod, it's an affirmation to the call of my heart, not the question on his lips.

I rush forward, past an all-too-still Charlena. I hope that

her new statue act is a reflection of her focus: that she's working on giving Kara and Gio those precious seconds of stolen time and nothing more. I order myself to home in on the same thing. I need to get through. I need to keep moving toward her fire, so achingly close now. I need to chase the storm that's so uniquely hers, its spices twinge my nose. One…step…at…a…

A giant cosmic hand suddenly shoves me forward. I grunt, all the air knocked out of me, while tumbling into the large room.

At first, I shiver. The temperature has dropped by at least thirty degrees. It smells a little better, though. And then, as I raise my head, even wonderful.

Incredible.

She's here.

So small but seeming even more so due to her hunched-over shoulders. From her defined shudders and soft whimpers, I can tell she's crying. Her slight form moves in and out of the lamp puddle in which she's kneeling. Her hair is a thick, shiny tangle against her shoulder, which is bare because her lush red robe has slipped a little.

She's gorgeous even in her sadness. With her cinnamon spice in my nostrils and her shimmering skin in my sights, I wonder if she's even real. I'm suddenly overwhelmed with the fervent need to step over and haul her into my arms. To kiss her with such possession, she forgets about who made her wear that robe or who's brought on her tears. More vitally, who violated her mind with his insidious touch.

I vow to right all his wrongs. To bring back her joy after

so much desolation. To light up her soul as I finally push sound up to my lips. The sound of one word alone.

"Kara."

CHAPTER 14

Kara

SOBS OVERWHELM ME. MINUTES pass as anger threads through the hopelessness I can't seem to shake. I'm banging my fists against the old library's shelves, tearing at the dusty tomes and adding to the mess of the room until I fall to my knees in defeat. Wiping at my unending tears, I take the smallest solace that I could still be with Hades and his minions, planning Maximus's defeat.

I take in a deep breath, then groan in frustration for taking my anger out on the books. They're not mine, but books have been my only companion at times. A wonderful comfort in bleak times when being a Valari—celebrated and sought after—was simply too much.

I begin the task of stacking up the casualties of my tantrum. I recognize a few titles in English. Most are in Latin. I open one, slicing my index finger in the process of turning the pages. Blood drops land on the fragile paper. I close the book quickly, only to expose the book beneath. Dark round droplets land on the book's emblem—a faded golden torch. Below, gold lettering reads Ἑκάτη in ancient Greek.

"Hecate," I mutter. "Goddess Hec—"

A pinpoint of burning light traces the outline of the emblem, rendering me speechless for a moment. Once the light completes its circuit, the cover loosens from its pages as if the book has taken a small breath and released itself to be opened. I reach for the cover's edge, eager to explore the contents of this already mesmerizing tome.

The pages, filled with combinations of symbols and words that glow as my fingers pass over them, is a golden sustenance I've never taken in before. It's as if a higher power took my bond with Maximus and translated it into chants and sounds and symbols that only I can understand.

I'm so busy marveling at the book and the energy coming off its pages that I barely hear my name. I falter for a second, certain it's my mind playing fantastical tricks on me. But I breathe deeply, borrowing from the strength that my veins draw in from the book.

"Kara."

But there it is again, rough as rustled leaves but steadier than the oak they fell from—effectively reducing me to the texture of a sapling. Even in the space I've found out of sheer instinct, I need just a few minutes of solace before trying to deal yet again with my new reality.

No. Not total instinct. The library beckoned as if I'd been by it a thousand times instead of a couple. It called as if I were meant to be here. It spoke to me just as the book has, making me forget where I am and why I even escaped in here…

Until now.

I look back up, expecting the horror of hell to press back down on me.

But instead see only beauty.

Even in the far corner of all the disheveled chaos, there's new light and mighty magnificence...

Because the room is filled with the glory of *him*.

I tremble and can't control it. I tear up again, and that's even more impossible to stop. Still, I'm certain that I must be dreaming again...

Until Maximus starts to stride over.

And I shake harder, as his every step cannon blasts along the walls.

Until he gets even closer.

And I breathe like some Victorian maid getting ready to pass out in her stupid corset.

It gets even worse as he pushes into the puddle of light that defines my little corner. I can see the cobalt rings of his irises again. I can smell him, so rugged and masculine and yet earthy and stormy, but I still don't trust that storm. This can't be real. This *can't* be...

But then there are the details I can't overlook. Through the wide gashes in his shirt, I gawk at his bloody and broken skin. Though there's a lot of pink, freshly healed wounds, it's simple to see that a beast tried to rip him apart.

Perhaps a monster with more than one head.

A predator he faced, along with so many other dark creatures and trials and storms, just for the chance to be here next to me again.

I know it now as truth.

Because I feel it from him as fact. As such a glaring refrain from his soul that I practically read it in the air as text. It's irreversible. Unmistakable.

I know him now. I *feel* him now. I experience every one of his vibrations—a mix of such potent need and endless euphoria, clipped at the end by that self-imposed control, that I can trust the moment in full now. I can open my heart to it. Especially as he clears the last step between us.

And I'm suddenly, *finally*, swept up into his perfect hold. Crushed tightly along his massive body. Wrapped in a shower of light and sparks and energy, possible only from the miracle of finally holding him again. Connecting with him. Rejoicing in the fusion of our energies and the light of our love, until it feels like time itself has halted…

Until, with the sweep of his kiss, it does.

I cling to him harder as I open for him wider, sighing as our tongues mix and our breaths meld. My blood heats as I feel his pulse, the very beats of our bodies matching each other. Aligning with our perfect fire. Our inexplicable electricity. The fusion that I experience with nobody but him. The connection that is ours alone, undeniable and impenetrable.

Except…not.

I pull away, sobbing in a flood of shame. I don't know how to tell him about what's happened with Hades, but it's worse to think about keeping it from him. I dip my head, doubling the motion as a desperate sort of prayer. Perhaps Maximus will understand, having been the first one to have the god tromping through his head. But what if he doesn't?

"Kara? Hey, look at me. It's really me this time, sweetheart. I promise you."

"I know."

I blurt it quickly, realizing how severely our time is surely limited. We have to make every second count.

"Then talk to me, beautiful." It's a command despite his velvety murmur. He cups the sides of my face and peers deeply into my eyes.

I want to just abandon everything and take long swims in those lush blue fathoms. I want to take permanent shelter in the strong surety of his hold. I yearn to do so many things that won't fit into the short moments we have. I must force myself to face the truth and recall all its awful detail.

"Hades... He..."

"What?" So much for the soft fabric of his tone. His words are as fierce as the new glints in his eyes and the indents at the corners of his mouth. "What did he do, Kara?"

"He...got in." I touch my forehead, hoping that's enough to convey my full meaning. Saying all the words feels like a massive impossibility right now. "I didn't want him to," I say with frantic desperation. "I fought him; I fought so hard...but then I fell asleep, and I had a dream that felt so—"

"Real." Just like that, his violence vanishes. His energy is different yet wonderfully familiar. I recognize it from a reality that feels so long ago. It's the way he gets in class, stroking his used copy of *The Divine Comedy* to the point that every female in the building suddenly wants to be old, leathery, and full of medieval poetry. I get it now because *I'm* at the center of that quiet but intense thought process. And it's already that addicting.

Still, I manage to murmur back, "Yes. *Real.* How did you—"

"Because it was my dream too."

My heartbeat thrashes. My gaze flares. His gaze rivets me harder as he rubs a thumb along my cheek. "I was there, right along with you. Somehow, I was able to see you...dressed in *this* thing"—he glances down, obviously unhappier about Hades's choice of wardrobe for me than I am—"until you got up from that big bed, and then—"

"Walked over to you, on that red lounger," I finish in an astonished rush. "That couch... I hadn't seen it in my room before..."

"Probably because it wasn't," he offers. "It was part of the room *I* was in."

"And where were you?"

I don't want to be so enthralled and curious, especially since it's a dangerous way of avoiding my true terror about this whole nightmare, but if I can't indulge it now, in the shelter of his arms, I also lose out. If, by some strange gift of the cosmos, we survive all this, I have to be able to remember it all.

A gift of the cosmos...that might have just been bestowed in the form of the book I found in the corner.

But at the moment, all of that is still just a few pages of nonsense to be stored at the back of my mind. All that matters now is Maximus and the few seconds we have left in this beautiful bubble.

"We were in the noble castle," he explains. "Getting in a quick rest."

I join my smile with his despite the tiny pang in my heart. My expression is right out of Gramps's book. How I wish I could see him right now. And Kell and Jaden...even my mother. "That place is actually real?"

"Can you believe it?" he returns. "No meadow, river, or seven walls, though. But Charon and Minos, with a few embellishments, are pretty much written to truth."

My jaw drops. "Oh, come on. You're just saying all this to keep me gasping."

He playfully kisses my nose. "Little demon, I have better ways of doing that."

His expression, so adoring and passionate, has me mesmerized for a long moment before his words fully hit me.

"Wait. You said *we* were in the noble castle. We...who?"

"What's shaking, little ladybug?"

Once again, I'm motionless except for some stunned blinks up at my lover, who's still wearing a mischievous grin. That's because he *knows* that no other voice in the world could have me scrambling out of his arms only to launch myself into others. As I do, to sob out with sheer elation. To hug in tight until it hurts. To endure, with so much joy, the breath-stealing clinch I'm given in return.

"Gramps." For a long second, I'm afraid to vocalize anything else. I don't want to ruin the dream. But I'm not so successful with tamping my tears. As they gallop out of me, he starts rubbing my back as if to simply soothe me through a bad case of the hiccups.

"One, two, buckle my shoe," he murmurs into my hair, and I burst with a snotty laugh.

"Three, four, lock the door." It's been at least fifteen years since I last uttered the rhyme back at him. It feels amazing now, especially as Gramps joins his light laugh to my watery one. "*You're* the one who got Maximus here?"

"Bah. Only the Vestibule and a couple of shady neighborhoods," he says with a humble shrug. "Your grandmother was the real hero, getting us the rest of the way."

Charlena appears behind him, but she isn't having any of the shrugging. Her posture is taut. "Duty is duty," I offer, letting her save a little more face. No doubt duty has been the key to her rise in stature here. The backbone that's pulled her out of the dreary mire that Hades showed me in the distance when I first got here. Was that only a day ago? A few days? It feels like an entire year sewn together by hopelessness and fear.

The same sensations that overtake me now, as the energy on the air gains palpable ferocity. Suddenly Charlena's sense of duty, not as my grandmother standing beside my beloved gramps but as a soldier of Hades, becomes frighteningly clear. That can only mean one thing. I push the conclusion to my lips while spinning back around to Maximus.

"Hades. He's on his way here. I feel it."

I curse myself for not expecting it sooner. I think about begging Gramps and Maximus to take cover or attempt an escape on their own, but neither of them look ready to do that. Gramps has already lifted his shoulders and planted his feet. Maximus's profile is painfully perfect, with his forehead set and the proud blade of his nose leading down to the firm line of his mouth. His jaw is clenched with such finality, I can visually trace its line through his dirty beard. From there, I can't help but view the tattered hole in his shirt, now torn even farther so the edge of his shoulder shows. But even there he's coiled and proud and prepared.

Outwardly, I shake my head. Inwardly, I'm screaming.

They're both ready to face another monster, just to save my life.

But this time, not just any beast.

The creature who calls himself the ruler of this realm. The god who's already seen inside Maximus. Now, it seems, more than once.

How many weaknesses can Hades exploit now? And what will happen to my own soul if I have to stand here and watch the deaths of the two men I love most in this universe?

I can't. I won't. So I back up and shut my eyes, unwilling to watch even the start of this play out. Refusing to give Hades even a glance as he sweeps into the library, flanked by what sounds like his whole captains' contingent.

For some reason, that's what makes me stand taller and open my eyes again. I'm a weak third in our war party, but at least three against eight—perhaps nine—sounds better than the odds Maximus and Gramps were originally facing.

"Gentlemen. Greetings. Glad to know you both made it here in one piece."

His salutation is such a boom, a lot of the torn books take flight and shed more of their pages. It's a good match for his new uniform, which looks like his tailor took fashion notes from train *and* orchestra conductors and then dipped the whole thing in sinners' blood.

"I didn't come all the way here for friendly banter," Maximus snarls. "So are we all good to just move on?"

Already, several captains bristle his way. Hades stands them down, his hands relaxed in the air. "If that is truly how you wish to play this out, then yes."

"Perhaps we can all agree to be civil," Gramps interjects. "After all, we wanted none of this."

The assertion earns him a curious but sinister look from Hades. "Says the fugitive who's been playing with my mercy for over far too long?"

Hades switches his view, flashing an accusing glance in Charlena's direction. "Ah, there you are. It's not like you to ignore a call of the captains."

She stiffens to tighter attention. "I already knew what you wanted. I figured I would stay a step ahead and find them first."

He smirks. "Clever. Always so clever. I was ready to deliver Kara to one of the others' districts—"

Her composure breaks. "You promised her to *me*!"

"I promised her to the captain who brought me Maximus Kane, which you'd know if you bothered to attend my meeting," he spews back. "And we both know I'll cast her to the ice below the loggia if that's what I want. Don't speak to me as if you can change that, Charlena, or like you deserve anything more than unending agony. Further"—he wheels back around, narrowing his eyes on Gramps—"you must have known how tenuous things were if you went rogue to find me not one but two lost souls. What a massive surprise this is, indeed. Giovani, a divine pleasure to see you again."

To my growing dread, Gramps rebuts that with an equally brazen regard. "Pleasure, eh? There you hell creatures go again, speaking of earthly mechanisms that you claim not to care about."

Hades's laugh is another wall-rocking burst. "Perhaps you temporals would be wiser to value those constructs more—most especially when standing before the god who can make sure you never have to be troubled with them again."

Gramps, clearly already expecting something like that, jogs his head higher. I have no idea what he's about to verbally add to that, but I do feel all the outrage that's going to drive it. Anger that won't be taken well at all by our host.

But my plan to cut his mistake short—by silently beseeching Maximus to step in—has struck a roadblock of its own. As soon as I turn to my breathtaking hero, he steals the air from me in new ways: with several gut punches of his own emotions. Frustration, impatience, and even murderous intentions are boiling near the surface of his composure.

Oh, no. Ohhh, no-no-no.

Where's my staunchly self-controlled Professor Kane when I need him most?

And why do I already know there won't be a quick answer for that?

CHAPTER 15

Maximus

THE DARK WORRY IN Kara's gaze says so much. But also asks too much. She's begging me for restraint, backing her visual plea with a vise grip hold around my forearm. But she's asking for the impossible. She has to see that. Hades isn't going to offer us tea service and a civilized summit. The only shreds of humanity in his skull are what he's stolen straight out of others. He's the Don Corleone of the gods, a savage in a silk suit. Getting through to the former won't be accomplished unless I'm willing to rough up the latter. And by now, Hades has to know I'm not afraid of a little dirt.

Yet even in this roaring wind-up of a moment, all my logical lamps are cranked on full. I'm no longer the skittish newb who sat down with him at Honey Bacchus's bar. I'm the half-god nephew who's had a steep learning curve in this side of the universe and has been fairly crushing it so far. Surely even he sees that by now. Even the god of chaos has to respect the power of perseverance and give it a place at his bargaining table.

"That got you feeling a little better, Uncle?" I insert into the silence that's oozed on for too long. "Now that you see we're all clear about who the big man in the room is, can we move on?"

The second I verbally dot it, a small hand digs into the back of my elbow. I'm not scoring points with Kara, as she's clearly conveying.

"*Maximus*." Her half hiss only gets her my outstretched hand, grabbing her in gentle admonition. As much as I want to give her more than that, I don't dare. Trusting Hades once cost me a chunk of sanity. The second time, the price was much steeper. Now, I'm not about to take my eyes off him.

My intensity doesn't derail his slimy serenity for a second.

"Cute." His charcoal gaze maintains enough of a peeved spark to keep the beast battalion squirming. But not for long.

They all jolt in their seats when the dark god clasps his hands at the apex of his stiffened stance. I almost expect a jewel-encrusted cane—or a fire-wrapped sword—to materialize beneath his stacked palms.

"Of course we can move on," he says, again with too much congeniality to believe. "This is home, nephew. I'm more than content if you are. Besides, we've been having some reasonable levels of fun around here lately." He tilts his head and scoots his gaze around to Kara. "Isn't that right, love?"

Now the captains aren't the only ones twitching. But

my violent shift likely has a much different motivation—and intention. Kara, already sensing it, tightens her grip at my elbow. This time, she hooks around the whole crook. My every blood vessel, exploding like ignited hydrogen, doesn't care. My vision is painted red. My senses are nothing but rage.

The stuff's so thick and potent, I barely notice when Gio lurches in, all but spitting in my face. "Stow it, son." He slams a harsh hand to my sternum. "He's baiting. You know this."

The last corners of my mind blare in agreement. The sections of me that remember every part of my woman that this monster has seen. Her naked body. Her bared mind. The heights of her ecstasy and the gloom of her despair. Shame that *he* brought her to in the name of his goddamned *fascination*.

The visions keep frothing, swelling into blacker clouds of rage, but I cling to a shred of perspective. Hades is anything but a simple character. He's been alive for millennia, which gives his evil more dimensions than I can fathom. He can't be underestimated, though that doesn't mean he can't be understood. And right now, understanding is one of the few tools I have left. If it gives me just one more weapon to outwit him...

I just have to dig deeper.

What's he after?

I mean, beyond the obvious choice of what's in front of him right now. If Kara is the ultimate treasure, he wouldn't still be so fully engaged now. He'd have left Gio and me to his capable horde and moved on. Even Charlena has already implied that we're just passing entertainment until a shinier interest comes along.

Right now, I'm assuming that shiny thing is named Persephone.

How much longer until the goddess of the underworld is back? If this place hasn't messed too heavily with my sense of passing time, I determine that their reunion must be imminent, on the day of the autumnal equinox. But that's assuming the tall tale of the ancients is close to true.

In the last week alone, I've been to a cocktail bar in a portable realm, watched hellish statuary transform into moving beasts, and been ambushed by my own flashback of life in Olympus. So buying into Persephone doing the earth-underworld commute every six months isn't my most massive stretch. It actually makes the next thought easier. I now see Hades in a brand-new light. He's just a sad, bored husband waiting for the love of his life to come home.

But with that assumption on the table, is he really going to risk that prize for some temporary amusement? Pawns he's going to forget once his true love walks through the door?

Waiting around for that answer isn't a good idea. No way are we going to figure out how long it'll take for him to throw us away. And he'll not have a moment more of Kara's thoughts so long as I'm here and able.

The resolve spurs me to take a protective step in front of her. My height and bulk already create an imposing barrier between her and Hades.

The movement inspires another smirk from Hades. "You truly think you can protect her?"

"I can. And I will." I roll my stance higher. "You've enjoyed your sick voyeur moments, haven't you? That's the only reason she's here, right?"

He smirks. "New experiences are always exciting. But even when they're *not* new, they're...useful."

I clench up both my hands. It's my only defense against showing him what I'd find *useful* right now. "You've had your fun," I spit out. "Now let her go home and we can be done with this."

"Hmm. Just like that?"

"This doesn't have to be hard."

He shakes his head with a deepening smile. "My word. You do have your father's sense of entitlement, don't you? You actually think you can bound into my kingdom and take *my* subjects. And what authority would you be invoking for that exactly? A lover's passion? A professor's intellect?"

I push toward him, fists still formed. "I'll fight every lackey you've rallied here if that's what it takes."

"And you think *that's* what makes you deserve her?"

"That's the difference between us, Uncle. I already know I don't deserve her."

His nostrils flare. "She's mine. Mine!"

The last proclamation rattles more books from their shelves. But by now, his temper only riles my own. Kara may not be mine to possess, but she's mine to protect. To love and worship and save from a vicious fate she doesn't deserve.

My muscles coil tighter. My gut clenches hard. There's

thunder in my ears as I take another threatening step toward him.

"Maximus, no. Don't be foolish!" Kara keeps fighting to drag me back, even tearing my shirt more with her furious effort. Part of it slips down one of my arms, but it doesn't matter. I'm everything at once—passion and adrenaline and exhaustion and utter fearlessness—because I see it all now. Hades and his full, undeniable plan. His scheme to whip *me* up like a volcanic meringue and then watch me froth over the edge right at him. For the sheer *fascination* of it.

Fine. I'll give him what he wants if he keeps his focus off Kara. I'll take the bait and entertain him with my rage. I'm already painting an invisible target on the middle of his torso, right where I'm going to smash my knee into his cold and calculating heart—

My offense makes psychological incisions he can't ignore. His upper lip twitches as our visual standoff goes on, confirming thoughts I've only harbored as hunches until now.

Until I'm suddenly thrown down to my back.

Deflected by a fire blast that's like a flamethrower burn, except it's still only Hades standing there. At least I think so. My view now consists of the library's gold leaf ceiling, as well as the pair of minions pinning me down. But not for long. Their weight, even combined, is already succumbing to my struggle. All I have to do now is plant my feet for some leverage and then shove up and—

"What the—" I'm suddenly choking hard. Then

bursting into a violent bellow. I pump my legs, kicking out—or trying to, as several spots along both those limbs are immobilized by shots of searing pain.

My protests only make the torment worse. I have no direct sightline at what's going on courtesy of the hell disciples kneeling into my ribcage and elbows, but it feels like someone or something keeps taking mini blow torches to my ankles, shins, and knees. Any second now, I'm positive I'll be smelling my charred flesh. When a minute passes and I'm still only inhaling stale dust off the floor and pungent sweat from everywhere else, a more gruesome truth hits.

That relief isn't coming.

This is hell, and I'm going to burn like this for as long as Hades dictates it.

"Maximus!"

Kara's shriek is like an echo, haunting the rational thoughts that still huddle in the corners of my mind. But they won't crawl out far enough so I can connect them to words. My throat is nothing but agonized clenches as my senses fight to process my physical torment.

Perhaps…if I can just look at her again…

Somehow, I rally enough strength to raise my head again—but my timing couldn't be worse. I refocus just enough to glimpse Hades dropping a finger, giving two more demons permission to go at me. They swarm in with gleeful cackles and snarls, joining their friends to clamp me down harder. I swear and grunt against their holds, but it's no use. Their grips are like stun guns, drenching all my muscles in paralysis. All the protests on my lips and stamina in my limbs are abandoned to a thousand shadows of grim, dark surrender.

And a million new horizons of scorching pain.

CHAPTER 16

Kara

I DON'T LET UP my protesting screams. They spill from me over and over again, but everything still moves too fast, beyond my control. In less than a minute, I've gone from tugging on Maximus to clawing at Hades's pawns, my nails tearing into their half-dead flesh like kids' clay. But it won't matter to these eternally dead creatures. None of it will stab harder, pierce deeper, or torture as brutally as this misery of a moment.

Maximus's roars take over the air. His agony sears my soul. The captains sear slits into his clothes, clearing the way for his fresh agony.

But it's not just the pain he's physically enduring. It's the harrowing helplessness that's twisting at his psyche…that's hauling him, inch by exhausted inch, toward the precipice at the edge of his sanity. The escape, like a welcome dream to him now, into nothingness. I know because I can feel it more acutely than anything else, even my own blinding fear.

"Maximus!" I shriek out. "Don't go there, Maximus. *Please* don't go!"

But while his head lolls over, responding as I invoke his name, his gaze is as vacant as a dead monitor screen. He looks right through me, lost to everything but the unending fires of his torture. But in the most central part of my awareness, in that inexplicable place so deep in my chest, I feel fire of a different kind. A spark of something so desperate and exigent, stretching out to the corresponding part of me.

It's him.

"Oh my God," I rasp, knowing it as utter fact.

Suddenly, beyond those empty screen eyes and the awful sounds from his throat, I can hear his voice echoing inside me too.

Kara.

With my heart tangled in my larynx and my hands wringing the tatters of his shirt, I force my head up and my gaze all around.

Come and find me, Kara.

I don't know where to look or what to do. I'm misplaced and terrified. Since the first day we laid eyes on each other, our bond has been palpable and powerful. We both suspected it before we even touched. After that first kiss, we knew it. We were both so sure of each other. So thoroughly led by our faith and belief in each other. My grandfather might have been his guide to physically get here, but Maximus's courage for the journey was driven by his tethers to me. And I persevered through the nightmare because of a hope that was tied to him.

A hope that's fading fast…

But isn't gone.

"Not yet."

I rasp it aloud because my spirit needs to hear it like that. Because I sense Maximus's does too. But the affirmation still feels pointless. Even struggling to my feet feels like trying to dock a broken ship in the middle of a raging squall. My heart is ripping. My courage is slipping. My mind is spinning. My instinct tells me to lurch forward, leap at Hades, and rip into his face the same way I've gouged parts of his minions.

But there's an instant disconnect. I yearn to do it but can't. The ugly truth behind that doesn't take long to come. There'd be retribution, swiftly delivered—and not to me. The love of my existence is still in Hades's ruthless custody. His captains don't make a move without his calculated permission. I shudder to think what would become of Maximus if more of his temperamental buttons were pushed. There's no way I can help unless it's to wreck Hades himself. *But how?*

Then I finally see it. Most vitally, I *hear* it.

Find me…

The last time he sent those words to me, we were joined in a half-conscious fantasy. One of the best dreams of my life—until it wasn't. Until Hades invaded my memories, down to their last detail. Until he looked at me with such voracious intent, like he planned to do so again.

So why should I be the one to deny him now?

I quickly set fire to the feeling. For this crazy plan to work, crazy is all I can permit in every synapse right now.

All the insanity of my frustration. The consuming darkness of my fury. The dizzy senselessness of my pain and sadness and loss.

It's not hard to bring them all back. After stumbling forward and dropping as close as I can to the savage fray, the sight of Maximus's straining neck and quivering limbs has me mentally reaching out, battling to soothe him in even the tiniest way. But it's no good. He's already so far gone. And I'm still so useless to him.

I hate this. With every drop of my blood and breath in my body, I hate it. He's been there for me so many times, and now I'm right here next to him, without a single weapon or power to help him in return.

All I have…is me.

But maybe that's enough. "Hades." I shuffle back toward him, still on my knees. I hunch my shoulders and bow my head. To save Maximus's life and sanity, I'll lick the dust off Hades's boots as this whole crowd watches. For now, I settle for giving the god a verbal version of that. "Please. *Please*…I am begging you…"

"And oh so prettily," the king finally murmurs, ticking up my hope that the wilder plan might be averted. He reaches down and cups my chin. "Do go on, love."

But then he has to go and repeat that.

Which turns Maximus into nothing short of a blood-baited animal. He roars and bucks, breaking an arm free from his paralysis. Another one of Hades's captains joins his friends in holding him down again. I can hardly bear to watch, but I do, funneling the helpless misery into the new fervor of my pleas.

"Why?" I demand. "*Why* are you doing this? Your quarrel is with me, Hades. *My* disobedience!"

"Brought on by your obsession for *him*," he spits back. "A compulsion he did nothing to thwart. An attraction he *welcomed*—"

"Because he knew nothing until it was too late! He had no idea the vow I was breaking."

He scoffs.

A shiver claims my body. I suddenly relate to Sisyphus, rolling the same stone up the same damn hill. Hades seems determined to punish Maximus for a situation he never sought out, no matter what I say. Or maybe Hades already knows the words I don't dare give volume to. That torturing Maximus is a worse blow to my soul than any persecution he can dole to me.

But until Hades physically silences me, I have to keep trying.

"I'm kneeling here before you, begging you to let me pay the price for my own wrongs. To serve my sentence. All of it. Whatever duty or penance you would have me do. Even if"—I gulp hard enough to cut off my breath for a long moment—"even if you want to encase me in the ice. Just please...*please* spare Maximus."

Every syllable now drips with my torment. With the anguish so great, I welcome its crippling stiffness in my limbs. I raise my head like a schoolgirl at prayer, hoping my suffering puts even a dent in the glowering divinity before me.

"You may rule a dark world, but you don't do it

unjustly," I say. "You discipline with reason. This detention you've enacted…this pain you're meting…" I slowly shake my head. "It's unnecessary and unfair. It betrays emotions that are far below you. Weaknesses you shouldn't have."

I swallow hard again. The allegations are beyond reckless and dangerous, but I don't care. But damn it, neither does Hades. He doesn't surrender a nick of his composure. Not a flash of fire or fury or even a glimpse of the patient gentleman who first welcomed me here.

"I'm still pleading you, with all my heart and soul. I'm asking you to consider, with any drop of the care and generosity—"

"No," he retorts, even motioning over another captain to become part of the brutal horde on top of Maximus. "You don't get any arguments or exceptions or points to make. No repartee or jokes or deft little observations disguised as witticisms. Understood?"

He squeezes my chin until I'm whimpering, certain he's about to crush my jaw. But I welcome the pain as equally as his wrathful eyes and hateful grimace. It's all part of the thickening mix growing exponentially inside me, as part of the plan I have to enact now. The risk I have no choice but to take. The last chance that I desperately hope will work. *I hope…*

"Under…stood," I manage to rasp, casting my gaze back down. The little sign of respect is perfectly timed, letting me stockpile more of the dark devastation that edges up from my soul and takes over from my heart. When I start trembling again, I almost order my senses to slam off. Grief and despair are impossible enough to get through when they're *un*invited. Am I actually *letting* this chaos take over me? Drown me?

Yes. For Maximus, I'll endure it all tenfold. Or ten times *that*. Whatever I have to do. Whatever chunk of my soul that needs to be given.

Hades mellows his touch into a firm slide along my cheek. "Good girl. It's so much better that you fully comprehend your place, Kara. You know exactly what it is I want from you in return. And I *will* have all of it. Very, *very* soon." He frames the other side of my face with his free hand, gruffly rubbing my skin as if to praise my submissive pose. I hate every second of it. "And perhaps, if you don't want your lover to keep paying that special fare, even sooner than that."

No way will fate ever deliver me a larger kick in the backside—or in this case, frontal lobe—and every electrified thread of gray matter attached to it. Everything about the moment is aligned. Every digit of fate's hand is shoving me forward.

And I let it.

As I lift my head again and rivet the intent of my stare into his suddenly scowling one.

As I seize his hands like a revenant, newly awakened from my grave—and carefully watch as he visibly jolts.

As I take as much morbid pleasure in crooning to him, "You mean we'll get there like this?"

And as I flatten his fingers over my temples—and let him have every hideous drop of the emotions in my senses.

Even the ones drenched in Maximus's torment, passing more of Hades's own evil right back into his veins.

"Careful," I murmur. "You may get exactly what you ask for."

Hades opens his mouth as if to speak, but no words come. For once, he's as gutted, sickened, and speechless as all this filth first made me. But most importantly, he's frozen to the point of immobility—though I don't expect that anomaly to last long.

Meaning I don't have another second to lose.

"Gramps!" I call out while rushing back to my feet. I'm grateful when he appears fast, steadying my nervous wobble until my adrenaline fully kicks in. It doesn't come a second too soon, giving me bravery that still feels so far away. "Stay here, next to Maximus. Get ready to help him. We don't have a lot of time."

Gramps rears back and shakes his head. "For what?"

"Maximus." It's all I can get out in reply. "Just...help him."

If this works at all.

But I don't waste the seconds to utter that. Every move matters now. Every breath, every intention, every insane instant of this far-fetched plan—which is actually starting to feel like all kinds of right as soon as I pivot and seek out the book that was speaking to me with such mysterious force.

I'm relieved to find the tome right where I left it, in the library's corner. I have to admit to being surprised. After just a few minutes of absorbing the words and symbols that felt written just for me, I half expected the thing to borrow matching magic and walk out of here. But I'm so thankful that it decided to stay, especially when the torch painted on its cover begins pulsing with gold light once more.

This time, I think I know why the book stayed for me. Perhaps why I found it to begin with.

For the briefest of seconds, I close my eyes and run a hand over a page. Then the next and the next and the next, waiting for something to make sense. Sensing it's going to crystallize with meaning the way a certain line of poetry in Dante's *Comedy* would. The act fills me the same way, as if I've reached into thunderheads and grabbed the lightning swaddled within.

Suddenly the words on the page are electricity in my veins. A blinding force in my soul. A feeling so perfect and right in my spirit—until the energy pulses down the lengths of my arms.

It races past my elbows and then my wrists until it builds beneath my fingers. It throbs there to the point of pain.

Until I bring out the words to set it free.

"*In the land of Amazon, goddess on high, pray you rise till we are nigh.*"

My eyelids flutter, and the world starts to flash. Between flares of consciousness, I notice key things—like the captains cowering away from Maximus, and Hades unable to do a thing about it. Though he growls and gnashes, his head rolling as if he wants to bellow an order, no sound emanates from the god I've wrapped in ropes of grief.

"*Many forms yet one light, your stars aflame to guide us right.*"

The world pulses brighter. Only vaguely do I realize it's because of the light that's throbbing at the ends of my fingers. It's as thick and gold as the torchlight I've just invoked: a warmth that flows back up my arms and then across my chest, my head, my mind. I'm on fire, but in the most beautiful way. The brighter my inferno gets, the dimmer the red rings are around Maximus's arms and legs. As I absorb it all deeper, my smile spreads wider. This feels... amazing.

But I'm not doing it alone.

I know that with the same harmony and heat that continue filling my limbs and overflowing from my heart. I know it because in that endless golden surge, I feel an additional flow. The power of the book...and the higher grace of its author.

"Hecate," I mutter, somehow knowing this to be fact. The revelation inspires more of her words to flow through me.

"*Fax accenditur superiores. Hecate declarat. Ego sum unus cum Hecate.*"

Intuition continues to call me, begging my lips to repeat it like they're burgeoning drops in my swelling storm cloud. I'm helpless to resist the clamor, knowing I have to honor this—whatever it is.

But I'm not lost to it. Not yet. I'm still acutely aware of every occurrence in the room. Of Hades fighting the harsh sadness that won't last forever. Of the beautiful man still too damn close to him, battling the aftereffects from the torture.

"Unholy mercy," Charlena erupts, slamming trembling

fingers to her temples. But she's not the center of my focus. Nobody else matters as much as the man who has my heart screaming in joy as he finally wrenches free from his shackles. Best of all, as he opens his eyes in clear consciousness.

Yet I don't falter my incantation for a second.

"*Fax accenditur superiores. Hecate declarat. Ego sum unus cum Hecate.*"

Maximus charges up to a high kneel, now ricocheting his confused gaze between Charlena and me. "What the— what's going on? Kara? Is she okay? Is this Hades's doing?"

"No." Charlena steps forward, seemingly unafraid of whatever magic I'm channeling from the auspicious book. "The torch burns higher. That's what she's saying. At least the start..."

When her voice clutches as if she can't vocalize the rest, Maximus takes over. "Hecate declares it," he adds with blatant awe. "I am one with Hecate."

"Hecate," Charlena murmurs, trembling from head to toe. "My word. How did she find it?"

"Find what?" Maximus surges all the way to his feet.

"After all these years." She flashes a meaningful glance to Gio. "Hecate's grimoire."

Maximus freezes. Oh, how I long to turn and wrap every inch of myself back around as much of him as I can. But I can't, stirred by this incredible warmth in my senses— and the sorceress helping to stir it. She urges me on. Guides me closer to our precipice. To the climax of this energy brew, blended of love and hope and perseverance, that's going to take us higher. So much higher.

"Holy…" Maximus starts. "A grimoire. *The* grimoire of Hecate? The goddess who's already invoked by everyone from Hesiod and Homer to Ovid and Shakespeare?"

Charlena gives a definitive nod. "And Kara's incanting her conjuration. Nobody here would dare wield the will of Hecate for any other reason."

Maximus responds with wild-eyed wonder. Even now, in the midst of the craziest experience I've ever been through or likely *will* go through, my stomach flips in pure feminine adoration of his rugged handsomeness. The only thing that'd make him more irresistible is a pair of glasses on the bridge of his nose. But I'll settle for the scholarly intensity that builds in his chest-deep growl.

"Hecate is an enchantress of the highest order," my grandmother continues. "She is one of the few who can countermand the All-father and get away with it. She's the goddess of the moon, ghosts…"

Maximus fills in for her purposeful pause. "Yeah. And of witchcraft."

CHAPTER 17

Maximus

KARA INVOKING HECATE—OR WHATEVER is on the pages of that tattered book—is a zero-to-Mach 5 revelation, especially while my body is still so shocked.

But Kara is *shining*. Glowing with whatever hidden forces turn her fingertips into pinpoints of firelight and spread her hair out like star-kissed angel wings. I wish I had forever to take in her glory but can't help assessing the real-time ticking clock that's at our backs. With every passing second, Hades is regaining his faculties. The last few of his demon friends push away from the walls, looking intent on helping but wondering how. I'm right there with them. I have no idea what kind of spell Hades is under or why. All I know is that despite my fondest wishes, it's not going to last forever.

As thoroughly and beautifully as this enchantress gig fits my woman, she's clearly as new to the revelation as I am.

Her spell might have interrupted my captors' efforts for a while, but can it get us all the way out of here?

If not, it might have to be my fists. I prepare for that as one of the captains from the perimeter finally charges forward, a shrill war cry on his lips. Luckily, his lungs seem to be his only weapon. I'm able to silence his shriek with a fast blow to his throat before taking down the rest of him with an elbow-fist pummel to his face.

The rest of Hades's minions are frozen in aftershock. That fallout doesn't last long. The seven other trained beasts stalk toward me now. Hades's face is still locked in abject grief, but his eyes are regaining their leering twinkle of celebration.

Beside me, Kara clutches the glowing book close to her chest. "*Fax accenditur superiores. Et ignem ipsum liberet. Hecate declarat,*" she whispers reverently.

I stare, entranced, as the most dazzling female I've ever known slides her hand around mine.

And then…I'm more than just entranced.

At once, she's imbuing not only my skin with that mesmeric gold heat. From every one of her determined fingertips, a different part of my senses is changed. The hairs along my arms are lifted by a wind so warm I swear I'm on Recto Verso's patio on a summer morning. The air smells the same way, like Sarah's eye-opener brew and a shipment of fresh paperbacks. I can even taste that coffee, bold but laced with a shot of cinnamon. I look over just in time to see Gio wrapping an arm around his granddaughter, smiling as Kara continues the powerful magical litany.

But my smile is bigger. Because sounds of the bookstore start to invade my senses too. All the things I miss so much and even those I never thought I would. The crackling roar of Sarah's bean grinder. The laughter of book clubs inside, dueling with traffic and scooters and crowds from outside.

In another second, they're brutally pierced. Hades's angry roar is like a boulder hurled through the shop's front window.

"No! You can't leave. I forbid it!"

I grip Kara tighter, helping her strike back. If we end up in a billion pieces of nonexistence, lost in cosmic limbo between realms, so be it. We'll be together.

But I'm hoping for a better outcome, as Hades's beasts start to blur until they're unrecognizable. Only Hades remains somewhat clear as he rushes toward us.

"No!" he snarls, charging like a crazed primeval beast. "Give them chase, you cretins! *Give them chase!*"

"My lord...but where?"

I don't know which captain has the balls to shoot back that question, because I can't see any of them anymore. Between one blink and the next, my sights are taken over by light. *So much light.* Once more, I wonder if this will be my forever fate, but that's fine too. Better than fine. Though I can't see Kara or Gio anymore, I feel them with me, moving through this nothing-yet-everything void. The side effect of the trip must be some kind of euphoria or a buoyant relief after what I've been through, because my smile is wider than ever. I've got her back. Finally. We're together again, no matter what.

Along with the light, there's now an indescribable rush of hope. But just as the contentment settles in, the brilliance begins to change. The light isn't so endless. It's taking on shapes. As it does, I'm conscious of Kara's fingers again. This is it. Five fingers, five senses. Sight is her last infusion to me…

And it's the best gift by far.

Because suddenly, magnificently, I'm home.

I'm surrounded by the smell of used books and fresh coffee. I squint my eyes against the glare of sunshine on a clean glass window. The air is alive with laughter, bike bells, *good mornings*, and a million other things that I always took for granted. Never again. Though the sensory bombardment almost feels like too much, I don't shut it off. Not by a drop. I want the whole cavalcade. Every detail that's *not* the moaning, morose, miserable bowels of hell.

Goddamn, I love LA.

I'm so happy, I almost start warbling the Bangles song playing softly over the store's speakers, a sure indicator of who's overseeing the business this morning. I'm glad to hear that Regina's busy chatting up a regular at the moment, though. I need the extra few minutes to get in some essentials, like breathing. Also, to lean over to where Kara's sprawled on the opposite end of the couch, still blinking dazedly. I collect her in my arms, clutch her against my chest, and kiss her until air isn't important anymore.

It's the best kiss of my life.

As I part her lips and stroke her tongue with mine, she's nothing but soft surrender and grateful moans. As the lyrics fill the air, about sun shining through the rain and easing the pain, I'm sure there's not a better track to welcome us home. *Home.*

We're really here. Really just necking on the couch in a coffee shop, like any other normal set of kids who just survived a hell dive.

The musing has me smiling against Kara's lips as we finally do surface for that necessary oxygen. When she stares up at me, brow crinkling with curiosity, I dip in and give her a simple brush on the nose. "You did it, my beautiful little demon," I murmur for her ears alone.

"*We* did it," she whispers, pulling on my neck with a firm hand. Her other one is still wrapped around her big leather book with glowing-fingered ferocity. "Maximus." Tears encroach on her voice, but her gaze is as clear and gorgeous as ever. "I was so scared for you. But somehow it made me brave enough to try. You gave me the strength."

I slowly shake my head. "All of that was in you, beautiful. You're more powerful than you realize."

She yanks on me again until our lips are mashing at each other once more. When she lets me back up, there's a smile on her lips that's new to me. It's dreamy but exultant. Aroused but celebratory.

"I did do it, didn't I?"

"And I'm so fucking proud of you," I concur, dropping into a low and possessive growl as the Bangles get into a new track about a love that's overdue. It's more serendipity, manifesting all the mixed feelings behind my own triumphant grin. Neither of us are normal creatures—

that much is a glaring truth now—so why should we have anticipated a normal love affair? But don't our human halves deserve at least a few moments of that? Aren't we past due for a hefty payment of mortal-style hearts and flowers and couch necking sessions?

Yeah. It's about time we collected on *all* that.

But just when I drop my head in again, intending to sweep my mouth over this woman's in a carnal conquering she'll never forget, Kara pushes me off and jolts to her feet. She still clutches the grimoire like it's also her shield, despite how her eyes are wide and her mouth drops into a stunned O.

"Gramps," she gasps out. "Oh, shit. Did he—"

"Right here, ladybug." The old man pushes up from behind one of the bookstore's big wingbacks. "And now I know how a space shuttle landing feels..."

"Oh God," Kara erupts while joining me to help him get centered in the big chair. "I'm sorry. So so—"

"Ladybug," he interjects, wrapping a hand around her forearm. "Can you do me a favor and cut yourself a little slack? You were in the midst of asking Hecate to help us escape from—"

"What in the bloody hell?"

Regina issues it with the best and worst timing. A second more and she'd have been walking in on the craziest story of the century—but would she have believed it? More definitively, is she filling in the blank for herself anyway? Do I still have hell muck in my hair and beard? Are the stains on my clothes as bad as their multiple rips and tears? Do I have no-sleep-for-days circles under my eyes? It feels like years since I last saw my own reflection. Even as we crossed the Acheron, I was fixating on the vision of Kara in the water, not on my own appearance.

"So?" Reg prompts, tossing her chin up with enough force to have all three of us stiffening. "Escaping from where, now?"

"Ermmm...not *where*." Kara beams a charming smile at Reg while swooping her book beneath a couch pillow. "It was *whom*. A big group of Maximus's new female fans. They spotted us when we were leaving the apartment, and—well, there they were, just waiting out on the sidewalk for us—"

"You were leaving?" Reg inserts again.

"Yes." Kara casually tosses her hair. "To come here, of course."

"In that?" Reg sweeps a look over my woman, not missing every tangle of her hair or wrinkle in her luxurious red gown. But Kara is incredible about rolling with even this. She strikes a pose as if every inch of her muss is a carefully laid plan.

"Sure. We weren't expecting such an audience, of course." She blinks with full authenticity, even as Reg gawks intently at us for a long moment. And then...

"Oh, there you are, ladybug. I'm so glad you outsmarted those media hounds." The comment comes from the smiling guy off to my right, who "enters" and hugs Kara as if he's freshly arrived at the shop. "And Regina Nikian, as I live and breathe! Once a certain little bird told me that you owned this place where she likes coming with Maximus, I knew I had to come and see all the fun for myself."

Reg accepts Gio's effusive hug with a bemused look. "Mr. Valari," she murmurs before giving herself an obvious mental kick. "I—I mean Giovani. Or—errr—"

"Why don't we simply go with Gio?"

He dilutes the awkward tension with the same ease that Kara just diffused the issue about her odd wardrobe. As a broader smile actually has Reg showing teeth, I'm able to take my first full breath in the last five minutes.

"Technically, I was never really your employer," Gio continues. "Anyway, it seems more fitting now to be your friend. I have a feeling these two will be keeping us on our toes for quite some time."

"That would be a nice thing, Gio," Reg answers, seeming more relaxed—at least on the surface. I'm not sure she'll ever trust the Valaris as far as she can throw them, including Kara herself, but for the moment, she's trying. I can be nothing short of grateful.

I try to tell her so with a meaningful glance. She accepts it but is clearly still a little confused. I don't blame her. Who knows what my communication really looked like. What I am most is exhausted right now, and I'm wondering how I'll stay awake during coffee and a catch-up chat with the guy I've just been gallivanting around hell with for the better part of a few days. A few weeks? How much time *has* passed anyway? I'm still without my watch, my phone, and all digital ways of checking.

Just when I tell myself that I really don't care and all that matters is counting the minutes until I can go home and sleep for three days with my woman, more music punches the air. A badly bellowed song coming from the hallway that leads in from Recto Verso's back entrance.

"Good morning to you! Good morning to you! We're all in our places with bright shiny faces, good morning to—"

Jesse stops as soon as he rounds the corner and drops his jaw. He doesn't alter the look while scouring all four of us. "Okay, pardon every bad double entendre here, buddy, but what the *hell* are you doing back here?"

And that's as subtle as a tsunami.

The giant wave of meaning that definitely doesn't get past Regina.

The kind of storm that rides the furious tides in her dark eyes, descending over the irate sneer on her lips, as she stares hard at Kara and me.

I swerve a look toward Kara, hoping she picks up the message in my gaze or the shout in my spirit. They're the exact same, so either is cool.

Anything you can pull out of those pretty sleeves without a massive set of incantations, my beauty—that doesn't *involve my lifetime security detail discovering I took a jaunt to the underworld without her?*

CHAPTER 18

Kara

JESSE SEEMS TO BE putting at least some of our story together. He rolls forward slowly, his gaze traveling rapidly over my disheveled state before noticing that Maximus and Gramps aren't presenting much better. For someone in the know, all we're missing are T-shirts that read *I just took a trip through hell and didn't bring back anything for you.*

I start laughing nervously. I even manage a half-believable blush. "Oh, no! We're so busted!"

Maximus chimes in, chuckling like he has any idea where I'm going with this. He attempts to hide his amusement as I dip my face into my hands as if to cool my faux flush.

"Wow. I'm so embarrassed," I mutter. "We were at a friend's party last night, and I guess we overindulged a little bit. We lost track of our driver and had to take a cab back to Maximus's place. But as soon as the driver recognized us, we told him to stop at the closest place we could think of before he got anything scoop-worthy from the trip. So here we are," I add with a little laugh and flourish of my hand. "Sorry, everyone!"

Reg doesn't join in the awkward smiles that are infectiously spreading through our little group.

Even Jesse plays along, shaking his head like a dad listening to his kids' mischief. "Well, I'll be as green with envy as the guy who missed the party bus. You're still drunk, aren't you?"

Maximus rolls his eyes. "As if."

Reg scoffs. "As if? You came in here with a splitting head two mornings ago, Maximus Kane. Don't tell me special firewater can't dunk you into the cups."

"Two mornings ago." Maximus blinks, confused, but quickly recovers with a rough laugh. "Uhhh, sure. Busted again by the barista who forgets nothing. I guess it's just been a wild couple of days." He exhales a tense sigh. "On that note, we'd better get back to my place before someone recognizes Kara."

Jesse rolls closer. "Or you, man. Your face is still on every gossip rag in town, you know."

"Let's go," Maximus suggests then. "I'll drive."

"I can drive," I insist.

Jesse shoots me a glare and bounces the keys in his hand. "Not a chance. Come on. Later, Reg."

Before Regina can open her mouth to object, he's spun his chair in a smooth one-eighty and started playing drum major for our little band down the narrow hall that leads to Recto Verso's loading dock and back entrance. I'm beyond thankful the guy knows enough to get us out of here fast, but what he doesn't know about the twists that brought us back here could fill half of Hades's library. Maybe more.

As soon as I debate spilling everything—like about how the trash in the alley dumpsters is a better smell than the despair of Dis—Jesse is rolling down the slight concrete incline leading from Recto Verso's back door. The rest of us hurry behind.

"So, forgive me. Can someone spill the proverbial tea for me, kids?"

"In a minute," Maximus replies, clearing the width of the alley in three long strides, then turning it into six on his way back. "What day is it? I mean, exactly?"

Judging by Jesse's initial reaction from inside, I'm already guessing that Gramps and Maximus's trip was a shorter hop than they all anticipated. But that hardly means anything. I have no idea how long it took them to coordinate their mission after I was taken. While so many aspects of my time in Hades's world will never fade in my memory, time isn't one of them. Every moment there felt like a year.

"It's Monday," Jesse supplies. "You didn't know that?"

"No watch, no phone, and I've been navigating underworld physics," Maximus explains.

"Which is why you need to start dishing some details. That was the deal, right? I stay here at headquarters, and I get a full download the minute you're back. Which, granted, wasn't quite as long as I was expecting."

As soon as they exchange another commiserating look, I'm beyond relieved. It's clear Maximus has finally chosen to confide everything to his friend, meaning we don't have to worry about a conversational tiptoe around Jesse anymore. It releases a weight I didn't even know was there—a good thing considering there are a few more to easily replace it. One in particular.

The not-so-tiny souvenir I picked up in hell. The book in Hades's library that refused to let me ignore it. The book, I'm beginning to realize, that isn't a book at all.

And I'm holding it because I understand it. Because it spoke to me in ways that it clearly doesn't to others. The recognition drives me to clutch the tome close to my chest, intensely protective of it. Yes, its magic delivered us from hell, but deeper instincts tell me that this book means more. Can *do* so much more.

Maximus clutches my hand tightly. I sigh, certain that I've fallen in love with him even more through the insanity we've just survived. But I'm as schoolgirl giddy about it as always, flashing a goofy grin while he tucks me close to his chest. Even now, coming to astonished absolution about what we've just done. Exactly where we've just come from.

When Maximus follows his clutch with a sweet kiss atop my head, I'm tempted to burrow all the way against him before peppering his neck with thankful kisses. I settle for resting my cheek on his pectoral and savoring the low vibrations of his voice as he riffs back to Jesse.

"As the guy who thought *you'd* be a dirty old man by the time I saw you again, nobody's more surprised by this than me, man."

"Dirty?" Jesse chuffs. "Says the guy with chunks of Satan-knows-what still stuck in his beard? Yeah, you got me on several levels with the post-credits doozie, professor."

"Hmm." Maximus chuckles. "How about we call it a late-breaking development in the story instead?"

I raise my free hand and wiggle my fingertips. "As the paparazzi queen, I will vouch for the gorgeous god next to me on that one."

"*Demi*god." Though Maximus ends it with another kiss into my hair, his voice is a testy growl.

"Semantics later?" Jesse cuts in. "Hellquest story *now*? Pretty please?"

Maximus hauls in a breath. His exhalation is heavy with conflict. I share the sentiment. It's not tough to figure out. It's not just about our shared weariness. It's about all the missing chunks of this chapter we still haven't figured out yet.

But at least I know a good place to start looking.

More precisely, a perfect person to start asking.

As if Gramps has plucked that thought right out of my brain—and right now, I wouldn't debate that for a second—he steps up to Maximus and me on this dusty asphalt with the same confidence he had on the red carpet at Piper's premiere. My eyes close of their own accord. It feels like ten years since my grandfather and I were in that hotel suite, getting primped and perfected for the judging eyes of the press and public. A decade since my biggest concern was staying upright in stilettos and making sure I correctly pronounced my dress designer's name.

I open my eyes to be just as stunned by Gramps eyeing Jesse with the same hey-bucko confidence that he'd give a cocky reporter during the step and repeat grind. His stubbled chin is high. His gaze is intense and attentive.

"Stories happen to be my forte, son. But you have to know the best place to start them before you can speak them."

At that, I reach around for his hand.

Gramps's return hold is firm, but now's the moment that there's unsteady moisture in his eyes. "You're not the beginning of all this, ladybug. But neither am I."

I tilt my head with a questioning look, and he folds his other hand atop our connected ones. Once more, my breath is skipping over on itself.

"You descend from a long line of divine sorcerers, granddaughter."

I process that for a long pause, though it doesn't feel long enough. On the inside, I'm whirling close to out of control. Pangs chase each other in my belly while stars aim for each other in my mind. "How long?"

Gramps lightens my load with a subtle chuckle. "Not all the way back to Hecate, though you'd maybe think so after what happened back there."

He casually thumbs back over his shoulder in a symbolic gesture, but Jesse eagerly cranes his neck at the chipped brick wall, following the trajectory. "Back *where*?"

Gramps continues like Jesse's merely whispered it. "To be honest, I'm uncertain just how far. But I'm guessing several centuries perhaps."

"Well, *there's* some good meat," Jesse mutters, demonstrating his contemplation by rubbing hands along his chair's wheels. "And certainly the most fascinating family tree of the day."

Gramps gives him a serene nod. "One I didn't even know I had until I was a little older than Kara."

"What?" I face him a little more fully. "You weren't aware of it at all? Not while growing up?"

He gives me a stare that's thick with tenderness. "It's magic, ladybug, not hard science. And even though we might have centuries of it in our veins, it manifests at all different life phases, in all different forms—or not at all."

I nod, already telling myself to move on from the next question that floods in, but my restraint is too late for my curiosity. "So…is *Mom*…"

"If she's gotten the manifestation, she's kept that announcement from me."

"Which would surprise no one." I roll my eyes.

Gramps lifts a hand to my cheek. "All that matters right now is that the gift did pass to you. You wouldn't have been drawn to the grimoire otherwise. Only witch's blood will open its pages."

From Maximus, there are no words at all. I feel and hear only the steady thrum of his focused support. And, as my thoughts collide atop each other like groupies at a rock concert, I'm profoundly grateful.

"Witch's blood," I finally stammer. "I might need a couple days to process that."

"What *you* need right now, young lady, is a couple days of solid rest."

"Already all over that one, sir," Maximus chimes in.

My grandfather eyes Maximus. "If someone hauled you out of the Acheron, would you call them 'sir'?"

Maximus chuckles. "Won't happen again."

"Wait." My muddled mind finally absorbs what they're actually talking about. "The Acheron?" I whip my gaze around. "You fell into the River of Pain? *All the way* in?"

"Basically." He sweeps a soft kiss across my furrowed brow. "You'll get the full story once you've gotten some sleep."

"But—"

He jacks up an eyebrow. "You going to come quietly, or are we going to be the downtown candid for the day for everyone? Because nobody in LA can resist a caveman with a screaming princess over his shoulder."

"Well, damn." Jesse fishes into one of the storage pouches on his chair. "As desperately as *this* Angeleno wants to watch that go down, maybe it's best that you take the truck home yourself."

"Huh?" Maximus scowls. "No more dedicated commandeer?"

"You've worn me out with the *Adventures of Maximus and Kara*," Jesse counters. "All this fresh adrenaline has made me realize how caffeine-deprived I am."

Maximus laughs. "Really?"

"What? A fella can't be expected to go home and just sleep after helping his buddy break into Hollywood Forever, can he?"

Before Maximus can quip something back, I push between them. "Hollywood Forever? The cemetery?"

"It was his idea," they utter in unison.

The fingers they stab toward Gramps are as well-synched as their indictment. He rocks back on one foot as if he's foreseen the development, and now I wonder if he really has.

"They're not wrong. But you're still not going to get the story until you're not stumbling over your own two feet."

I'm drawing breath to huff out another protest about their collective obsession with my exhaustion, when my foot catches on my gown. I nearly topple to the pavement, but Maximus's quick reflexes save me in time.

"Oh, yeah. Nap time, little demon," he soothes, hoisting me all the way up off my feet. But he stops and turns before heading for his truck, which is snugly parked next to Reg's Mustang in the shop's reserved space off the alley. "Can we give you a lift, Gio?"

I recognize the small burst of emotion with his words, but I've also had the advantage of sensing my grandfather's melancholy since it started back in the bookstore. Perhaps Maximus has too. The two most important men in my world have just shared a bonding experience like no other. There's a very good chance Maximus now has insights into Gramps that I'll never imagine.

"Kind of you to offer, son, but I like how Jesse's thinking right now," Gramps answers. "A cup of joe and some sunshine might be just the ticket for my morning."

"You sure?" I tilt my head to scrutinize him deeper. He's already waving me off with a dismissive frown.

"Don't you start fussing, ladybug. I may enjoy my hermit ways most of the time, but I haven't gotten around this city for over fifty years on my good looks alone."

"Your transportation isn't what I'm worried about." I press my own hand to the middle of his chest. "*Gramps*. Come on, it's me."

He tugs my hand away. "Then you should know *me* better."

"What I know is that I've never seen you look at someone the way you looked at my grandmother in the library."

He drops my hand, but in his eyes, I see the truth. He's busted and not denying it, which draws out the ache of my own heart, but I wonder if Jesse's coffee-and-sunshine medicine isn't the best prescription for his dilemma, after all.

"Go on," Jesse urges, affably shooing us away. "I'll keep him out of trouble."

Seemingly satisfied with Jesse and Gio's plan, Maximus turns us back around to head for his truck. Every step he takes is a forceful show of his determination, so I don't even try to protest anymore despite the questions that pelt my brain like lightning-struck pebbles. I don't know where to start on prioritizing them all, so I pluck the one that's burning the hardest.

"Do you think my mother knows? I mean, about Gramps being a…a…"

"You looking for the word 'warlock'?" Maximus gently offers. He takes my hand and kisses my fingertips before turning over the engine. "And, no, I have no idea if your mom has a clue about it."

As he peers over his shoulder to back his truck up, I readily drink in the gorgeous contours of his beloved face. I'll never forget all the hours I spent grieving, thinking I'd never see it again. Never be close enough to reach my fingertips into his warm beard or marvel at the blue brocade in his intense eyes. Most importantly, to feel his soul opening to mine, letting me know that any and every question I have right now is completely okay to vocalize.

"It would explain so much…if my mother knew. She's always in a snit because of our abilities. Maybe she's always seen those as early signs of our mystical halves."

"And maybe they actually are," Maximus notes.

I don't argue the point, despite wanting to. It all makes too much sense, no matter how thoroughly it rewrites the past. *My* past. The stories we've always been told about Hades ordering Gramps to mate with Charlena because he wanted to diversify the demonic bloodlines. Though it's still technically true, it's also not the whole truth.

"You think that's how Gramps made it out?" I venture as Maximus slows for the left turn onto 7th. "I mean, the first time. When he was completely by himself—if he was called to open this thing as strongly as I was—maybe that was when his manifestation came on too. Hades probably witnessed it and saw a great chance for taking advantage of a cheeky young warlock."

"Viable theory." Maximus nods, despite the deep lines across his brow. "It even justifies why he's more interested in you than he should be." He stops the truck at an intersection. "And why he likely isn't going to slink off into his shadows about this."

When he finishes with a pointed glance to the book in my lap, I bristle. "So I *shouldn't* have taken this? Though it clearly shouldn't be in his possession at all?"

"Do you know that for a fact?"

"Do *you* think it belongs in Hades's personal library?"

He scrapes a hand through his hair. "I'm saying we don't know enough yet."

I huff, feeling contrite about my tired testiness but work on calming down before apologizing. "There's just so much I need to talk to Gramps about…" *And he's back at Recto Verso, just enjoying the morning with nothing else to do…*

My brood is cut short by a flow of sincere compassion from the man behind the wheel. "You'll get that time with him, beautiful. Very, very soon. I promise."

I'm already primed to push back on his promise. To make him commit to a day and time that we'll go to Beverly Hills for a long sit-down with my grandfather. But as we enter the darkness of the garage at his building—gloom that doesn't resonate with misery and smell like eons of decay—I reluctantly accept how right he and Gramps may be about the percentage of connecting synapses in my mind.

This time, I'm more than happy to obey as Maximus quietly dictates me to stay put after he parks. I'm even happier when he ducks into the cab to lift me out, not lowering me until we're standing at the wide door to his place on the top floor.

As soon as he opens the door, tears sting my eyes all over again.

Home.

We're really here, surrounded by all the little things that mean I can breathe normally again. The brick wall in the kitchen and dining nook. The sunlight in the flowers on the balcony. The smell of leather couches and a thousand books.

All the pleasures I had to say goodbye to.

All the joyous hellos my heart speaks again.

All the ways I want to crumple to the floor in sheer joy. And, after setting the grimoire on a side table and then stumbling a couple more steps, I do.

"Little demon." Maximus grits it out while slamming his door. Within seconds, he's on his knees next to me. His keys jingle as he lets them tumble, filling his hands with my face instead. "Kara. *Sweetheart.* What is it? Tell me..."

Everything. All the things. Happy. So happy. Oh, Maximus...

But that's not what I say. Because I don't say a single thing.

Because suddenly, I don't want to tell him all those things.

I want to *show* him. So much of it. No, *all* of it. I yearn to show him in the most real, most raw, most pure way I know how.

And I show him so...by lifting my head and offering my lips to his in a carnal offering of a kiss.

CHAPTER 19

MAXIMUS

I SHOULDN'T BE LOVING this as much as I do. I stopped her from lingering with Gio so we could come back here and sleep for the next two to twenty-three days—not so we could devour each other after stepping through the front door.

But right now, I can't think of anything but consuming her. Every succulent, delicious inch. Every fiery, sexy drop she'll give me. Perhaps a few I'll just take for myself.

I make sure she knows that as soon as I break off the bond of our kiss but not the connection of our eyes. Kara feels me already, smiling up into my face as I steady her ascent with my hands on her waist. But she doesn't let me stop there, already popping easily onto her toes and then up against my torso, her legs clutching around my waist. As I move my grip to her silky thighs, I use the chance to bury my tongue in her mouth once more. God*damn*. She tastes like sunshine and spices and fire.

She tastes like she's all mine.

But just for good measure, I make damn sure she knows it.

Her lush little whimpers vibrate through my mouth as I claim her without stopping, rolling my head to ensure I'm delving as deep as she'll allow. I can't get enough of taking over her. Of needing to mark her in any way I can. As if Hades is going to burst in here any second and—

No.

It's not just my silent resistance. Hades wouldn't tread back into the territory of a son of Zeus this soon, especially knowing Kara's now armed with a spell book powerful enough to launch all three of us out of his custody.

For right here and now, we're safe. We're together.

And it's my every intention to soon make us one.

I know that Kara's picking up that very vibe once she releases a full moan. The sound is like angels' song in my senses as I backstep across my living room, toward my bed. The thumps of my dogged steps are wrapped by the swooshes of her gown, its voluminous folds still dragging along the floor.

But not for much longer.

As soon as we get to the platform that supports my bed, I stop and let her slide back down to her feet. As she lowers, sunlight slats in across the room, highlighting specific parts of her astonishing beauty. I get a peek of her slender calves. Another marveling caress around her waist. A breath-grabbing glance at her cleavage. Even a brand-new observation of the heart-like taper of her chin.

Fuck.

The word pours out of me as I take advantage of the mattress behind me and sit back onto it. Kara stays on her feet, brushing her knees along the fronts of mine while she nervously fingers the robe's big collars. Never once do our gazes drift apart. She's got visual access to my whole soul, just as I do hers.

Good thing, because right now my soul and body are on speed dial to each other.

And if I'm correctly interpreting the smolders in her breathtaking browns...

"Damn. My sexy, sweet little demon."

Kara pushes in a little closer. But just a little. Our knees are tightly pressed now, instead of the teasing brush-bys.

"My stunning, fearless demigod."

I close my eyes for a second, taking her reverent words in like they're really a prayer. With my lids still shut, I finally utter, "Can you do me a favor?"

"Anything," she whispers. "You know that."

"Take off that damn robe so I can finally burn it."

Forget the angels' song. The most awesome sound of my afternoon is the heavy drop of that cursed garment to the floor.

The next moment, I open my gaze to the day's most perfect sight. For that matter, its most magnificent and incandescent too. I could waste time on at least a hundred more adjectives for that list, but as my gape roams over more of her nudity, I become a raving idiot in matching proportions.

"You debating whether to drench it in gasoline first, Professor Kane?" she softly quips. "Because I can help with that decision."

"Later," I hear myself rumble. There's a bit of interference in my mental feed now. Under normal circumstances I'd call it arousal—but this isn't a normal circumstance. This is me craving to cover this incredible female in as much of my passion as I can, as soon as I possibly can.

"Come here," I husk, tugging at her hip. My other hand braces her waist, gentling her fall all the way against me. But that's all I'm agreeing to be gentle about. The more I taste her, touch her, and fondle her, the deeper my fires extend for her. The harder I throb for her. The more that every part of my senses craves to experience more of her.

I tell her exactly that with the brutal invasion of my kiss, ensuring she feels it all when I let go of her waist to wrap a hand around her nape. Though she's the one on top, she easily succumbs to how I hold her in place. In return, she gets the rough tremors of my body beneath her weight… and the full confession from my helpless cock, betraying who's really in charge right now.

But my fiery little minx seems to want more proof. She sits up, eyeing me from head to toe as she does so. During her journey, a sanguine smile spreads across her lush red lips. The expression gets even more gorgeous as she pulls up her hands, palms toward the ceiling. Slowly, she lowers one—a movement that corresponds directly to the motion of the zipper on my khakis' fly.

My lungs start madly pumping. Her eyes go wide as

my body denies all my self-control efforts. It's springing through the gap in my crotch, confirming her effect on me in dark, pulsing glory. Those come courtesy of the tears in my pants that correspond to the spots where Hades's minions subjected me to their burning torture. My new flinches and flexes cause the fabric to rip wider, exposing more of those tender areas to the air again. I grimace from the minor pain, though it's transformed into a smile as soon as Kara's fervent rasp hits the air.

"*Maximus.*"

But I'm back in the land of sobriety once her underline of sadness sets in. Though I've never fully looked away, I examine her with deeper intent. Her shoulders have sagged. And those are definitely new tears in her eyes. *Not* joyous ones. Not at all.

"I can't bear what they did to you."

I wince again from the agony in her voice. "What they *did*, sweetheart." I fight to control my own voice from cracking. "It's in the past. I survived, and so did you. That's all that matters now. Kara…*Kara*, what're you—"

She probably hears me but is choosing not to listen. Not as she makes me go tense and still, from the moment she leans down and presses a reverent kiss to the highest burn mark on my right thigh. I'm knocked for such an amazed loop, I almost forget that the woman already has me as hard as steel for her. This isn't helping—but it's not exactly hurting. Especially not as she pulls at my khakis, lowering them to the point that she can see the next burn down on my leg. Once more, she bends over and brushes the silky bow of her mouth to my angry skin. And once more, it feels...

Warm.

Worshipful.

Wonderful.

But definitely not magical.

I'm as sure of that as I am my own breath, and that in itself brings a different revelation. I'm healed and humbled in ways I never imagined by this sweet, soft offering from her heart as a woman and a woman alone. For just this moment, as she strips me, she's peeling layers back from herself too. Honoring my suffering with her adoring kisses. Comforting my body with her careful touch. Looking at the scars that still darken my flesh and exalting them as my heroism, not my failure.

That truth hits me with more certainty than all the others, blinding and beautiful, as she grazes her mouth between the two scars on my calf. Though I'm clear about her purpose now, as well as her need to finish it, I almost order her to stop. The way she sees me...the millions of ways she's retaught me how to see myself...is overwhelming.

Life-changing. Heart-changing. I don't know how to give it all back to her. How to show her my awe. My reverence. My love.

But more than that. So much more.

The feelings keep growing and swelling until I feel like a hot air balloon, ready to burst and fall from the sky of my sanity. But that's also not going to happen. I command it to myself, over and over. I'm grounded right here, bound to the most breathtaking creature in all the cosmos, and she's painting my skin with her perfect kisses. She's restoring my soul with her enduring strength.

And now, thank God, she's retracing her sensual trail... back up my other leg.

None of my feelings disappear, but they're sure as hell blindsided. At the moment, I'm grateful. It's easier to stir them into a force with which I'm happily familiar. The ache for her in my blood. The fire for her in my balls. The stretch for her along my cock. It has me shifting and moaning, ready to beg her for relief...

Until she gives me something better.

"Kara!"

It bursts from me as she seals her lips over my tip. Then again as she takes all of me into the wet heat of her mouth. And it's good. So. Damn. Good.

She releases me from her tight hold but not from her seductive service. With her lips playing along my veined length, she croons, "Looks like I finally found you."

"Thank fuck," I laugh out, though the next second it's tumbling from me in a taut moan. But not for long. I'm back to speechless euphoria once she engulfs my crown in her mouth again and then lowers that wet heaven all the way down once more.

I'm nearly gone at that second but clench myself back, holding out for the bigger prize. The much better homecoming present. The treasure I seek while calmly pulling her up and then not so calmly flipping her over. Once I move over her, leaning in to plunge my mouth against hers, I forget the word *calm* ever existed.

When we finally break apart to gulp in air, my pulse is hammering and my cock is aching. Both give me the fortitude to form intelligible words of command at my lips.

"Make room for me, little demon. I need to be a part of you, right now."

CHAPTER 20

Kara

READILY, I PART MY legs for him. Greedily, my core weeps for him. Joyously, I welcome all of him.

There's no hesitation about his primal thrust. Nor the one after it. I'm grateful and glad, filled with him until I forget there's a world beyond us. This is my new fire and glory, the only hell and heaven that matter anymore. And Maximus is my new ruler: the king of my soul, the holder of my heart, the hero of my survival.

I love him so much.

But I long to give him even more than that. The surrender of my body. And the whispers, from so deep in my soul…

"Maximus…"

He captures my tears with his full, warm lips. "It's okay," he assures between his long thrusts. "I know, sweetheart. I know."

But how can he? How can he comprehend the fullness

of this desire, the size of my love? Yet as he lifts his face until our eyes lock again, I see that it *is* possible. In all the rich striations of his blues, I see the force of my desire reflected right back at me.

"It's all yours," I tell him in a thick rasp, and the edges of his lips kick higher.

"I know that too," he murmurs.

"Then take it." I curl my heels against the firm planes of his backside, begging for his deeper invasion. "Take it until I can't think anymore. Until I can't—"

My own sharp sigh is my interruption. He's done it. Swept me to the place where even words aren't enough and all I can do is burn for him. All I can comprehend are flames that consume me from the inside out. I watch them, layers of orange and gold reflected against the dark intensity of his own gaze, and I'm lost to their power. To our connection. To the union of our bodies, rocking in a rhythm as old as time but as bright and brilliant as our love. And hot. So searing and glaring and hot…

Until my body's not enough to contain it anymore. My heart's aching and pulsing with all the devotion I hold for this beautiful man. Words push themselves into being because holding them in any longer seems impossible.

"Oh, Maximus. I love you. So much…so much."

My heels pull him in deeper. My hands find their way to his shoulders, where I dig into his steely muscles with a force beyond my control. I hate even thinking about hurting him any more, but as I grip him tighter, his hardness pushes at the confines of my core.

The places, so deep inside, that begin to push back.

He hovers his face just inches over mine. Boring that cherished cobalt gaze into mine. Thrusting his mighty, magnificent body into mine. "I love you, Kara. I'll never stop."

Denying his truth is impossible.

Pleasing him is incredible.

I'm shattering into a billion particles of passion. Of pleasure. Of ultimate fulfillment. Maximus is there with me, all his pieces chasing mine, until our groans and shudders dominate the air. Until our ecstasy and unity become a new incantation of their own. Except I doubt there are any words, in Latin or any other tongue, to express the completion of every sense I can still comprehend. I'm conscious of every inch of Maximus, still fitted inside me, but beyond our atmospheric envelope, the world is a haze of inconsequential nothingness.

Only after my heartbeat slows and my body relaxes do I let more awareness back in. It enters in small pieces as Maximus rolls to his back and tucks me against his side, our bodies still slick and warm in the patches of sunlight that sneak through the apartment's tinted windows. It's so perfect to lie here in a languid puddle, simply reconnecting with the sensory fabric of the city. Compared to Dis, the dust and din of LA is the world's most divine symphony.

Very soon, it's the aria that lulls me toward the heaven of deep sleep.

*⁎

"Hmm?"

I'm still so groggy, I have no idea if the mumble spilled from Maximus or myself. I'm not sure it matters, since my head won't stop whirling. I swing a glance at his bedside clock. It's late in the afternoon, but I feel like I only nodded off for a quick nap. The sensation intensifies to the point that it seems the whole room is swaying—on a very unsteady axis.

That's when I fully open my eyes and realize that it is.

And that the axis feels big enough to extend to the street outside. Maybe the whole city.

"Oh my God," I mutter, but I can barely hear myself past people yelling and the blares of at least a hundred car security horns. "Maximus." A shock of adrenaline makes me sit all the way up. "Is this—"

"Earthquake." He pulls me close as he lifts from the pillows too. "A decent rock party too." The timbre of his calm words against my ear is the perfect reason to stay where I am, even before he goes on. "We should stay put. This is a support wall, so we're safer riding it out here."

His order is justified by the new sounds that filter in at us. Crashing glass. Swishing trees. More alarms, violent and loud, this time from the building's own hallways.

"Riding it out," I echo. "But for how long?"

At once I admit the absurdity of the question. Neither of us knows that answer, despite having been through this kind of thing before. During a temblor like this, five seconds always feel like five hours. Finally the quake's energy fades. We're silent for another long pause, waiting to make sure the peace holds. The hanging light over his dining table still sways. The dishes in his cupboard cling to some quiet clatters. But then, as one of his larger books slides defiantly off its shelf, the two of us cave to spurts of nervous laughter.

He gently busses the side of my temple. "You all right? Nothing around here knocked loose?"

"Hmm, yeah," I reply, using the hard slab of his muscle to push up so our gazes are level again. "But you might want to check *here* too."

I demonstrate my meaning by fitting my lips to his. I go so sweet and soft at first, but the growly shiver from his throat is like a panther playing with the yarn of my self-control. At once, I'm unraveled. And, with so many leftover jitters still left to burn, uninhibited.

And, so suddenly and sharply, inflamed. In one specific area of my anatomy…

Without any more thoughts or doubts, I swoop myself up and over until I'm straddling my dazzling demigod. As the center of my body aligns with the same part of his, he becomes a seism in his own right. My gasps blend with his groans as his thighs flex against mine. He digs his hands into my waist, dictating the sensual slide of my cleft along his urgent hardness.

But just when I hold my breath, ready for him to fit our flesh together, he makes me stop. His hands flow up, over my ribcage and breasts and neck, until he's framing my face with the spreads of his long, firm fingers.

"You're my magic, Kara," he declares in a rough husk. "Right here, right now, just with me. Just like this."

I lean my cheek into his palm. "And you're my earth-shaking god."

When he reacts to that with a low snarl, I make him endure my giggle before getting ready to correct myself. I'll love every inch of this magnificent male until the end of my existence and beyond. And yes, he's going to get all *that* in words too.

Except as I drop my head to make sure he hears every syllable, I lose my balance and tumble against him.

No. I'm knocked off-kilter—by the second slam that rocks the apartment. That, from the sound and look of things beyond his seventh-floor windows, quakes the whole city again.

"Whoa, baby." This time, he's the one with the jest in his voice.

In the enclosure of his hands, my shoulders shake. I press my face tighter into the crook of his neck. "*Another* one?"

"Probably an aftershock," he soothes. "You grew up here. You know how it goes." But as the quake goes on, easily twice as long as the first, he modifies, "Okay, maybe the *other* one was a foreshock…"

I want to believe him, especially as the walls begin to groan and his fallen books get a few more friends on the floor. But I'm still roping my hands around his neck and clutching him like we'll be the ones to be thrown down next, despite our secure position in the middle of his big bed.

"You're right," I say, trying to breathe easier as the shaking subsides. "I don't know why I'm being so silly." I even attempt a short laugh while drawing the sheet tighter around us both. "Growing up, I even used to think quakes were fun."

Maximus cocks a stunned brow. "And now I *know* you're the most unique woman I've ever met."

I laugh. "Rerek would make them fun, believe it or not. And they were one of the few things my mother couldn't control."

"And now?"

"Now I realize how little *I* can control."

A third convulsion takes over the ground so far below—and has me lurching back to the safety of his arms.

Outside, the sky gains strange shadows. My sensible side reasons that we probably slept most of the day and it must be nearing twilight, but my something-doesn't-feel-right side is back at some DEFCON stage that hasn't been invented yet. I grip Maximus harder, not caring that I'm on the verge of hyperventilating like a drama diva half my age. Sirens howl through the eerily quiet streets, as if everybody in downtown is hunkering with their loved ones just as I am.

Waiting...

For what?

As soon as the next jolt hits, I know. As soon as the boulevards below aren't so still anymore. There are louder alarms and sounds of steel hitting pavement, along with frantic screams and shouts. Prayers are moaned out in at least ten different languages. I can't understand most of them, but some phrases tug at a person's gut in any form. Cries for help and mercy and forgiveness.

Words my own heart pleaded not long ago, when I looked out from a cold window over an underworld city.

"Maximus." I say it because I need to. Because just his name empowers me. Confirms to my mind that everything is going to be okay, despite how so much of my nervous system disagrees. I show him as much with the lift of my head, the force of my gaze, and the new pressure of my hold around his shoulders. "Tell me the strangest string of tectonic slips to ever strike this city are just a coincidence with our first day back from...*there*."

That's the part I can't say. That I may never be able to vocalize again in my life. And I'm flooded with gratitude for the man beside me, who already tells me how deeply he understands with his soft but persistent kiss.

"Let's get up and turn on the TV," he suggests. "I'm sure the local stations already have updates about what's happening. For all we know, this was a quake followed by some disaster on the Metro line, or some massive power grid thing..."

"That's not making me feel any better."

"Kara." His voice is as steadfast as his kiss was, matching the powerful ease with which he reaches into his dresser, whips out a pair of black sweats, and pulls them on. "Whatever's going on, we're going to be okay. I promise."

I tuck in my arms, fighting a new shiver. "I appreciate that, but I still don't feel any better."

He leans over and seals my lips beneath his again. His

hair forms a curtain around our faces, and I long to pull it into place and never let go.

But all too quickly, he's rising back up. Along the way, he presses something into my hands. "Here. You can wear Mr. Fluffy."

I laugh lightly. "Mr. *What*?"

"My favorite T-shirt. Mr. Fluffy. He's all yours."

I open the garment, which I already dub as the best tent I'll ever wear, and let a new giggle out. Sure enough, there's a lavender cartoon rabbit embossed in the middle of the black cotton—and he's brandishing an evil grin and a loaded crossbow.

"Do I dare even ask?" I snicker while throwing it on.

"Nothing's off-limits to you, little demon," he answers. "But just for the record, Mr. Fluffy is *not* my *Call of Duty* handle."

"Thanks. So good to know."

Even better to know is all the information that Maximus finds from one of the city's news teams. It's absurd to admit it, but suddenly the reporters who are normally dissecting my personal life are now my best friends with their coverage of what's happening, including maps of the half dozen faults running directly under the city, as well as their granddaddy to the east, the San Andreas. I'm even fine when geological experts are summoned to chime in about liquefaction, landslides, and tsunami warnings.

All of this I can completely deal with. And I can keep coping because not one of them has mentioned fires erupting from unexpected places or a mysterious figure in a crimson three-piece stalking up Olive Street. That assurance, as well as the fortifying man who hasn't let me go for an hour and a half, keep me settled next to him on the couch with a reasonably normal heart rate. After a little, I'm even smiling as he pulls a blanket out of the nearby storage chest and wraps us together in warmth.

I snuggle into Maximus's side with a contented sigh, telling myself this is all I need—until my stomach informs me otherwise in the form of a long snarl.

"Damn," he mutters. "Did you eat at all while you were...there?"

I shrug, appreciating the uncomfortable hitch in his query. "My appetite was the last thing I was worried about, you know?"

His lips compress as his gaze softens. In his own way, he *does* know—and I'm beyond tempted to kiss him because of it.

Before I can act on the impulse, he says, "Let me see what I've got. Might be just peanut butter and jelly."

My answering groan is thick with ecstasy. "Yes, yes, yes, please." The idea of sinking my teeth into all that favorite goo from childhood is even better than listening to the news experts drone on.

But Maximus is only halfway to the kitchen when another quake has the building, and him, reeling. He swears softly before backing against the support wall. "Stay where you are, Kara. It's a big aftershock."

But it feels like nothing of the sort. Three more seconds go by like years as I roll up in the blanket and burrow against the cushions.

The fault lines have decided they deserve their own war game handles.

And are going to celebrate that fact right now.

For the better part of a minute, I actually do wonder if strange societal factions have decided to go to war—or a worse scenario, involving the god in the crimson suit. It feels like someone's tossed a bomb against the building, with the windows shattering, the horizon weaving, and a bunch more of Maximus's books now flying to the creaking floor.

"Holy *crap*," I rasp while covering my head with both hands. I curl up, expecting chunks of the ceiling to hit me any second.

Eventually, the building stops swaying. The walls settle. One by one, the alarms in the streets below are silenced.

I gulp hard, not moving. The quiet guts me nearly as deeply as the quake did.

"Kara?"

"Still here," I croak.

Maximus releases a relieved whoosh. "Good. Me too."

I peek around the edge of the couch to watch him push back to his feet. When he spots me, he dips his head to the side and smiles.

"You okay?" he murmurs.

"If I said I've never been better, would you stand there for a little while longer?"

"No. I'd say I don't believe you." He chuckles it out in response to my little come-hither stare. But the next second, his brows draw together. "You're really pale. Are you sure—"

A phone buzzes incessantly. Since I'm certain mine is

still in my purse back at Rerek's hellmouth beach house, I look around for Maximus's device. As soon as he pivots and eyes the screen on the butcher block next to him, his own color drains by several shades.

He grabs it quickly, activating the call as well as the speaker.

"Mom?" he queries. "Hey. Are you—"

"Maximus," she cuts in with bold bluntness. Maybe that's a mother thing, not just a Veronica thing. "Oh, thank God. You're all right, then? Where are you? At the bookstore? It sounds so loud."

"I'm home. Looks like the last hit might've taken out a few of my windows."

"But you're okay?" she demands. "You're not hurt at all?"

Maximus gives me a private peep show of his adorable eye roll. I crawl a little higher on the couch, propping my chin on the back edge. No way am I going to miss a second of this. I haven't met Nancy Kane yet, but from the pictures he displays around this place, I grasp the irony of her charge. The woman is barely bigger than me, and she's concerned about *his* welfare?

"I'm fine. I mean it." He steps over to stroke a big hand over the top of my head. "Are *you* okay? You're at home, right? Monday's your day off."

But it doesn't sound like she's at home. Especially not as her end of the line is suddenly muffled, giving me the impression that she's speaking with someone besides Maximus.

No, not speaking. Yelling.

"Mom?" he demands again. "Hey. Are you—"

"Max. I'm so sorry. It's just...getting crazier here."

"Here *where*?" A deep V forms between his brows. "Is everything okay?"

"The first responder agencies are setting up disaster response centers across the city. They sent out a text asking for volunteers. Didn't you see it? One of the biggest centers is here on campus. At Alameda."

Maximus's expression darkens. "I haven't been on my phone much today. We've just been glued to the news since everything started shaking."

"We? Are you...with Kara?"

There's tension around her tone, but she hasn't exactly spat my name like a cuss word. It's more like a demand. An urgent one.

"Why is that important?" he finally asks.

"Please, just answer me, son. Is Kara with you right now?"

Maximus cocks his gaze in my direction. I answer him with a consenting nod.

"She's right here. Why do you want to know?"

"Because they just checked in a new patient here." She pauses, giving away her vacillation between professional calm and sympathetic worry. "Kara...I'm sorry, honey. It's your sister, Kell."

CHAPTER 21

MAXIMUS

"THANK YOU, MRS. WORTHINGTON," I say into my cell as Kara yanks the strings taut on one of my old pairs of gym pants. Though the workout gear is bleached out and shrunken past fitting me again, she turns it into a trendy-baggy look by pulling up the leftover pant strings and cinching a knot where Mr. Fluffy's crossbow cocking stirrup should be. "I guess *I* owe *you* the cookies now," I tell my neighbor after she promises to be up here in a few minutes with all the materials to board up my busted windows. The woman is hiding a superhero cape somewhere, I'm sure of it.

But right now, Mrs. Worthington can't be the only hero in the building. As soon as Kara finishes getting dressed, I have to step up and be hers.

The vow spurs me forward, rushing to cover the space to the spot where I ordered her to stay put. She has nothing more than a thick pair of my socks to protect her feet, so I don't want her padding through unexpected broken glass.

But protecting her only starts at the bottom of her feet. Nothing between them and the follicles in her scalp is past my concern. With her shoulders trembling in my grip and her eyes glimmering with impatient agony, I double down on the promise.

"Damn it," she whispers. "Why don't I know a spell for just blinking us there?"

I squeeze her tighter before dipping my head, compelling her stare to stay on me. "Pretty sure you'd need more than twenty-four hours of practice to pull that off."

"Can we just get going? Do we have to wait for your neighbor to come up?"

"Mrs. Worthington has a spare key," I say while clasping her hand in mine. "So let's do this."

"Thank you, Maximus," she rasps against my arm. "*Thank you.*"

But the fervency of her voice still isn't matched by her breaths, even after we get down to the garage and hurry into the truck. During the quick but stressful drive to campus, she's still jittery and unsettled.

I let her fidget, hoping she receives my reassuring mental wavelengths as I navigate the debris-strewn streets. Luckily, LAPD is out to direct traffic and keep a sense of calm, but as we get our first up-close views of the physical damage from the quakes, it starts adding up to an eerie homecoming.

By the time we pull into the parking lot closest to the Alameda Arena, where the response center has been set up, Kara's more controlled on the outside, despite the anxiety still churning in her big brown eyes. Though I know she's anxious to jump out and get to Kell, I reach over and firmly pick up her hand.

"Everything's going to be okay, beautiful."

She nods but hardly means it. "Even you can't promise me that."

I frown, wishing I could disagree with her, but she's right.

Her nervousness doesn't prepare me for her lithe dismount from the passenger side of the truck. The effect is strengthened by how she pauses in front of the truck's grill, waiting for me like she's standing on a red carpet in an evening gown instead of her baggy-chic ensemble.

If I could take a longer moment to admire her fortitude, how she's holding herself together despite the crap numbers that keep coming up for the dice tosses of her life, I'd take it. But I have to settle for getting back to her side and hoping my fierce kiss to her forehead adequately does the job.

Just in case it doesn't, I squeeze her hand and murmur, "You can handle anything that comes your way. You've been to hell and back. Literally."

"So have you."

I nod solemnly. "I guess that makes us a pretty good team." I pause, taking in the worried contours of her face. "In case you didn't already know it, I'm not going anywhere."

She accepts that with a brief clench back at my fingers, right before we enter the circle of frantic energy that surrounds Alameda Arena's front entrance. The building, which easily accommodates thousands, is a good choice to relieve the capacity load from the local hospitals.

That being said, the crowd at the entrance fits every frenzied dystopian movie I've ever seen. First responders of all sorts are hurrying back and forth, threading through the mobs crowding the marquee monitors that would normally advertise college events and traveling theatrical shows in the arena. Tonight, they display a terse grid that's filled with peoples' names, along with their admission time and treatment status.

When we near the outskirts of the crowd, Kara starts popping up on her toes. "Damn it. I can't see a thing."

"Maybe I can help."

The offer, from a female off to my right, is vaguely familiar. I turn and study the pleasant smile of the woman who's stopped next to us, feeling lousy that I don't recognize her. The situation clearly isn't the same from her end, because her smile stretches farther toward the short, red-tinged curls that are kept back from her face by a sparkly brass headband. The hair gear is the only notable thing about her basic black attire, consisting of a T-shirt with *Staff* emblazoned on the front, black leggings, and functional flats.

"Professor Kane. I'd say it's nice to see you again, but given the circumstances..."

"Professor Levin." Kara gets my thankful glance as she pivots and greets the law professor with the strangely shiny eyes who first chatted with us on Saturday night. "You're helping out tonight?" Kara nervously asks, eyeing the smart pad in Erin's grasp.

Erin replies by twirling a stylus with a flourish. "They

need everyone they can get. If the situation weren't so awful, I'd be enjoying the chance to get out from my paper-grading mountain."

"No kidding," I reply. "But nevertheless, you've got a good soul for being out here to help."

Erin swooshes her hand, as if to give me a Hollywood-style *Oh, stop.* "Please, let's not get ahead of ourselves here."

I take a second to simply stare, wondering if I'm correctly reading her kidding-not-kidding subtext. But before I can zero all the way in, Kara gestures again at Erin's screen. "Do you have an updated list? I'm desperately looking for someone."

Erin gives her an empathetic look. "I'm not sure, but maybe we can give it a whirl. Who are you looking for?"

We're interrupted once more, this time by a commanding tug on my elbow. I whip around with a glare before opening my arms and crushing our interloper in a ferocious hug.

"Mom."

I bury my nose in her ponytailed hair. It smells like it always does: something fruity that she grabbed on special at the drugstore because she liked the cute packaging. Her embrace matches mine for the lung-crushing factor, but she leaves me in the dust when it comes to emotional intensity. But during the seconds she'd normally take to pull back and examine my face for everything from exhaustion to insecurity, she's already swinging away to haul Kara into a Nancy Kane Special of a clinch.

"Hi," she finally says. "I'm Nancy, and I'm sorry we can't be doing this over large glasses of wine and a cheese plate. God knows we'll need plenty of that kind of thing when this is past us."

"So happy to meet you. I'm...Kara."

"Hello." Erin offers her hand between the two other women. "Erin Levin. I'm a professor here too."

"Oh?" Mom shakes Erin's proffered hand but keenly narrows her gaze. "Are you in the literature department with Maximus?"

Erin shakes her head. "I'm filling in at the law school."

"Ah. Okay."

But weirdly, my mother's tone communicates the opposite. At once, I try to decipher that unnerving change. The sociability, spread so thin on a base of suspiciousness, isn't like her at all—even if it dissipates as rapidly as it's arrived.

"I'm sorry we don't have more time for introductions, but I need you two to follow me," Mom says with renewed purpose. "This way."

As we walk along a shadowy path along the side of the building, Mom glances back a few times to make sure we're keeping up.

"Is Kell really here? We didn't see her name on the intake boards." I'm worried about getting Kara's hopes up, but I also don't want her to endure unnecessary stress if Kell is safe and well.

"We kept her off deliberately," Mom explains. "For a thousand reasons you can both fill in for yourselves."

"Yeah," I mutter, feeling dumb for not putting that one together myself. "Nothing like a media mob to make your jobs harder. Thank you, Mom."

"I've got your back forever and always, beautiful boy."

Kara gives me an affectionate side-bump without breaking our pace. "Your awesomeness is starting to make some sense, Mr. Kane."

I smile until we stop at a door marked *Maintenance Staff Only*, where a campus security guard is stationed. He jabs his chin toward me in friendly recognition before tapping his key card to open the portal for us.

At once, we hurry into a big room that has us squinting against its glaring brightness. Only after my eyes adjust do I realize the effect isn't just me and the gloomy settings to which I've acclimated the last few days. The building's wide fluorescent bulbs have extra help from huge, portable surgical room lights that are slanted over half a dozen gurneys. From two of the beds, there are sounds of victims groaning in pain. Three other bays are quiet save for the somber beeps of monitoring equipment. From the sixth bay, which is closest to us, there comes the sound of…

Humming?

It's a woman. I'm able to pick out that much.

Kara beelines toward the drapes that hide the hummer. "Kell? Hey Kell, are you—"

Mom pivots, clearly already expecting my little demon's reaction. She halts Kara by grabbing her elbow, though her stare lays down even more authority. "Calm down," she orders gently. "You can see her. I've already told her you were on the way. But we should discuss some things first."

"Things?" Kara's tense with attention now, anxiously

searching Mom's face. "Like what?"

"Do you have a private physician? I mean, for the family?" The hue of Mom's gaze deepens from a summer sky to an autumn twilight, a change that always irked me as a kid. It means she is hiding deeper truths.

Kara hesitates but only for a few seconds. "Yes," she offers quietly. "We always have."

Mom nods, her lips tight. "I suspected as much. When her labs came back…" She releases an exasperated sigh. "Well, you probably know what I'm going to say. Her blood work alone would have taken a team of scientists to unravel given the appropriate time. Thankfully there's been no time to speak of, and no one has grown too suspicious. It's been beyond chaotic, so I've been able to keep the doctors distracted with other patients."

"Oh, no." Kara's eyes widen as realization clearly hits her. No doubt she's resolving Kell's health emergency with whatever she knows about the Valari family's medical secrets. "How serious are her injuries?"

"I'm afraid she's fractured her leg. She's stabilized, but I can't release her to you in her current condition."

"Fractured it? How badly? Will she need surgery?" Kara presses—at the same moment that Kell jumps the humming to outright singing.

Mom shakes her head so hard, the curls in her ponytail bounce. "I don't believe so, but I'm not the doctor. That's the issue. I've been trying to keep them away."

"I understand. Is there any way you can try to have her released to us? I don't want to jeopardize your license, but you've likely figured out most of the real story here. I can help her much more if I get her home."

"I get that. I do." But Mom finishes it with a heavy sigh. "It's going to be risky but possible. I'll do my best to make her records—I don't know—disappear, I guess."

I want to hug my mother all over again for the blithe humor that she's always pulled off better than me. But Kara beats me to it, hauling Mom into the kind of effusive embrace that only women seem capable of.

"Thank you, Nancy." Tears push in at the edges of her whispered gush. "I'm going to pay you back with that giant wine soon."

As Mom pulls back, I'm pretty sure there's a distinct sheen in her gaze too. There's a warmth in my chest now, watching my mother already accept the woman I worship as a daughter of her heart.

"You'll get no argument from me on that one," she effuses before indicating toward the draped-off area from which an off-key pop ballad is rising. "Now can you two try to get her to hit the mute button before someone decides to thoroughly check her chart?"

I send Mom off to work her paperwork magic with a fast kiss on the cheek and a smile that threatens to break my face.

As soon as I follow Kara to Kell's bedside, the expression vanishes.

Despite Kell's cheeky private concert for herself, she looks painfully small and weak in the big rolling bed. She's much paler than I've ever seen her. One of her legs is practically twice the diameter of its mate and suspended high thanks to a mobile traction stand. It also looks like they're pumping her with medication and fluids through an IV line.

If Kara picks up on my concern, she hides it with shocking serenity. Her whole composure is the same way. It's as if she purposely let all her trepidation unspool before now.

"Kell," she murmurs. "What happened?"

Kell rocks her head back on a laugh. "It's just a few bumps and bruises."

While her sister's leg is heavily wrapped, much of her exposed skin is scuffed and bruised, leading me to silently echo the question.

What the hell happened?

Kara loosens her hand from mine in order to fully envelop Kell's. "We're working on getting you discharged. Dr. Doug can treat you at Mom's. But I need you to relax until we get the paperwork in order."

Kell snorts again, taking us in with glassy eyes. "Relax?" Her voice edges on a slur. "Oh, trust me. I'm *relaxed*. Whatever's in this IV drip is pretty awesome. But *not* as awesome as a martini. Oh, that would be sooo goood. With two blue cheese olives, please."

"Okay. Ssshhh, now."

Kara resettles her sister's hand on the thin sheet covering the plastic medical mattress. The motion distracts Kell enough that I'm able to lean over and lift her blanket. Her clothes are ripped in several places and covered in a thick layer of dust.

"Kell." I lower the blanket but raise my scrutiny, taking inventory of the continued damage up the left side of her body. "What happened? Do you remember anything?"

The question prevails in calming her again—perhaps too much. As Kell's expression dims, Kara's fills with complete despair.

"I...I don't want to." Kell laces it with a loud whine.

"Honey." Kara whispers it like an apology, probably hoping to encourage her sister to do the same. "Please. You have to. Especially if..." Her voice halts as her breath does, and her shoulders hunch with awful tension. "Especially if this was a deliberate act." She brushes her hand across Kell's worried brow. "Sister?" she urges. "Was it? A *deliberate* act?"

Immediately that stress level invades me too. Working to put together the pieces behind whatever ordeal Kell's survived, not once have I considered she's been a victim of intentional violence. But perhaps Kara can already sense what I failed to suspect.

"Tell me, Kell," she grits out. "I can feel you trying to hide it, but *why*?"

Kell looks up at her with strange new lucidity. "You. Know. Why," she says with unexpected vehemence.

"No," Kara snaps back. "I *don't* know. Does this have anything to do with Arden?"

"Maybe. Maybe not."

Kara stiffens. "What does that mean? Wait. Are you *covering* for him?"

"Maybe. Maybe not." Kell punctuates the taunt with a poke of her tongue in Kara's direction.

My little demon isn't amused. "Since when was Arden Prieto so important to you?"

"Hmm," Kell retorts. "Since the day he became my fucking incubus?"

"Prieto." My interjection is a dazed mutter, as if saying it like that will make the word less nauseating. Doesn't work by a longshot. "*He* did this to you?"

Kell grimaces. "Let's just say, one thing led to another."

"Why don't we *just say* other things too?" Kara counters. "Like what exactly led to you being so broken and bruised like this?"

Her sister flings back with a frustrated sound from somewhere down in her throat. Kell doesn't have a shortage of them in her arsenal. "After the first round of quakes slammed, they let us out of classes. I stayed a little longer because one of the girls in my guitar class was freaking out."

"And?" Kara urges.

"When I finally left the Aquila Building, Arden was waiting on the steps for me," Kell says. "He did *not* look happy." She stabs a new stare up at Kara. Though her mouth twists slightly, her eyes are filled with flares of strange fire. "But he wasn't there because of me at all. Guess who he *did* want to talk about?"

I press closer to Kara, sensing she needs my physical backup in addition to the mental. If we were all just normal masses of flesh and blood, I'd still be aware of the agitation tumbling out of her. I'm practically taking a bath in the stuff myself when she finally stammers a reply.

"Arden and I barely communicate now. The last time I

even said two words to him was at the Gold Circle dinner. Since then…"

"You know, I've been wondering that myself. Where *have* you been, big sister? And don't tell me you've been holed up at Maximus's place, because I will smell that lie on you so fast—"

Kara blinks hard. "I don't know what you mean."

"You heard me," Kell charges. "Where have you been since Saturday night, Kara? Because if even half of what Arden told me is right, you've got one hell of a ruthless god *still* after your soul—and a lot of explaining to give everyone in this city."

A harsh tremor claims every inch of the woman next to me. It spills into her breaths, which are again nothing more than shudders, while she struggles to hold her posture despite her sister's accusing appraisal.

Kell shrugs. "Then I guess you could say the conversation got a little *heated*."

Kara's stillness is worse to witness than her shivering. "What?" she finally rasps. "My God, Kell."

"What are you saying?" I interject. "That *Arden* did this to you?"

"Arden only started it. The fault lines finished it. Call it a win for your new pal, Hades."

The mention of Hades and Arden in nearly the same breath forces me to walk away before my nerves get hold of the chaos that's spinning my head.

Damn it.

Whether Prieto came by his underworld update

through honest means or not, he reacted to that privilege by taking his frustration out on Kell—to the point that she paid an agonizing price for it, inside as well as out. That thought alone has sparks arcing between my fingers during my frantic escape onto what looks like an employee break patio.

At once, I start a furious figure-eight around the four round tables positioned beneath a stretched canopy cover. The lights from my fists flash in and around the wrought-iron furniture, then up along the arena's outside walls.

But the sparks aren't just providing a safe outlet for my rising anger. Reluctantly, I accept the secondary duty of their white-hot sparks. The comprehension they're igniting in me. The possibilities they're making me face, no matter how painful or blinding.

If Hades is already on such a rabid hunt for Kara again, what does that say about the coincidence of all today's damage? Is the City of Angels actually being rocked by pure demonic destruction?

And if so…what's going to come next?

CHAPTER 22

Kara

"**K**ELL."

I yearn to regain her attention by shaking her with more than my voice but don't dare. It's already nearly impossible for me to stand here and fake my overall composure. In the deepest recesses of my gut, I can already feel the accuracy of her indictment. The double underline to Arden's rash action, whatever it was.

"*Kell.*" I settle for leaning over and circling one arm around her midsection. Though I'm careful about any injuries I don't know about, I still give her ribs a firm tug. "Hey."

A rough sound vibrates in her throat before she squirms. "What?"

"Look at me."

"Why?" I'm not her older sister by a lot of years, but they're enough to pull rank when I have to. And this, right now, is a *have to*.

She finally sighs, but it's too long and heavy to have me celebrating.

"Please tell me the truth."

Her body takes on tension. "Maybe *you're* the one who should be telling the truth right about now."

I take my turn with a long and meaningful sigh. "Okay." And do her one better by working on my gentle diplomacy. "About what?"

"I think you know what. Arden told me you went… there." She swallows hard. "I was worried something like that might have happened. Mom claimed to know nothing. I tried and tried to get a hold of Jaden to see if he had any idea, but to no avail."

A gut punch of alarm whips my head an inch higher. "You haven't talked to Jaden lately?"

"That's what I just said," she snaps. "And I just kept having this feeling…"

I release a low groan. It doesn't communicate a lot but enough to validate her intuitions—and confirm my trepidation. If Arden's underworld insiders have been doing their work, he must have discovered I was a guest of honor, however reluctant, in the bottom circle. He might even have the scoop about Maximus and Gramps's rescue mission being a massive success.

But he hopefully doesn't know why. And I *really* hope he doesn't know how.

I suspect, though, if Arden gave Kell even a whisper about what I did with the grimoire, she'd have been all over me with that from the second I entered this place, pain meds flowing or not. I'm so relieved about not having to justify all that yet, my composure is infused with some much-needed patience.

With my hand still semi-tucked around her middle, I hitch up to sit next to her on the gurney. Our gazes meet, exchanging shades of brown that are different by such tiny variations. I swear, sometimes the effect is like looking into a matching image of my soul. And other times, like now, it's not. Kell and I can see each other, but we're also lost to a billion separate thoughts. That's okay too. It's our ease, being able to fly around the same cages as each other. We're synched the way sisters often are, but even more so due to our gifts. As I sense her spirit loosening and relaxing again, she tilts her head and wriggles her nose.

"Well?" she prods. "Come on. What'll it be? You know you're still wearing *Eau de Underworld*, right? Bet you could easily sneak back in and give your little sis a fun-filled tour."

I purse my lips. "It's not a place you even want to joke about, okay?"

"Oh, I'm not joking."

Despite her charge, she rubs a few fingers atop my free hand, so subtle and sweet, conveying a different intention than her jab. It's such a mesmerizing mix of affection and derision…but I'm not about to let her off the hook because of it. Definitely not now.

"Damn it, Kell. Tell me what Arden said. You need to tell me, because if I keep writing that script myself…"

For a second—just one—I consider how many of my

own violent sides would be rearing right now had Arden inflicted damage on her that wasn't so easily repaired by her demonic DNA. My soul is already knotted in the spiritual version of the stomach flu, feeling so much of what he's done to beat her down inside.

"Please, sister."

"It was very nearly what I just said." She halts her strokes along my knuckles as the corners of her eyes pinch and their centers glaze over. "I was outside the Aquila Building. Arden showed up. Before I opened my mouth, he started ranting about you and Hades and a million more underworld no-noes you'd somehow heaped on top of the first one."

"Why would he waste his time complaining to you about it?"

"Because the jerk thought I was in on it somehow. He accused me of helping Maximus and Gramps jump. Like I'd know the first fucking thing about it." Kell rolls her eyes before closing them briefly. "Then he started going on and on about some book, over and over again, like I'd have a better idea what he was talking about if he screamed it a hundred times. Honestly, I felt like I was in an interrogation room and he was the bad cop—only I never got to meet the *good* cop. Anyone ever tell the clueless wonder that you only get a confession when the good cop's involved too?"

She's giggling about it now.

I'm not.

My bloodstream turns so cold, the stalactites and stalagmites are sharpening each other. I finally stammer out, "A...book?"

She keeps chuckling about the memory, even as my stomach plummets. "He would not let up about it. Kept telling me I knew where it was. That it belonged in the underworld and you had no right to take it." She blinks slowly—before sniffing toward me tentatively. "Do you know anything about that?"

At once, I step back. I shake my head, forcing myself to believe it so Kell won't pick up on the lie. "What happened after you argued?"

"Then another one of the quakes hit. It sent lots of people scattering, except Arden. He thought he'd use the moment and create a 'happy accident' to get me talking."

After a few seconds, I shove aside my mounting ire to speak. "What did he do?"

Kell cocks back her head with a sad smile. "The quake was strong enough to rock the statue. He gave it a little extra push."

"The statue?" I search my recall for the one she's talking about. "The big concrete treble clef in the courtyard outside Aquila?"

Kell clicks her tongue. "That's the one."

"That thing's ten or eleven feet high."

Kell shrugs. "It was cracked near the base. He's strong and fast enough to give it the momentum it needed. Thankfully it didn't kill me. Then he'd have to marry Jaden. Imagine how peeved he'd be then!"

She starts snickering wildly at her own joke, but again I don't join her. I can't.

Through several long seconds, I scramble through the

confused brambles of my brain. If I had to paint a visual of them now, they'd look like the stark, snaking vines that covered so much of Dis. The despair that fills me now just thinking about Kell having to defend herself against Arden and that gigantic concrete slab... My heart inches hideously close to the feeling I had then. The emotions that are impossible to revisit. Not now. Not so soon. *Please...not ever...*

"What's wrong now?" Kell coos.

"I'm disgusted, okay?" I finally say. "Disgusted and dismayed and furious. He had no right to make those accusations. You're blameless in all this. You have been since the beginning, and now—"

My rising intensity has her smacking the back of my hand. "Okay, adjust the equalizer settings, please. I thought you wanted to keep a low profile here. Or do you actually *want* everyone in the building to get an earful of the real Valari secrets?"

I focus on counseling a bunch of calm to myself. But the rage burns higher inside, producing a red haze at the corners of my vision. But I'm more than just angry. I'm sick with guilt, oppressed by helplessness. I was cuddling on the couch with Maximus when my sister was getting assaulted by her incubus. "I'm sorry," I mumble. "He's despicable. A belligerent bully."

She slides her hand into mine again. "Yeah, he is. But there's nothing we can do about it. The important thing right now is—"

"Making sure you never have to see that heartless

bastard again." I ball up my hands from the first second of her eye roll.

But Kell persists with a declaration that matches her firm handhold. "You need to send that fantasy off in the dream balloon right now, sister. Arden may be a heartless, despicable coward, but he's also got the pedigree from the powers that be. We both know what that means."

I drag in another sharp breath. "There's got to be another way!"

"There isn't. You're not making anything better by pushing that agenda. I mean, haven't you caused enough trouble for yourself already?"

Suddenly she's not gazing at me with affection.

"Kell…"

She ignores me, rolling to her side to further sever our connection.

"Come on. I don't want to fight about this."

"Then let's not," she retorts. "I'm really tired, K-demon. Why don't you go check on Maximus? I'll have his mom find you when I'm close to getting sprung."

I hate admitting it, but her suggestion has merit. I can only imagine what fate Maximus is concocting for Arden as we speak—and as much as I'd love to get in on that plan, messing with him further is not a brilliant concept right now. Via just the few details Kell has supplied, it's obvious Arden has tight inside tracks all the way to Dis, perhaps to Hades's inner circle itself.

No. Not *perhaps*.

Probably.

Which makes him an enemy best kept at arm's length but alive—whether any of us likes it or not.

CHAPTER 23

MAXIMUS

"ROOM FOR ONE MORE at the table?"

Kara's murmur supplies the final dose of sanity that I need for turning off my finger lightning. As she sits beside me atop one of the break tables, I try to calm the small squall that's still whipping at the edges of the patio.

She loops her arm beneath mine and rests her cheek on my shoulder. I sweep my head down to taste her…needing her spice more with every passing second. I'll never stop craving this gorgeous, fiery female…

Her breath catches at the last minute, ramping my desire by the key notch that'll keep the rain steady for at least another few minutes. Neither of us notice. Just like that, we're totally lost in each other again.

But reluctantly, I bust our bubble back open. There are things we have to talk about, and I don't know how long we'll have to do it. Not after everything I've just been mentally turning over.

"Do I even want to know what Arden pulled now?"

"She's his fiancée, but I'm afraid that doesn't mean much to a full-blooded demon." Kara lets out a heavy sigh while brushing some errant hair strands away from my face. "He also knows about the grimoire."

I grit my jaw. "How do you know?"

"Because he accused Kell of knowing where it was. He thought she might have helped you cross over too. When she vehemently denied both, he resorted to more brutal measures to get the truth out of her."

"Did you tell her about it?"

She shakes her head. "Are you kidding? If I tell her anything right now, she'll be shouting it into the streets all the way home. When the time is right, I will."

I claw my free hand through my hair. "Good idea. What do we do about Arden?"

"Right now? Not a damn thing. Kell seems...resigned. She won't retaliate, and she won't want us to either."

"Come on. I know incubuses are bred to be predatory, but Arden Prieto is a worm dressed in Gucci. He can't get away with this."

She interrupts by molding her other hand over the top of my forearm, gripping with clear purpose. "Maximus, I don't have a choice. I'm the reason she's entangled with him now. It's hard to argue with her. If she wants to figure this out on her own, I have to let her. She deserves my respect for her decision, even if I don't agree with it. At all."

I don't answer her verbally. Instead, I shove up from my perch, needing an outlet that isn't going to have me causing a blizzard across LA tonight.

"Maximus." She presses a more intense plea into it now. "Please come sit down ag—"

"You know what?" I spin back around. "Your mother's obsession with the Valari legacy is costing more each day—and you, Kell, and Jaden are paying for it. I'm sorry, Kara, but I refuse to stand by and watch that become the ultimate price. Something has to be done about him. I went head-to-head with Cerberus not that long ago. I can handle Arden."

I mean every word while immediately wishing to take them all back. I must look like a grandstanding idiot, though Kara's reaction is saying something else. Something way more.

"*Maximus.*" She whispers it this time. But not in rebuke. She's gasping it…from revelation, or maybe even shock.

What has her gawking so hard over my shoulder? I seek the answer by swinging my sights in the same direction. Once my stare is filled with the force that's really bearing down on the patio, I wheel around all the way—and assume I'm now copying her with my stunned awe. And a dash of dread.

It's Zeus, steadily strolling toward us. While his open-necked shirt and casual slacks have me taking easier breaths, the clothes are the only insouciant element of his demeanor. Gone is the guy who seemed fazed by nothing and noncommittal about everything. He's a thunderstorm with legs, and his turbulent expression backs the point to every degree.

"Hello, son," he grits out.

"What are you doing here?" I demand.

"Nice to see you too," he deadpans. "Though if I'd known you were going to go and punch every one of Hades's triggers at the same time, I'd have asked the Hellenics to scoot their wine festival to a more convenient weekend."

I rocket a brow nearly to my hairline. "It's not like you've been standing by to help."

The accusation doesn't land the way I hoped. In his steely gaze, I finally glimpse the intimidation factor for which he's so famous. I *sense* it, but I don't *feel* it.

"You understand why I couldn't get involved," he answers tightly.

"And you should understand why I had to."

"To the point that you had to dive into hell yourself?" His nostrils flare. "With the warlock who already finagled his way out of the place?"

I fold my arms. "At least he showed up. He went the distance with me. He gives a damn."

No matter how strong the craving to lean over and shake this point into dear old dad, I already know it's going to be no use, so I stow the instinct.

Z cants his head as if his eternal neck bones need cracking. "You make it sound so innocent. So simple. Except by doing what you did, you've now unleashed my brother's greatest wrath in centuries. I've explained this to you. These are the ramifications when a realm isn't enough to hold a god's fury."

"And Hades is furious." That certain truth comes out of Kara in a rasped sob.

My own tension quadruples. I hate that I can't just turn, scoop her close, and seal her away from the horror of this revelation, but I don't dare look away from my father.

Past his grim expression, he doesn't offer a shred of light on its source. His only change is a brick of a sigh that precedes a bed-of-nails growl.

"My brother's not one for losing gracefully." He includes Kara in the small sweep of his glance. "You've probably already figured that one out."

"So now he's reciprocating," she fills in. "And all of LA is paying for it."

"There has to be a way of opening up a new dialogue," I say to my father. "He can't really mean to demolish the entire city."

"And the dozens around it," Z informs. "As well as parts of Vegas and everything in between. No one knows where it'll stop."

I narrow my scrutiny. "So my point stands better made. Two of the globe's leading cities for championing all his favorite causes… Is he really all about ruining them with one diabolical punch? What's the purpose in that plan?"

Z tosses back his head with a hearty laugh. "You think his ego considers *plans*? Son, if that were the case, history would be free of half its floods, fires, and freak weather catastrophes." He's not laughing anymore. Once his head lowers, he's even baring his teeth in a rare display of vitriol. "I'm aware of my temper and its notoriety, believe me. But Hades makes my passions look like crochet projects."

"Passions?" I'm tempted to be the one brandishing the

laughter now, but his grimace sobers me fast.

"Right now, we can't afford to—"

He interrupts himself, violently swallowing the rest of his words. His blatant stress has me startling along with Kara. When he's looking over our heads in much the same way Kara just gawked past me, all the oxygen in my own system seizes. For an insane second, I'm actually lost about what to do next. Pretending I'm ready for a hand-to-hand battle with Hades is as huge an illusion as it was in hell. If he's brought minions with him, the situation will be worse.

"By the Pleiades," Z murmurs huskily, breaking the panicked silence.

I follow his gaze to the woman approaching us with fast steps. The inside of my brain seems to be working at reverse speed, grasping the full impact of this moment way too late. There's nothing I can do to stop it from happening. Nothing I can do to warn Mom about the emotional meteor headed directly at her…

"Okay, you two. I managed to process Kell's paperwork and got a new doc on the rotation to sign off the discharge without checking all her stats." Mom spouts it while flipping efficiently through the pages on her clipboard. "So Kara, as her requested next of kin and designated driver, you just need to sign—"

When she looks up, the clipboard slips from her grasp and clatters to the pavement at her feet. Her fingers start to tremble. Her chin starts to wobble.

At the same time, I'm certain my father is about to shed tears in front of me for the first time in my life. He looks like someone knocked the wind out of him.

That someone being Nancy Kane.

"Zeus."

He responds by pushing air out through his nose, prompting a rough swallow down his taut throat. But at the edges of his unsteady lips, there are tremors of joy. They can be nothing else. As a man, I'm certain of it. As his son, I'm moved by it. Grateful for it. There's strength in a parent showing their tears to their children. I've seen enough of Mom's to know.

"Nancy," he finally says.

His reverence doesn't dent her. She backs up with her arms folded tightly. "Wh-What are you doing here?"

He shakes his head as if he can't make sense of her words. "You're more gorgeous now than the day we met."

"That's not an answer," she says. Her tone is cold and her posture is just as stony. "What the *hell* are you doing here?"

CHAPTER 24

Kara

IF MAXIMUS AND I were still in our delusional bubble about the earthquake swarm, I'd be entreating Mother Nature for another temblor this second. But Hades stands clear of the fault lines for now, leaving Maximus and me to figure out proper focal points that *aren't* his parents laying eyes on each other for the first time since his boyhood.

I shamelessly gawk at the two people who are still blatantly magnetized toward each other, whether they want to admit it or not. The wave of their energies is so strong it could be my own. Heaven knows, the feeling is far from foreign with Maximus in my life now.

"I can explain, *leaina*."

"I'll take the explanation without your fancy Greek, thank you."

I bite my lip to hold in a giggle. Two magnets, no doubt. Except one clearly doesn't want to be realigned.

After all this time, maybe Nancy Kane isn't mesmerized

by the handsome king of the gods. Still, they already remind me of a couple from a big budget musical, drawn together with such dazzling destiny that everyone on stage freezes or fades to the shadows. It's difficult to watch Maximus's mom beholding the adoration that Z has kept so fully aflame for her and tossing it into emotional ice water. Maybe she's just nervous, but that's not what I'm picking up at all. Her aversion is like blown glass that has yet to cool. It's hot but cold. Formidable but fragile. But ready to break with one bad twist…

What does she know that we don't? What other secrets could she possibly be holding back? The fact that all of Maximus's early memories have been taken from him heightens my need to know more. Regrettably, we're not likely to get them from her now. Her resolve is one of the most adamant auras I've ever detected.

"You mean Maximus hasn't told you what's happened?" Z tacks on a look of such implication and aggravation, my human side winces.

Nancy's jaw clenches. "What do you mean?"

To his credit, Z pointedly hesitates. There's not even an indicting glance toward his son. Perhaps he already knows that Maximus will fess up first.

Because, of course, he does.

"Kara was in danger, Mom." He firms his stance while meeting her gaze. "So I had to go and get her."

The woman races a startled gaze to me. "Danger? In what way? Are you all right?"

"I'm fine." I rush it out, already contrite about causing

her such concern. I forget, with frightening ease, that this is how most mothers blast their worry. Then I realize, with equally terrifying clarity, that I'm not sure I could have dealt with twenty-two whole years of it. "I really am, Nancy."

"But not long ago, she wasn't," Maximus says. "Which was why I had to walk through hell and get her back."

Nancy pales by a shade before dropping heavily to one of the round benches. At once, she's plummeting her head into her hands too. "Oh, God."

Maximus approaches her, a hand outstretched. His remorse makes my chest twist. "Mom—"

She throws a hand up, her palm like a stop sign. "*Don't.* Just...give me a second, okay? This isn't like you just snuck out to Jesse's for World of Warcraft, damn it."

Maximus remains crouched next to Nancy, with his hands stretched over his thighs. Whether on purpose or not, he lifts his head with a beseeching look—that lands right on his father.

Z, clearly buying into his own press, adapts a stance as if he's brandishing a scepter topped by a gilded eagle. "Listen to your mother, son."

As if the eagle has gotten form and swooped in on us, a violent sound breaks the air. After a second, I realize it's Nancy's sharp laugh. "He's been doing just fine without your help for over ten years."

I can't pretend that his punctuating glare doesn't freak me out. Even Maximus jolts at this glimpse of his father's notorious temper. But Nancy's already giving back as good as she's gotten, lurching back up and practically matching him toe-to-toe. She's a lioness in mint green scrubs, mentally tearing down that eagle's ego before Z knows what's coming.

"If you don't want to hear the truth, then you should go back to where you came from. In fact, I think that's for the best."

"I'm not going anywhere." Z drops his hands into his slacks pockets, a casual motion that doesn't fit the mood of this moment. I want to cheer as Nancy jogs up her chin, officially leveling her blues with Z's. Though her syllables vibrate with just-try-me grit, her face trembles with just-take-me need.

The perception isn't just what my gut feels. It's what my heart knows and my experience confirms. Nancy Kane is fighting a battle that's just not winnable. She's in love. The best and worst kind. The forever kind.

But she's trying to resist...valiantly. She even adds a flippant shrug to her fake nonchalance.

"I mean, we're having a bit of an emergency here. Just in case you couldn't tell or anything." She waves toward the building behind us. "I know it's a stretch, asking you to look at situations strictly about us lowly mortals, but—"

"Nancy."

"Believe it or not, and for your permanent record, there are a lot more of us in this city alone than all of you up on Olympus. So if you really want to make yourself useful—"

"*Nancy.*"

She clenches to a stop, matching the heavy-lidded look he's wielding now, as he steps closer and dips his face to within inches of hers. When Z's intention is glaringly clear, and even Maximus is swearing because of it, my own mouth pops open. I guess the almighty of Olympus is a bigger cowboy than I thought. But thankfully, a smart one. He backs off within seconds of getting her palm print across his cheek. His own expression hardens with resolve.

"For *your* permanent record, I'm here exactly because of this *lowly* situation," he responds tightly. "Which, very soon, isn't going to be so cleanly cut and put away."

Nancy gulps hard. "Oh?"

"Everything that's happening… This isn't the fault lines all deciding to have a bad day at once."

"No." Maximus shifts uneasily. Sighs just as heavily. "It's Hades becoming the poster child for unchecked petulance."

Z swings around with a piercing look. "You'd be wise to keep those remarks to yourself, lest they're overheard by the wrong parties. I think you've aggravated him enough, don't you?" He accepts Maximus's glower as enough of a reply to continue his terse briefing. "On his best days, he's a tethered beast. If you care for this realm and those in it, the goal is to keep the tether stable."

The logic in my mind forces out the words on my lips. "And the status of the tether now?"

I expect it's the exact question Z wants, but he hesitates to respond.

Maximus fills that gap with a heavy sigh. "Hanging on by a thread, I'm guessing."

Z returns that assessment with an unnerving stance, rubbing his thumbs along his forefingers in maddeningly casual circles. "You want to test the theory by tightroping on the thread?" he drawls. "Or should we get things moving by talking about how we're going to deal with this now?"

The declaration has me breathing easier, especially as Maximus's expression opens up. It can't be easy for him to take off his blinders about Z and acknowledge the benefit of his experience over the hurt from his absence. But maybe a bigger recognition is dawning for him too. The black-and-white memories from our upbringings seem to gain more gray scale nuances as our journey goes on.

"Okay, you're right," Maximus concedes. "Movement is essential. But where? My place is out now. So is Kara's house."

"And just about anywhere else on the continent." Z cocks his head, still too steady and calm for comfort.

Maximus dips a respectful nod. "What do you have in mind?"

"No." Nancy jerks Maximus back by the crook of his elbow, exposing the new overlay of her intent. "Just no. We don't need him to save us! All these years, we've done it on our own and have been just fine. Right?"

Maximus tugs his arm in, bringing her hand closer. "Mom." He gently slides a hand atop hers. "All these years, we've never had to deal with something like this."

Her mouth compresses. "But that doesn't mean we can't," she rasps.

"You don't know who you're dealing with, Nancy," Z says. "Hades will rob a baby from its mother if it serves his whims or glory. Just as easily, he'd kill it."

"And you wonder why I got *our* child out of your world when I did?" she snaps.

The god's countenance goes rigid. "You mean the world that's going to be his safest sanctuary now?"

"Whoa." Maximus's posture seizes up. "Wait the hell up. What're you—"

"No," Nancy spews. "Absolutely not. I forbid it."

"He's a grown man now. He can make up his own mind—"

"To tell you he refuses to follow you to where you tug the leash just because you slam on a crown every once in a while!"

Z hauls in a long breath. "A crown isn't what designates me as king."

"And your DNA doesn't designate Maximus as your puppet." She's in Z's face once more, skewering him with her glower. "You can't make him go. You *won't* dictate his decisions!"

Z pushes back into her personal space. He doesn't blink or flinch. "Even if I leave right now and take *you* back with me?"

I yearn to hug Nancy. My soul already cracks with just one thought of Maximus rushing off to Olympus. A demon, even by half, belongs less in Olympus than a demigod in Dis. And we barely survived that ordeal.

"Nancy, you *won't* be able to hide from this now." Z swings his stare back around at Maximus and me. "He doesn't want to see just a little suffering. He'll exact the pain in every way he can."

"So your solution is to tuck us away in Olympus?" Nancy counters. "Because that worked so well the first time?"

There's an awful extended pause. Z doesn't seem deterred by her challenge. Not by any detectable inch.

"We can figure something out," he finally states. "But until then, at least you'll be safe."

"*Safe*. In what exact sense of the word now?"

The question is a velvety murmur, but it impacts my nerves like a fork on glass—until I tense at a new sound. We all spin toward an outer gate on the patio—an access route that's locked off to the public by a menacing padlock.

Somehow, Erin Levin has managed to get past it with ease.

I don't ignore that part. I can't afford to. Especially because she's strolling closer and closer, her smirking gaze never leaving the king of the gods.

Like she's met him before. Lots of times.

"Erin. Hi." Maximus's attention finally fixes on the new person in our party. "You lost? Are you looking for someone?"

The professor slides her gaze between Maximus and Z like a serpent slithering through marsh grass. She's watching…deciding…savoring… And now it's beyond unsettling. As every second goes by, she's less and less the sweet but shy woman from the silent auction room at President McCarthy's party.

But that impression fades beneath the worst realization that hits me.

I'm completely deaf and blind about her aura. Especially as she circles her shockingly intense stare right around at me. The blue and green shades of her irises don't appear so sparkly anymore. They're marbled and saturated, surrounding unusually huge pupils.

I gasp and shift back toward Maximus, desperately needing his strength. Because Erin Levin isn't who she appears or claims to be. I feel that much in my bones. A second later, with Z's recognition, I know it as fact.

"Megaera." Zeus's growl has never sounded more like music to me. "You have no business here."

Every muscle in my body tenses painfully. I share a knowing look with Maximus.

Imagination offers too many possibilities to my brain. Is she an emissary for Hades, come to drag me back to the world that'll kill my soul long before my body perishes? Or has she come to enforce some other brand of justice?

Z twists a hand as if yanking on a pet's leash.

Erin hisses, her neck extending toward Z with the sound. "*You* have no business here."

"Do you dare reprimand me?" Zeus jerks harder on the invisible chain.

Erin—Megaera, whoever she is—cries out before dropping to the ground. From that position, she twists her head, spearing Z with the gaze that's gone from startling aqua to terrifyingly bright turquoise. A small scritch vibrates from her throat, hinting at a laugh but never getting there.

"I am your Fury!" she lashes out. "I have every right to be here, meting out justice by your law. Am I not at your service as the punisher of lies, infidelity, and broken oaths? The power *you* have given me to punish all who sin in such a manner?"

"The power with which you've barged in here on behalf of your queen instead of your king?" Z bellows. He flings his hand down as if tossing aside the leash, but the female on the pavement seethes in deeper torment.

"Would you have me pardon those who've broken a sacred oath simply for their heritage?"

"Enough. Explain yourself!"

Somehow, the Fury struggles into a proud but quivering kneel. Despite her terrified trembling beneath the seething stare of her king, she clearly digs deep for a well of arrogance. She licks her lips, as if anticipating the reaction she'll incite with her next words.

"Don't worry. Her Majesty proposes a compromise. Maximus is your bastard, after all," she croons.

"If Hera has sent you with a message, deliver it now before I send you back to her," Z spits. "*You* can figure out how to explain you've failed your mission."

Megaera resettles her shoulders and proudly lifts her head. She doesn't move from that stance but cuts her glare over and jabs it into Maximus. And then into me. "You have perpetuated the sin of broken promises. Knowingly neglected your given vows."

I'm gulping on bitter, raw nerves before she's even done.

At the same time, Z is pulling the trigger on a withering glower. "And as usual, my loving spouse believes her palace party line before checking the facts." He sidles forward. "You can slither back to your queen now and tell Her Majesty that if she lays a finger on my boy—"

Megaera throws her head back, hissing out a long and gleeful laugh. Even on her knees, the Fury seems to hold on to some semblance of her power and purpose.

Slowly, she levels her gaze to Z's. "My queen wishes you to know that Maximus Kane shall never set foot again in Olympus. Not him, his mother, nor his demon lover. If you dare attempt it, trust that they will know sudden and swift deaths. Hera will show not a shred of mercy."

She draws out the last word with a savoring smile before holding up one hand, her two longest fingers extended.

"So I swear it—and very happily so."

CHAPTER 25

MAXIMUS

MY LUNGS PUMP WITH enraged air. My muscles are bound by ropes of nearly painful tension. At once, I wonder why. It's not from shock or betrayal at Erin's revelation but from much deeper feelings. Darker discomforts. An overriding conflict between yearning to fight or flee. To run or destroy.

My thoughts float back to the fuzzy memories I have from my days in Olympus. Should I return to the villa as Mom keeps bidding me or lash back at Clymene and her snickering herd with all the force I can summon from my seething body?

A low, livid snarl unfurls from me. Satisfaction sets in watching the sound sink into Megaera like my own teeth, but the feeling is fleeting. The decades in between are like blips to her ancient soul. The only reason I'm important is because my existence validates hers. Another bastard to go after, further stamping her meal ticket with the gods.

"Leave."

Only a word, but it surges my senses like a victory cry. I'm not even saying it for the smirking woman at my feet. I'm demanding it for the boy who silently begged Regina for the chance to shout at them so long ago on the lawn in front of the villa in Olympus.

"You've delivered your message," I emphasize with my teeth locked and my jaw gritted. "And now you can get out."

And this time, I accept what I should have so long ago, during all those years of making Mom so sad and frustrated with my constant demands for information. Sometimes the past isn't *once upon a time*. Sometimes *I don't remember* has to be good enough.

The resolve should feel good but doesn't. Even as Megaera complies, coiling into a tight ball on the ground and then dissolving into desert dust and disappearing completely, I struggle to accept my new insights. But my head and heart return nothing but a sense of strange emptiness, especially through the long silence that stretches after the Fury vanishes on the wind.

Finally, Z grits, "Don't worry. Hera's meddling can only go so far. I'm not her simpering husband. I'm her *king!*"

His roar causes ripples in the lingering puddles on the ground and even makes Kara stumble back by a step.

The only unfazed one is Mom, who pins him with a cold stare. "And you wonder why she sends spies instead of emissaries?"

My father clenches his formidable jaw. "She isn't the

anointed ruler of the kingdom. She has no jurisdiction over those welcomed or denied there."

"Of course not, dear." Mom flashes a saccharine smile to match the tone that earns her his harsher glance. "Oh, come on. She's more subversive than that, and we both know it."

"Which means that for now, we're going to table the subject." I step up, gathering Mom beneath my free arm. "Just like we're going to say *thanks but no thanks* to the golden gates pass, Pops."

This time, my parents give up a joint jolt of reaction—though likely for different reasons. Mom verifies it by intensifying her stare, scanning my face with open curiosity.

"How…did you know that?" she queries. "About the gates?"

"Hey, you know me," I say with affection. "Probably read it somewhere."

But the cover is for her ease alone. How *did* I suddenly know that?

But is it that important right now? Not when I'm too damn worried about my father fighting me on this. With a casual blink of his eyes, I could be standing in the land of glowing playtime balls on the lawn in front of our private Olympus villa. No way. I won't accept it. Not now, when I'm unclear about what realm Megaera's really slunk off to.

Even without her in the mix, there are too many other factors to consider here. Priorities I can't and won't ignore. Reg, Sarah, and Jesse. Gio and Kell. Jaden, who's hopefully escaped from Rerek's custody by now. Crazily, I even consider Veronica. Leaving them now, knowing the full brunt of Hades's wrath is likely still to come…

I refuse.

I don't yield the decision, despite the silent thunder of Z's fume.

Somehow, Mom gets that. She pops a hand to her hip and an approving chuff to her lips. "Good call. Same call I would've made."

Z's glare gains miniature lightning bolts. "When all I want to do is what *you* haven't allowed me to? To protect you—"

"Like you *never* did." There's a give in her voice that doesn't match the pride in her frame. "Not even when you thought you were." She shifts as if to shield me from his fiercer glare, despite how my beard grazes the top of her head. "You didn't believe me then, and I don't expect anything different now. All I ask is that you let us go in peace. We're going to collect Kara's sister from inside, and then we're going to decide, as the family we are, how to figure this crisis out."

There's little change in my father's tumultuous bearing. Of course, there's still the not-so-small matter of how we're going to handle whatever's coming next. Clearly, Hades doesn't know the meaning of graceful resignation. His vendetta has already been marked by the heavy tolls on Kell, Jaden, and half of Los Angeles. How far will he go before it's enough? How deeply will he tear into our family, friends, and city?

A moment of light interrupts my brood. Kara's deep-brown velvets are so soothing in her acknowledgment of my torment. But most of all, and especially now, so complete in her comprehension of the support I need to feel. The sincerity I need to see.

The plan I need to hear.

"I know where we have to start." She turns, layering a hand atop mine in the junction where Mom is still tucked against my side. "Let's get out of here."

*✳

This isn't the way I envisioned entering the Valari mansion for the first time. It seems entirely too empty and quiet, but I'm glad. Concentrating on jostling Kell as little as possible, especially up the wide stairs to the second and then third floor, is a solid excuse not to focus on all the stuff Kara's given up for me, over and above the obvious. An atrium with a retractable sun shade? A bathroom with a glowing waterfall next to a lagoon tub? I don't even glance into the numerous walk-in closets as Kara guides me into a bedroom that clearly eclipses the square footage of the apartments of my early childhood.

Kara switches on a nightstand lamp as Kell, who's been softly mewling in my arms since I got her out of the car, gains semiconsciousness. Gently, I lower her to the sheets and pillows.

"Kara! K-demon, baby! Karaaa!"

"I'm right here," Kara murmurs while sitting on the mattress beside her. She runs an equally careful hand over Kell's hair. "How are you feeling?"

"Mmm. Is it martini hour yet? Shaken not stirred, please."

As if on cue, the mansion sways from a new jolt to the earth three stories below. "Oh, never mind. *Don't* shake!"

"It's okay." Kara folds Kell's hands between her own. "Try to get some rest."

Kell sighs and beams a dreamy grin. "I love you guys."

Once Mom returns from the bathroom with a cup of water, we share a chuckle about Kell's tipsiness, but Kara's brow crunches. If I'm reading her correctly, it's not all from concern. No doubt she's still whipping herself inside, feeling responsible for the "accident" that would've killed her sister in a more mortal scenario.

"We need answers," she mutters angrily, surging back to her feet with a stiff jolt.

As the charge stamps the air, Mom's already stepping over. "You're on it," she states. "And I'm on her. Don't stress about a thing."

I swear to every god and demigod, including myself, that even if Kara and I were on our way back into hell, getting to see her and my mom hug with such affection is like transforming my chest into a sun deck.

As soon as Kara turns and heads for the door, she mutters from tight lips, "Okay. Let's do this."

Not more than a minute later, I learn that *this* means knocking on the door of her grandfather's casita. Here we go again with trying to figure out Hades's crazy schemes, starting on Gio Valari's doorstep. Most unsettling of all, here *I* am, having to accept that if Gio can't help, I could lose Kara completely.

And this time, there won't be rescue do-overs.

Thankfully I'm distracted with a burst of gratitude at seeing Gio's face. He's still scraped-up from our scuffle with Cerberus, but in all other regards, he's the same affable grandfather I introduced myself to, in this very same spot, only a couple of days ago.

At once, Gio seems overtaken by the same rush of relief. He shuts his eyes tightly while grabbing his granddaughter into an adamant hug.

"Kara. Thank every power, you're okay."

"Yeah." A few tears encroach on her voice, but she's mostly firm and strong while surely squeezing the man to the crushing point. "I am, mostly. Are *you*?"

"Of course." He rocks back and gives her a friendly chuck on the chin. "Your gramps isn't *that* old and ossified yet."

She grimaces. "Stop saying things like that. If you weren't here…"

"You'd be just fine," he soothes, before jogging his twinkling regard up to me. "Especially with this fancy dog fighter around."

I laugh. "You ever going to let that go, old man?"

"Probably not, young buck."

Our banter aside, Kara's already homing in, like she needs to and should be, on the reason we're standing at his doorstep with our proverbial hats in hand.

"Gramps." She locks her intent stare with his, wrapping her hands around his elbows. "You have to know why we've come."

Gio turns his hands over to cup the bottom curves of

her elbows. "I've got a few working theories, yes. As soon as I got home and found this place ransacked and then learned from Dalton that Arden Prieto had been through every inch of it…"

He drops his hands back down to his sides, where they spread and blaze like electric talons. The veins leading to them, along his wrists and knuckles, look like glowing red snakes.

"I'm so sorry, Gramps," Kara murmurs. "But I think I know what he was looking for."

"Of course. He wants that damn grimoire. Well, his boss does anyway. Tell me you still have it?"

Kara nods. "I do. It's—"

"Don't tell me," Gio says. "No point. You should have it. I wouldn't trust anyone else with it. Protect it, Kara. Anything Hades wants that much has to be powerful beyond anything we can imagine."

He takes a second to gather his breath, and Kara uses the time to seemingly round up her own wits. But every second that clicks by is feeling too valuable to me. Too important to waste.

"We've talked to Zeus."

I go ahead and say it. No sense in holding him back from the shock, which he displays by instantly jacking up his head. The red streaks fade from his wrists and hands, leaving him looking a little older. A *lot* more drained.

"I thought he was keeping his distance from all this," he mutters.

"That was before Hades started breaking everything in LA."

"Hmphhh," he grunts. "Makes sense."

As his grimace harshens, so do the rapid in-and-outs of Kara's chest. "Please, Gramps," she echoes with double the desperation. "Can you help us? Do you know at *all* what will stop Hades this time? We have to find a way to—"

The rest of her words are sucked out by a massive rush of air across the backyard.

Across the whole block.

Across the whole *city*.

And there's no more finding anything, as the wind howls through the nearby canyons, blasts across downtown, and screams up into the hills—before amalgamating into a tower of furious energy in the middle of the swimming pool.

The swimming pool?

The wonderment practically washes me in consolation, until I remember exactly how Gio backdoored me into hell in the first place. And all the ways that fate delivered its glimpses of Kara to me.

This spectacle isn't a glimpse of anything.

The atmospheric dervish is a violent centrifuge for everything not directly rooted, glued, or nailed down. Every leaf off the hedges. Every petal of every flower. Even the martini glasses and drink coasters from the poolside bar—

Until, as if it's all been kindling for a massive bonfire, there's a fiery flume atop the aqua water. The tower, spiking at a good twenty feet high, compresses as swiftly as it flares. The column of my throat tightens in equal measure. Through the thick flames, I start glimpsing things. A shiny, dark-red suit. A head topped with slick black hair. A stance full of arrogance and command.

All the components that are coalesced by that vicious crucible...and materialize into *him*.

CHAPTER 26

Kara

A S THE FIRE OF his formation turns into morbid smoke, my vital systems flee the other way. My veins are ice. My breaths have a below-forty windchill. Clear thoughts are more impossible than breaking ice with a toothpick. As Hades approaches, stepping across the water and then up over the lip of the pool, I can't see or smell or hear anything but the pitiful moans and desolate tundra he's here to take me back to.

After flicking droplets of water off the shiny leather of his shoes, he rolls his polished onyx gaze back up to us. Maximus hauls me hard to his side. His hold is protective to the point of punishing, but I don't care. A handful of bruises are better than being a captive of hell again. If Hades succeeds this time, it'll be forever. An eternity in that place, serving at my grandmother's will in her desolate district. Unless everything that's happened has nullified Hades's offer…

No. No!

But I have to confront the possibility. I can't stand here and watch entire cities topple in the name of my selfish needs.

"You here to give us a talent show or talk about how we can resolve this without harming more innocent people?"

Maximus's challenge, and the keen mind that's sparked it, make me burrow tighter to him. Savoring his warmth and strength for every minute I can.

Hades takes the moment to smooth his crimson tie and prepare his urbane comeback. "Well, that's up to you, Professor." And then he cocks a black brow. "I can call you that now, yes? *Professor?* Considering we're...here?"

He sweeps a hand toward the LA metropolis, with the flickering lights and scattered fires of this widespread catastrophe. I already feel Maximus's inner conflict. He's ready to blow up, verbally or physically. Maybe both, neither good.

"Your lordship." Gramps intones it like a practiced courtier, managing to convey respect but disdain at once.

Under other conditions, I'd be flowing a thousand percent gratitude toward him for saving Maximus from himself, but at what cost? If Hades hauls him back to hell with me, I don't know if I could survive the misery.

"If I may respectfully ask—" he goes on.

"You can't," Hades barks. "And be grateful I didn't set all the captains on you when I could have, vagrant." He doesn't stop to even afford Gramps a glance, instead funneling more of his black focus on me. "I only made certain to keep special eyes on this place, anticipating you just might have visitors. Thanks in *no* small part to my loyal staff." He flicks a pair of fingers at the main house's entrance.

Shock flares my eyes.

Arden isn't the one standing there to absorb the intensity of my betrayal and hatred.

It's our butler, Dalton. The steward who feels like he's been with us forever, always watchful and diligent, never seeming to tire of his duties or us…

Well, now I know why.

For the first time, I notice the similarity between his uniform and those worn by Hades's captains. My jaw falls and my heart aches to think that our rapport over the years amounted to this—his brutal betrayal.

I grip Maximus harder. My mind flips frantically through hazy memories, demanding to know why I couldn't sense Dalton's deceit earlier.

He dips his head in a polite salute to his master. "My pleasure, my lord. As always."

Though Dalton's refined accent is still in place, it's wrapped in smoky layers that revert my mind back to the prison of hell. At once, it's almost like I'm back there. I shiver, so cold and degraded, wondering if I actually am.

Hades could make that happen fast. He did before. But I fight that awful surrender, clinging to the long, strong fingers that still bind my shoulders. I reach and cling to the mighty muscles of the man still by my side. He keeps me from giving up, no matter how hard Hades starts to stretch for my mind and soul. But he can't get in. Not without the third factor. Not without being right here next to me, sealing the deal with his touch.

"Now, Kara." The glass of his composure is still rough with frustrated edges. "Let's not make this another silly dust-up. You'll surrender with a smile and save your city, your family, and your friends, or you'll watch them all burn while you're kicking and screaming."

"*Enough.*"

I stare hard at Gramps. His tone is also like glass, but without a rough edge in sight. In contrast, my mind is cracking in a hundred directions. The fissures split wider as he pulls in a long but calm breath.

"The deal is a soul for a soul, correct? In one way or another, you've been robbed, and a soul is due to settle the debt." He squares his shoulders and lifts his chin boldly. "So take me back instead."

"Gramps!" I scream it now. "*No!*"

Hades cuts us both off with a ruthless chuckle. "Now why would I make that choice, old man?"

"I'm the one who escaped the underworld, even knowing I belonged there. I was heartbroken and alone, and I used my magical gifts to open passages that I never should've had access to. And yes, you punished me for that, but was that ever really fair to anyone? My own daughter? All three of her children?"

I want to yell at him again but can't. I even want to hit him, but my muscles are heavy to the point of uselessness. Every bone, ligament, and tendon is weighed down by a dread I've never known before. A sadness that has no bottom.

Scenes start to play in my mind. I don't want them, but they keep coming. Gramps with a fuller beard and not so many wrinkles, cheering as I take my first steps. Then Gramps sitting on my pink comforter, making up a story about a princess warrior to chase my nightmares away. Seamlessly, that becomes Gramps in the underworld library, arriving to rescue me from a worse nightmare.

"I've been living on borrowed time, and I think we all know it." Gramps offers a humble shrug. "Besides…I've now realized that I have some unfinished business in your neck of the cosmos."

He's pulling something out of the pocket of his khakis, but my gaze is blurred by a teary fog. I blink angrily, clearing up the view in time to see the object: the elegant ring he's always kept locked away in his office cabinet. Protected there…but not neglected. It's a family piece. I know that much because the diamonds and rubies are cut so similarly to the ones in my earrings. Yet once, when I asked why he always maintained it though never wore it, he gave me an answer that felt cryptic at the time.

Not anymore.

Through my tears, I force myself to speak the words that he gave me.

"You said you were saving this for a special princess," I whisper. "In a faraway land."

Gramps sucks in another breath, clearly battling the many layers of his own conflicted feelings. "And now I've got to go and give it to her."

The rasp in his voice and the sheen in his eyes makes

me feel small and huge at the same time. Connected but hating it. Happy for him but miserable for me. I hate my selfish grief but can't do a thing to hold back its awful flood.

"No."

As soon as Hades intones it, my every emotion hits a strange hold button. My throat closes. My chest pinches. On Gramps's and Maximus's faces, I view the same tension.

"No," the god repeats, nearly drawling it with arrogant serenity. He folds his arms and tilts his head, making me think of an executioner contemplating his axe's best strike point. "Don't get me wrong, Valari. Your offer is touching, but I don't accept it."

Officially, I give up the idea of ever breathing again. For that matter, even speaking.

Gramps jams the ring back into his pocket while pressing forward by several steps. But it's Maximus who jumps first to voice objection to the verdict.

"Why not?"

Hades lifts his most sickening smirk. "For every reason you just gave me on a platter." He nods at Gramps. "Technically, you've already paid the penance for your crime. It'll give me no satisfaction to watch you suffer for it all again. Further, you're going to be my true property, forever and for good this time, in just a handful of years. You're the milk and the cow and damn near the steak already, Gio."

With equally decisive intent, he tracks his stare back to me. As his irises glitter, my stomach drops.

"But *this* fearless and fascinating creature…so maddening and mesmerizing…"

"Is no longer yours to play with, Hades of the Underworld."

The ethereal interruption on the air has my head snapping up and my gaze searching the sky for the voice. Maximus does the same, joining me in trying to make sense of yet another intrusion into this confrontation. It feels like it's coming from everywhere at once. In my nostrils, suffused by myrrh and juniper. In my eyes, still examining the stars as if they're about to become sparkling rain. In my ears, vibrating with evocative bells and musical trills.

But most of all in my blood…which pulses exactly like it did when I first opened the huge grimoire in the underworld library.

And it intensifies as I take in a sight similar to how Hades formed atop the swimming pool. But now the flames are like whirling ice shards, giving off a light mist that chills and enthralls me at once. I can't look away, especially as the light tower condenses and solidifies into an actual figure. A woman.

A breathtaking one.

She's tall and graceful, with flawless sepia skin and dark-blond curls that tumble around her proud shoulders. She's wearing a brilliant green dress with flowing layers that accent her strong curves and long legs. Her chest sparkles with gold necklaces of different lengths, each supporting a gemstone-encrusted pendant.

After one glance, I recognize nearly all the symbols on the assorted jewelry. My fingertips tingle from where they brushed the same shapes on the pages of the grimoire.

From where they used them to store psychic energy I'd never experienced before...

"Oh," I finally manage to whisper. "Wow."

"What's happening?" Maximus steps out into a defensive stance. "Who are you?"

I press a restraining hand to the muscles of his forearm. "It's all right." At least I hope it is.

Maximus narrows his gaze.

Hades follows suit, for different reasons altogether. "Hecate."

She meets his harsh greeting with a look of pure serenity. "Hades." Her voice is silken on the surface but solid as a claymore beneath. "If these were different circumstances, I'd say it's a pleasure."

"The hell you would."

That earns him an impish grin from the goddess.

"What's the meaning of this?" he snaps. "As you can see, I'm a little busy, and you're intruding."

Her full lips part to release a subtle laugh. "Since when did I need an invitation to come visit? You should know by now, I can come and go as I please. And I'm quite sure you already know why I'm here."

She pauses, almost as if making room for Hades to answer if he's willing. But he's still stewing deeply, which she also seems to have expected.

"Kara's blood has opened the grimoire," she states. "You know what that means. She's proven that she's one of us. As such, you cannot abscond her to hell at your whim ever again. You will answer me now, Hades, to indicate you fully understand my words."

Despite craving to turn for the pleasure of watching Hades's reaction, I don't. It's enough to hear the profanities that punch out from the rest of his furious mutterings.

"Hades... You cannot claim her. Neither can Zeus. You can keep throwing this temper tantrum of yours, or you can accept her fate and move on to new conquests."

He twists in place, seeming to stare off at his handiwork over the horizon. Destruction and mayhem. Hell on earth. When he finally speaks, I can hardly hear him.

Hecate clears her throat. "What was that?"

At last, a few decibels louder, he spits, "Yes, *yes*. All right? I understand. You can have her. I'm... well, frankly I'm bored of her anyway."

"Wonderful news!" As the high enchantress nods, a warm wind picks up the ends of her hair. The stars themselves seem to shimmer in those long shiny curls, securing her place in my esteem as a fully welcome voice stealer. I'm beyond grateful that hers still works, though. With a forceful jut of her chin, she addresses Hades again.

"So now you will accept Giovani Valari's generous offer for compromise and return to your world without harming any more humans on the way."

"On this trip only!" Hades spews. "I'll not agree to any permanent standdown about the feckless creatures in this pathetic realm. *You* already know *that!*"

"And you have not let me forget," Hecate placates.

"Then you say it too," the god demands.

"You will not be bound to your word beyond your

next return," she calmly complies. "But if you keep dancing around the subject, you shall also be making your next journey alone, without *any* soul to add to your legion." She rocks back with fluid grace but adds a jump of her expressive eyebrows while eyeing him anew. "Do you accept Valari's offer?"

"Fine," he mutters. "I accept."

"*No.*" All my vocal cords activate in the same screaming rush. "No. Please!" I overcome my church girl awe, bolting toward Hecate with hands coiled in entreaty. "Please." I fall to my knees. "I'm begging…as one of you now…spare my grandfather!"

"Kara." Gramps is down in the grass beside me, hands on my sob-racked shoulders. "Hey, ladybug."

"Stop it," I sob but am lunging into his arms just as quickly. I turn my head in, breathing in his perfect smell of biscotti and chamomile…already knowing this will be the last time I do. All my appeals aren't getting me anywhere. "Please, Gramps," I whisper anyway. "Can't we just stop everything? Can't…we…"

"Don't think there's an incantation for that one, my sweet girl." His murmur is the calm in my storm. The rock that's always been there. But even now, I feel that boulder slipping in the rain of inevitability. Succumbing to forces we can't fight. Not now, anyway. "This is the best way. The right thing I should've done a long time ago." A heavy sigh quivers through him. "But if I had, the world would never have you. So maybe I really was following the right path all along."

My grief presses harder at my lungs. My tears swell more in my throat. Everything hurts. I wrap my arms around his neck, trembling from the pain. "I'm scared."

"And that's okay," he whispers. "Scared is a good force—as long as it still *is* a force and keeps you moving. Don't stop now, Kara. Your journey is just beginning. And what an adventure it's going to be."

"You don't know that," I cry softly. "You *can't* know—"

"But I do." He pulls away but not far. He's still close enough to press a loving hand to my cheek. "I see it so clearly, in all the light of your new confidence...the brilliance of your new strength."

I sniffle hard. Then scowl with equal force. "My new..."

"You know what I'm talking about," he affirms. "You know it because it gave you the boldness to not just open that grimoire but to learn from it. You know it because you see it reflected back a hundredfold every time you look at Maximus."

There's a point I'm already set to believe, but Maximus moves in as if I need the extra proof. And it's absolutely all there. I soak it up from every formidable angle of his face, every adoring facet in his stare, every support beam in his mighty posture. Most of all, I feel it from the depths of his heart. All his adoration. All his love. All his commitment.

I compel myself to fortify my own composure. After the hugest inhalation of my life, I lift my gaze back into a lock with my grandfather's. "Find a way to send messages from time to time?" I utter. "Please?"

"Of course." He drops his hand from my face, using it

to point at the center of my sternum instead. "But if you ever really need me, all you have to do is look here."

I jerk my head through a pair of reluctant nods. "I know, Gramps. I know."

He hauls me into a new hug, and this time his grip is just as fierce as mine. "I love you, ladybug."

"I love you too. So much, Gramps. So, so m—"

But it's already too late.

My tears are plopping into my own lap. My arms are wrapped around nothing but air.

Until…they're not.

Maximus is here, filling my embrace and pressing close to my heart. His arms enfold me. His lips are warmer than the brilliant light from Hecate's continued presence, surrounding us like a blessing…though at once, even before she speaks again, I realize the metaphor isn't just theoretical.

"*Quod tuum est*," she decrees, flowing out one hand. "*Et tu es eius. Exposita est in mundo.*" And then the other.

As I turn my head to give her a reverent nod, Maximus murmurs, "What? Is it a new incantation?"

I brace his jaw in my sprawled grip while pinning all my focus back on his incredible demigod beauty. "Not sure. But I'd like it to be."

One corner of his mouth hitches up. "Oh yeah?"

With an answering smile, I supply the translation. "*He is yours. And you are his. It is written in the cosmos.*"

His gaze darkens as his face gentles. It fills my heart to bring him some small comfort after all we've been through together. Ordeals, I clearly sense, that haven't yet ended.

What an adventure it's going to be...

I'm not at the point of embracing even half of Gramps's enthusiasm yet, but Hecate's words help me agree with him about one point already. I'm stronger now. Ready to handle more of it.

I feel ready to handle anything.

And somehow, in so many ways, I know I'm going to need it. Now more than ever—especially as the layers of Hecate's dress seem to flow up, defying the stronger wind, giving form to ghostlike figures that sway gently over her shoulders. Incarnate spirits, sharing her features but with different shades of skin and hair, join her central figure in raising flowing fingers toward me, which fills me with a new vision. A realm that's still only haze and fuzz in my mind's eye but is so blindingly different from hell that I already know what I'm looking at.

"Kara," Hecate bids, a thankful pull back to reality.

If that's what I can call this, standing before one of the world's highest enchantresses, next to my demigod boyfriend.

No. Maximus isn't even that anymore. What *is* he now? What are *we*?

Written in the cosmos...

I'm not sure what that means, but I cherish the sound of it. But not nearly as much as I cherish *him*. There's so much of my love now, consuming my heart and guiding my soul, even as the high goddess goes on with a declaration that fills me with more fear than anything else.

"Kara Valari," the goddess declares. "You are of the earth. Your blood sings with the fire of the underworld, but your soul declares the words of the high spirits. The gift of magic flows from you now. You belong to no god. No realm. Do you know what this means?"

I swallow hard and shake my head. Because it means everything and nothing at once. It's too much to take in. Whole worlds of revelation to accept in my heart and mind.

"You're a bridge now, Kara. The bridge between worlds. And so much more." She offers me another serene smile. "And I will guide you between all of them."

I realize that I'm smiling now too, until a sobering thought intervenes. "But Maximus..."

"Is more essential to your journey than anyone or anything else," she imparts. "Even the grimoire. Your fates are intertwined and always will be."

As much as her words thrill me, I hold back with hesitation. I look over to Maximus, wondering if he's clutched by the same dilemma. If we thought our relationship was moving at warp speed before...

But as my gaze lands on all the gorgeous contours of his face, I smile. I'm pretty sure I've never seen him look so happy. His eyes are gleaming. His head is high. He's the man of my every dream, even the ones I never knew I had.

He tenderly cups my cheek before lowering his head. As his lips brush mine, he consumes my breath, my thoughts, the very beats of my heart. In return, I give him everything in equal measure: the ache of my soul, the gratitude of my spirit, the passion of my body. All of it. He has it now. He'll have it forever. I tell him so in the most meaningful declaration my lips can create.

"I love you so much, Maximus."

"As I love you," he promises before dipping his mouth to the union of our hands. "Where you go, I go." Somehow he knows I need the levity of his fast wink. "Let's do this."

Before I can give him my wholehearted agreement with another kiss, Hecate reaches out her hands, one toward Maximus and one toward me.

"Then come with me. We have so much to do."

COMING SOON

BRIDGE
of
SOULS

BLOOD OF ZEUS: BOOK FOUR

ALSO BY MEREDITH WILD

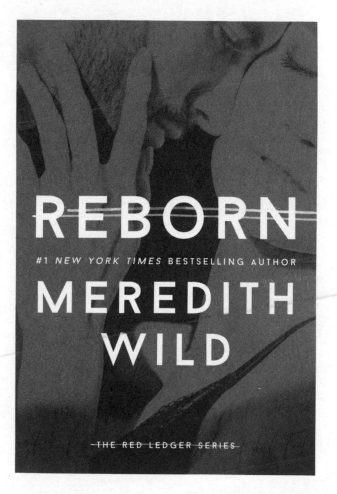

Keep reading for an excerpt!

TRISTAN

Sweat beads down my back. My heart beats slowly, like the pendulum on an old clock. Adrenaline rushes don't come easily for me. As I circle to the rear of the building, memorized details project onto the bright-white screen of my mind.

Isabel Foster. American. English teacher. Aged twenty-five.

Marked for death, she'll be extinguished within the hour. I register the faintest measure of relief that her lover—or the man who desperately wanted to be—is now out of the picture. Collateral damage isn't uncommon, but I prefer to avoid it if I can. God knows I have enough blood on my hands.

I scale the metal stairs in the darkness, mentally mapping my journey from a brief assessment of her living arrangements days ago. The week of Carnaval is already loud and dangerous. Her death will be one of dozens of others reported by the morning.

I peer into her apartment through the glass doors that open from her second-floor balcony. Nearly every light is on. I withdraw my gun from the holster hidden under my shirt. With practiced deftness, I spin the silencer onto the end until it's secure.

Opening the door from her balcony, I pause when a low sound comes from the bedroom. After a beat, I slip inside, leaving the door open a crack for my inevitable departure. I glance around the living room that leads into a small kitchen. My brain captures snapshots that my photographic memory will store forever, whether I want it to or not. A thriving bromeliad on the window sill. A framed photo of her with her parents. An old purple crocheted blanket strewn over the back of the couch. None of it matters. Tonight will be the last night she draws air.

With that final thought, I move toward her nearly closed bedroom door. The gap reveals my target, but instead of taking action, I halt my advance. Where I didn't care about the sounds of my approach seconds before, now I still my breathing and freeze my motions to become totally silent.

She's on the bed. Her chestnut hair fans out on her lavender pillow, and the sheets are tangled around her ankles. With one hand, she's massaging her breast through the sheer black fabric that clings tightly to it. The other hand is hidden under her panties. Her position reveals details I couldn't have appreciated when I watched her from afar—graceful, toned legs, a line of unreadable text inked along her rib cage, and a smooth, firm stomach decorated with a tiny silver ring pierced through her navel. The pinched look on her face is one I haven't seen before. Not even with her boyfriend. A fascinating mix of anguish and rapture.

With her eyes closed and her position on the bed,

she can't know I'm here watching her pleasure herself. The pendulum of my heart swings a little faster at my predicament.

Her beauty doesn't give me pause. A nagging instinct that I know her from somewhere else doesn't give me pause either, though perhaps it should. My weapon hangs heavily at my side now as I entertain both a slow burn of arousal and a rare moment of empathy that I'm about to end her life in the midst of her ecstasy.

I trace my fingertip over the cool metal trigger and attempt to rationalize my hesitation. Then I swiftly resolve to correct it. But not before Isabel's body arches. She wraps her fingers around the edge of the mattress, taking a handful of sheet with her. Her movements quicken, and she sucks in a breath. I'm growing hard, cursing myself with every passing second for my inaction.

Fuck this.

I grit my teeth and lift the gun, lining the barrel up precisely to ensure a quick, painless end.

Her body undulates unevenly as the orgasm rolls through her. She trembles and moans, and my groin betrays the pleasure it's giving me too.

Her lips part with a loud groan and then…

"Tristan…"

My name leaves her lips and fills the room like a gunshot.

I freeze, and the pendulum stops.

Continue Reading in *The Red Ledger: Reborn*

Keep reading for an excerpt!

REECE

She's got the body of a goddess, the eyes of a temptress, and the lips of a she-devil.

And tonight, she's all mine. In every way I can possibly fantasize.

And damn, do I have a lot of fantasies.

Riveted by her seductive glance, I follow Angelique La Salle into a waiting limo. A couple of friends from the party we've just left—their names already as blurry as the lights of Barcelona's Plaça Reial—wave goodbye as if she's taking me away on a six-month cruise to paradise.

Ohhh, yeah.

As an heir to a massive hotel dynasty, I've never wanted for the utmost in luxurious destinations, but I've never been on a cruise. I think I'd like it. Nothing to think about but the horizon…and booze. Freedom from reporters, like the mob that were flashing their cameras in my face back at the club.

What'll the headlines be, I wonder.

Undoubtedly, they've already got a few combinations composed—a mix of the buzz words already trending about me this week.

Party Boy. Player. The Heir with the Hair. The Billionaire with the Bulge.

Well. Mustn't disappoint them about the bulge.

As the driver merges the car into Saturday night traffic, Angelique moves her lush green gaze over everything south of my neck. Within five seconds my body responds. The fantasies in my brain are overcome by the depraved tempest of my body. My chest still burns from the five girls on the dance floor who group-hickied me. My shoulders are on fire from the sixth girl who clawed me like a madwoman while watching from behind. My dick pulses from a hard-on that won't stop because of the seventh girl—and the line of coke she snorted off it.

Angelique gazes at that part with lingering appreciation.

"*C'est magnifique.*" Her voice is husky as she closes in, sliding a hand into the open neckline of my shirt. Where's my tie? I was wearing one tonight—at some point. The Prada silk is long gone, much like my self-control. Beneath her roaming fingers, my skin shivers and then heats.

Well…shit.

If my brain just happens to enjoy this as much as my body…I sure as hell won't complain.

Maybe she'll be the one.

Maybe she'll be…more.

The one who'll change things at last.

Even if she's not going to be the one, she's at least *someone.* A body to warm the night. A presence, of *any* kind, to fill the depths. The emptiness I stopped thinking about a long damn time ago.

"You're magnificent too," I murmur, struggling to maintain control as she swings a Gumby-loose limb over my lap and straddles me. What little there is of her green cocktail dress rides up her thighs. She's wearing nothing underneath, of course—a fact that should have my cock much happier than it is. Troubling...but not disturbing. I'm hard, just not throbbing. Not *needing*. I'm not sure what I need anymore, only that I seem to spend a lot of time searching for it.

"So flawless," she croons, freeing the buttons of my shirt down to my waist. "*Oui*. These shoulders, so broad. This stomach, so etched. You are perfect, *mon chéri*. So perfect for this."

"For what?"

"You shall see. Very soon."

"I don't even get a hint?" I spread a smile into the valley between her breasts.

"That would take the fun out of the surprise, *n'est-ce pas?*"

I growl but don't push the point, mostly because she makes the wait well worth it. During the drive, she taunts and tugs, strokes and licks, teases and entices, everywhere and anywhere, until I'm damn near tempted to order the driver to pull over so I can whip out a condom and screw this temptress right here and now.

But where the hell is here?

As soon as I think the question, the limo pulls into an industrial park of some sort. A secure one, judging by the high walls and the large gate that rolls aside to grant our entry.

Inside, at least in the carport, all is silent. The air smells like cleaning chemicals and leather...and danger. Nothing like a hint of mystery to make a sex club experience all the sweeter.

"A little trip down memory lane, hmmm?" I nibble the bottom curve of Angelique's chin. It's been three weeks since we'd met in a more intimate version of this type of place, back in Paris. I'd been hard up. She'd been alluring. End of story. Or beginning, depending on how one looks at it. "How nostalgic of you, darling."

As she climbs from the limo, she leaves her dress behind in a puddle on the ground. It wasn't doing much good where I bunched it around her waist anyway. "Come, my perfect Adonis."

Perfect. I don't hear that word often, at least not referring to me. Too often, I'm labeled with one of those media favorites, or if I'm lucky, one of the specialties cooked up by Dad or Chase in their weekly phone messages. Dad's a little more lenient, going for shit like "hey, stranger" or "my gypsy kid." Chase doesn't pull so many punches. Lately, his favorite has been "Captain Fuck-Up."

"Bet *you'd* like to be Captain Fuck-Up right about now, asshole," I mutter as two gorgeous women move toward me, summoned by a flick of Angelique's fingers. Their white lab coats barely hide their generous curves, and I find myself taking peeks at their sheer white hose, certain the things must be held up by garters. Despite the kinky getups, neither of them crack so much as a smile while they work in tandem to strip me.

I'm so caught up in what the fembots are doing, I've missed Angelique putting on a new outfit. Instead of the gold stilettos she'd rocked at the club, she's now in sturdier heels and a lab coat. Her blond waves are pulled up and pinned back.

"Well, well, well. Doctor La Salle, I presume?" Eyeing her new attire with a wicked smirk, I ignore the sudden twist in my gut as she sweeps a stare over me. Her expression is stripped of lust. She's damn near clinical.

"Oh, I am not a doctor, *chéri*."

I arch my brows and put both hands on my hips, strategically guiding her sights back to my jutting dick. I may not know how the woman likes her morning eggs yet, but I *do* know she's a sucker for an arrogant bastard—especially when he's naked, erect, and not afraid to do something about it.

"Well, that's okay, *chérie*." I swagger forward. "I can pretend if you can."

Angelique draws in a long breath and straightens. Funny, but she's never looked hotter to me. Even now, when she really does look like a doctor about to lay me out with shitty test results. "No more pretending, *mon ami*."

"No more—" My stomach twists again. I glance backward. The two assistants aren't there anymore, unless they've magically transformed into two of the burliest hulks I've ever seen not working a nightclub VIP section.

But these wonder twins clearly aren't here to protect me.

In tandem, they pull me back and flatten me onto a rolling gurney.

And buckle me down. Tight.

Really tight.

"What. The. *Fuck?*"

"Sssshhh." She's leaning over my face—the wonder

fuckers have bolted my head in too—brushing tapered fingers across my knitted forehead. "This will be easier if you don't resist, *mon trésor.*"

"This? This...*what?*"

Her eyes blaze intensely before glazing over—with insanity. "History, Reece! We are making *history*, and you are now part of it. One of the most integral parts!"

"You're—you're batshit. You're not forging history, you bitch. You're committing a crime. This is kidnapping!"

Her smile is full of eerie serenity. "Not if nobody knows about it."

"People are going to know if I disappear, Angelique."

"Who says you are going to disappear?"

For some reason, I have no comeback for that. No. I *do* know the reason. Whatever she's doing here might be insanity—but it's well-planned insanity.

Which means...

I'm screwed.

The angel I trusted to take me to heaven has instead handed me a pass to hell.

Making this, undoubtedly, the hugest mess my cock has ever gotten me into.

Continue Reading in *Bolt Saga Volume One: Bolt*

ACKNOWLEDGMENTS

This book, this series, and this very special world of Maximus and Kara would not exist without the creativity, passion, and enthusiasm of my co-author. Thank you, Angel, for being my teammate on this project and for pushing forward when life was holding me back.

Special thanks to the entire Waterhouse team, for their patience and support.

Thanks, Mom, for always giving me the pushes when I need them most. And for reminding me to take care of myself too.

— Meredith

So much gratitude to the amazing Meredith Wild, for inviting me along on Maximus and Kara's journey. What an honor and privilege it is to create this with you.

Creating in the age of COVID has been an adventure, to say the least. I'm so grateful to the friends who have talked me off of a few ledges and been there with all the virtual hugs: Carey Sabala, Cynthia Gonzales, Victoria Blue, and Martha Frantz. Thank you, goddesses!

So much gratitude to the amazing team at Waterhouse

Press. I learn every day from your talents, passions, and support. So thankful for every one of you!

The Payne Passion nation: you are such lights in my world. Thank you for everything, Paynesters!

— Angel

ABOUT MEREDITH WILD

Meredith Wild is a #1 *New York Times, USA Today*, and international bestselling author. After publishing her debut novel, *Hardwired,* in September 2013, Wild used her ten years of experience as a tech entrepreneur to push the boundaries of her "self-published" status, becoming stocked in brick-and-mortar bookstore chains nationwide and forging relationships with major retailers.

In 2014, Wild founded her own imprint, Waterhouse Press, under which she hit #1 on the *New York Times* and *Wall Street Journal* bestseller lists. She has been featured on *CBS This Morning* and the *Today Show,* and in the *New York Times*, the *Hollywood Reporter, Publishers Weekly,* and the *Examiner.* Her foreign rights have been sold in twenty-three languages.

Visit her at MeredithWild.com

ABOUT ANGEL PAYNE

USA Today bestselling romance author Angel Payne loves to focus on high-heat romance starring memorable alpha men and the women who love them. She has numerous book series to her credit, including the action-packed Bolt Saga and Honor Bound series, Secrets of Stone series (with Victoria Blue), the intertwined Cimarron and Temptation Court series, the Suited for Sin series, and the Lords of Sin historicals, as well as several standalone titles.

Angel is a native Southern Californian, leading to her love of being in the outdoors, where she often reads and writes. She still lives in Southern California with her soul-mate husband and beautiful daughter, to whom she is a proud cosplay/culture con mom. Her passions also include whisky tasting, shoe shopping, and travel.

Visit her at AngelPayne.com

Photograph © Regina Wamba